FINAL DECREE

For my parents,
who taught me the value of hard work.

ACKNOWLEDGMENTS

I'd like to thank the many people who have encouraged me over the years, especially my husband, Benton, and my mother, Betty Bittner, who taught me the love of reading. For their constructive criticism and support during the writing of this book, I am indebted to Margaret Anderson, Mary Armeniades, Laura Elvebak, Julie Herman, Ann Jennings, Shirl Jensen, Bob Miller, Linda Posey, Chris Rogers, Ron Scott, Amy Sharp, Charlie Soparker, and Leann Sweeney. Special thanks to two of Houston's renowned family law attorneys - to Pat Lasher for encouraging my interest in writing and to Randy Wilhite for providing me with my first computer on which to write.

FINAL DECREE

by Kay Finch

To Kathy —
Hope you enjoy !
Kay Finch

Top Publications, Ltd.
Dallas, Texas

You can catch more flies with honey,
So you better find some now.
You think you're gonna get your way,
I really can't see how.

CHAPTER 1

Some investigators turn down divorce-related work, but I get a perverse satisfaction from putting the screws to a guilty spouse. Late Friday afternoon, I flipped through photos of a client's unfaithful wife whose clandestine meeting with the other man had taken place in the primates section of the Houston Zoo. My best shot featured the couple in a lip-lock, a treeful of curious squirrel monkeys looking on. As I admired the picture, Hank Williams belted out "Your Cheating Heart" on my office radio. How appropriate.

Footsteps tapped down the marble-tiled hallway outside my open door. Company coming. Gathering my unruly hair into a presentable ponytail, I clamped it in place with a large clip. I stuck the prints back into their envelope, just as the yelling started.

"Suzanna's not getting away with anything," a man thundered, "especially not my son!"

Jeez. I reached across the desk to crank down the radio volume.

"I'll make her regret this day, by God. Do whatever it takes. Just nail the bitch!"

My good friend, divorce attorney Wade Alexander, appeared in the doorway. Impeccable as always in a well-cut navy suit, he held a manila folder in one hand. Wade's unannounced appearances aren't unusual because his law firm is right down the hall. Today he was shadowed by a man in scrubs and a white lab coat.

"Got a minute?" Wade looked apologetic.

"Why not?" I said, even though this was obviously a client-from-hell case.

Wade didn't give me a chance to change my mind, smiling and motioning for the man to enter my office.

"Dr. Edward Kemp, this is Corinne McKenna. Corie, Dr. Kemp is a new client. Just served with divorce papers this afternoon. Hearing's in two weeks."

Kemp. The name sounded awfully familiar. I stood and rounded the desk, my hand extended.

The doctor checked out my khakis and T-shirt, giving me the same nod of disapproval made famous by my mother, chief of the wardrobe police. He studied the McKenna Investigations placard on my door before stepping inside to glance around my one-room office. His gaze lingered on the bookcase, taking in the stacks of country-western CDs, a framed photo of me shaking hands with Alan Jackson, and my collection of "how-to" songwriting books.

He glared at Wade. "You're trusting *her* with my case?"

What was his problem? He didn't think investigators were entitled to have a hobby? Or was I simply the wrong gender for the jerk? I lowered my hand, no longer interested in shaking his. Plopping into my chair, I grabbed a fresh tablet and a pen and scribbled the date along with Kemp's name.

"Relax, Doctor," Wade said, losing the smile. "Have a seat."

Kemp muttered something unintelligible, reluctantly settling into one of the chairs across from me. He ran a hand through his kinky brown hair and pushed wire-rimmed glasses up on his thin nose. Though he had shut up for the moment, his face still held an angry purplish tinge.

Wade sat next to the client and cleared his throat. "Dr. Kemp, when you hire me and the firm Alexander & Glover we like to make some judgment calls. Corie specializes in domestic cases. She's worked closely with our firm for many years. I'm telling you she's the best person for the surveillance. If you'd rather hire other counsel, say so now."

"Don't be absurd," Kemp said. "Of course I want you to represent me. And I want this whole thing over, finished, as soon as possible."

Wade held up a hand to interrupt his client. "We're a *long* way from the final decree. As I've already told you, the hearing is for temporary orders only. Use and possession of the house, cars, temporary custody—"

"And I told you *I'm* going to have custody of my son!" Kemp's white-knuckled hands gripped the chair arms.

Cringing at the thought of some poor boy having this guy for a dad, I wrote "Fat Chance!" on my tablet.

Knowing Wade as well as I do, I detected the strain behind his calm facade. "You and Suzanna will probably be named joint managing conservators," he said. "She'll have the right to establish your son's primary residence, unless we show a good reason she shouldn't have that right. That's why we need Corie on the case." He pushed back his chair and stood, handing me the manila folder. "Now, I'm running late for my four o'clock, so I'll leave you in her capable hands."

Gee, thanks.

"Don't worry," he told the client. "Corie will dig up the evidence we need to present your case."

"Just so I get my boy." Kemp gave Wade a dismissive nod, then turned and shook his finger at me. "Make damn sure we find out what she's been up to. I want everything photographed, logged, labeled—"

"*Doctor* Kemp." I picked up my tablet and slammed

it back down on the desk. The tactic earned me an even deeper scowl, but at least the man was quiet.

Pasting on a sickeningly sweet smile, I reached over to flick the radio off. John Michael Montgomery was singing "I Can Love You Like That," absolutely the wrong tone for this meeting.

"We need to start at the beginning." Skimming Wade's notes, I realized where I'd heard Kemp's name before. He was the orthopedic surgeon Mother worshipped for putting her back on the River Oaks Country Club tennis court in record time. It'd take a lot more to impress me.

I gazed at the doctor, working to maintain a neutral expression. "Tell me why you think Suzanna needs to be followed."

"She goes out several nights a week, that's why," he answered without hesitation.

"Out?" He made it sound like she shouldn't be allowed to leave the house.

"That's what I said—out." Kemp threw his hands in the air. By now his complexion looked as though he'd spent three hot, sunny days on a sailboat without sunscreen.

I tried to summon up some patience. "And when she goes 'out' she leaves you at home with little—" I glanced at Wade's notes. "With little Edward?"

"No," Kemp said. "We have a live-in. She either leaves Eddie with the old lady or takes him along. I'm not sure." He shrugged.

I twirled my pen, confused. "So, you and Mrs. Kemp are already separated?"

"No. I just got the damn divorce papers today." Kemp drummed long, thin fingers on his chair arm.

"Oh, you must be on call evenings at the hospital."

Kemp didn't confirm or deny my statement. "I'm a busy man. When I'm out at night, I phone home to check on my wife. Lately, she's never there when I call. She's out screwing around somewhere."

"I see." What a jerk! Obnoxious men like Kemp always remind me how lucky I'd been to marry someone like David. I fingered the sterling silver locket he'd given me on our last anniversary before his death.

"Did you hear me?" Kemp said. "I want to know exactly what she's up to."

"I get the idea, Dr. Kemp, and I have enough information to do the job." Not that the prospect thrilled me. "Do you have a photograph of Suzanna with you?"

The doctor took his wallet from the pocket of his lab coat. I watched him flip through the plastic sleeves, passing up several pictures of attractive women. He stopped at a beautiful blonde cuddling an adorable infant. The baby wore cute Mickey Mouse overalls and a miniature red baseball cap.

Kemp pulled the photo out and slapped it on my desk. "That's the slut," he said. "Keep it."

I hadn't liked the man from the start, but his statement turned my dislike into loathing. Suzanna Kemp was, after all, mother to his son. The picture of the little boy grinning at her tugged my heart strings. I couldn't help feeling sorry for both of them.

When Kemp finally left, his footsteps fading off down the hall, I thought about recent cases that had left me with a good feeling in my gut. Tracking down a stingy husband's hidden assets. Smoking out a deadbeat dad. Taking those pictures of the two-timing wife at the zoo.

I stared at Kemp's divorce petition, then picked up the photo of his wife and son. The only good I could see coming from this case was that it might inspire lyrics for a good gut-wrenching country music hit.

He has a lot to learn about women,
Things he really oughta know.
If he doesn't lose that attitude,
They'll all get up and go.

CHAPTER 2

Not five minutes after the doctor left, Reba Hofstetler burst into my office, dark eyes blazing.

"Now there's a man who oughta be hog-tied and thrown off a shrimp boat in the Gulf." Rhinestones glittered on the collar and cuffs of her black suit jacket as Wade's secretary planted hands on her hips. Only Reba knew where to shop for office attire that could double as evening wear for a night at the Grand Ol' Opry.

"Referring to Edward Kemp, by chance?" I said. When Reba's on a tear, she doesn't need encouragement, so I kept my opinion of the new client to myself.

"Damn straight." She smacked her double-wad of pink bubblegum. "The ass barged in with no appointment, demandin' to see Wade. Who does he think he is?"

"Looked to me like he just stepped out of an operating room. Probably knows as well as we do a lawyer's not likely to turn away a doctor's money."

"Guess you're right." Reba huffed, plopping down in the chair Kemp had vacated. "Wade *did* drop everything to meet with him. I would have set up an appointment for next month. Let the doc fume for a while."

"He did overreact a bit, didn't he?"

"Overreact? The guy was about to bust a gasket. Thought I might have to take drastic action." Grinning, Reba pulled a small pearl-handled revolver from her pocket.

I rolled my chair back from the desk. "Reba! What are you doing with a gun in here? Are you nuts?"

"No, I'm prepared. The clients are the loony ones."

"True," I said, "but now *you're* overreacting."

"I don't think so. Nobody's happy when they come to see Wade. They show up with hormones flyin', testosterone off the charts, ready to fight to the death over stupid stuff. You should have heard the couple this morning, arguin' about who gets custody of the goldfish, for Pete's sake. One of these days a nut case is gonna go postal on us. I'm convinced. That's why I keep this little baby at the office." She playfully aimed the gun toward me.

I ducked. "Will you put that thing away?"

Reba flipped her blonde curls behind an ear. "You scared of this tiny thing? You should see the big sucker I have at home."

"I'll pass."

"Anyway," she said, slipping the revolver back into her pocket, "Kemp's a maniac. Even worse than Leroy."

Reba's a career divorcee, and I lost track two or three ex-husbands ago. She must have seen the confusion on my face as I tried to remember Leroy.

"Broke all my crystal throwin' it into the fireplace," she prompted.

"Right," I said, leaning back in my chair. "But I have a feeling Kemp's more like the ex who took all those weekend trips to Vegas, different woman every weekend."

"Number four," Reba said. "But he was a hunk, girl. Kemp's nothin' to look at. Who'd want to hang out with him?"

"Lots of women follow my mother's philosophy," I said. "She'd be delighted if I brought home somebody with Ed Kemp's income statement. In fact, I think he's the doctor she's been praising for fixing her bad shoulder."

"Well, if your mama thinks Kemp's a nice guy, you better be extra careful next time she tries to set you up."

"No joke," I said. Thwarting my mother's matchmaking attempts is a constant battle.

Reba checked her watch. "Yikes, it's after five." She jumped up. "Friday night with The Stetler Girls. I sure was hopin' you could rehearse with us this week."

I frowned. "I filled in for Denise one time. Just once, and only because she had that emergency appendectomy. I am not, read my lips, *not* joining your band."

"But, Corie—"

"Don't start with 'The Stetler Girls' are the next 'Dixie Chicks' argument. It won't faze me." I folded my arms over my chest.

"C'mon, Corie. You have a dynamite voice."

"Mother didn't send me to voice lessons so I could join a country music band. Trust me."

"Don't go pretendin' you give a hoot what she thinks," Reba said. "I know you too well."

"Then you also know I'd rather stay behind the scenes. I like to write lyrics. You and I can keep on collaborating. But *you* go out and perform our songs. Without me."

"Okay, okay." She reached the doorway, then turned around, a cat-who-ate-the-canary look on her face. "I'm puttin' the finishing touches on 'You Were Wrong, Now You're Gone.' I guarantee we'll get the attention of all the big boys when we go to Nashville next month."

"When we *what*?"

My reaction time was too slow. Reba's high-heeled boots clattered down the hallway in a run. The law firm's back door banged shut before I made it across my office. Great. Reba's sly enough when it comes to "our" country music career to feed me tidbits, knowing I'll balk when I hear her full-blown plans. Our songwriting is a hobby as far as I'm concerned—no way do we have anything worth peddling to an agent.

I grabbed my purse and locked up, wondering how Reba planned to convince me to make a trip to Nashville.

Where are you goin' this dark, lonely night?
Tell me, I can't wait to see.
You're keeping lots of secrets, girl.
Don't be keeping them from me.

CHAPTER 3

By six-thirty I was on the job, not thrilled about spying on Suzanna Kemp, who I already envisioned as the aggrieved spouse. But, hey, every once in a while I'm wrong.

I'd parked in the driveway of a vacant house three doors down from the Kemps' brick home on Sunset Boulevard in West U. A black Saab the client had identified as his wife's sat in the driveway. Security lights on the eaves illuminated the front yard. I switched on my tape recorder to document the date, time, and case information.

November had been mild so far, but tonight there was a chill in the air. I settled back in the bucket seat and pulled my flannel shirt closer, inhaling deeply. David's scent still clung to the fabric, or was it my imagination? I could still picture him wearing the shirt the night before he died. Two long years ago.

I sighed, pulling out the small cooler I'd packed with food for the stake-out. Eating usually staves off depressing trips down memory lane. That and music. I punched the radio buttons, tuning in George Strait's snappy fireman tune.

Two peanut butter sandwiches, some Oreos, and a Coke later, a tall form wearing white warm-ups emerged from the house. I grabbed my binoculars, focusing on the slim blonde who walked down the driveway and climbed into the Saab.

I hit the record button again. "Eight p.m. Subject is in

her car. Here we go."

Suzanna backed out of the driveway and punched the accelerator, heading for Kirby Drive at a fast clip. My Ranger pickup quickly closed the distance between us.

A familiar surge of excitement took over, the thrill of the unknown. Surveillance can be boring, sure, but I'd take it any day over the Junior League and Garden Club meetings Mother was trying to involve me in back when David suggested I do some work for him and his partners at the law firm. One of the things she'd never forgiven him for.

Following Suzanna onto 59 South, I hummed Willie Nelson's "On the Road Again." We were soon on the 610 Loop, passing the exit to The Galleria. So, this wasn't about shopping. We drove for miles, and I was about to conclude Suzanna had left the house only to make Ed jealous when the Saab's turn signal flashed and she got off at Yale.

I coasted along the feeder road, falling farther behind so she wouldn't notice me. An old dented Monte Carlo, rusting around the edges, slowed beside me, the booming rhythm of rap music threatening to bounce my truck right off the street. Suzanna took a left, drove about a mile, then turned into a parking lot.

Warehouses lined the lot. I slowed, watching her car crawl deeper into the darkness, past a row of trucks belonging to one of the businesses. Curious. I continued down Yale, looped around at the next street, and headed back. Her car was almost out of sight, so I doused my lights and turned into the lot, pulling the Ranger into a space where it would be partially hidden in a large van's shadow.

"We're in a warehouse lot, near Yale and Crosstimbers," I recorded. "Place looks shut down for the night. Deserted. I doubt she's here for a quickie."

The woman had surprised me. Why would she come to this particularly bad part of town, alone, at night? I checked out the building in front of me. Not the sort of place the Kemps would rent to store excess household goods. Had she found out Ed secretly rented a place? Interesting idea, but why here when there were nicer places much closer to his part of town? Dropping the recorder into my jacket pocket, I headed after Suzanna on foot, camera and binoculars hanging around my neck and a flashlight in hand.

Each section of warehouse space had a set of six steps leading to an office door adjacent to a loading dock. Using the stairs as cover, I moved from one set to the next, hoping to catch up to Suzanna without being seen.

Her Saab was parked at the back of the lot. Through the binoculars, I saw her standing at the last office in the row, bent over the lock. A dim bulb above the door lit the entry, and the almost-full moon helped light the area. A curtain of long blonde hair obscured Suzanna's face. Like me, she had a camera strapped around her neck.

Okay, I theorized, maybe Ed's hiding assets here and she's taking pictures to use in the divorce case before he moves them. Pretty farfetched, but anything's possible.

She tried several keys before finding one that fit, then disappeared inside the dark building. I inched across the pavement, wanting to follow her, but without knowing the layout inside that didn't seem like a smart move. I reluctantly sat on the steps two doors down and waited, watching litter blow across the lot.

"Subject entered the last office door on the left," I said into the recorder. "No number visible on the door. No identifying signs. No other cars in sight." My eyes had adjusted to the darkness, and I could make out signs on the warehouses facing me. Regal Carpet, Torrey Electric, Bryan Services.

"Check with the client," I recorded. "Maybe wife's involved in a business he didn't mention."

A few minutes later, Suzanna emerged from the building. She wasn't carrying anything as far as I could tell. I slid off my concrete perch and ducked into the shadows. As she stood under the overhead light to lock the door behind her, I lifted my Nikon, focused the zoom lens and snapped a picture. The automatic time and date feature would document the excursion for Ed Kemp. The audio tape was for my own use when I typed up my report.

I waited until Suzanna was headed out of the lot before sprinting to my pickup. I would have liked to get inside, but I could return another time. For now, I'd better see what else Mrs. Kemp had planned for the evening. As we backtracked our route, I suspected she was on her way home.

I hit a speed-dial button on my cell phone to call Wade at the office. He's such a workaholic I knew he'd be there.

"Still on the job, I see."

"Look who's talking," Wade said, teasing. "How's the surveillance going?"

"Interesting. She went to a warehouse. Looks like we're heading back home, and it's only nine-thirty. I wonder how long the good doctor stays out screwing around."

"Lighten up, Corie. I admit Ed's not going to win any congeniality awards."

"Understatement of the month. Good luck finding character witnesses for the custody fight."

Wade ignored my remark. "Where are you now?"

"59 entrance ramp. She sure boosted my curiosity. The warehouse is on Yale Street. She went straight there, but only stayed about fifteen minutes. I'll keep you posted."

"Be careful."

I hung up the phone, smiling at his concern.

Suzanna exited the freeway, zigzagged through traffic then hung a left on Sunset. Going home, as I'd guessed. The

Saab pulled to a smooth stop in the driveway. If Kemp expected me to turn up evidence of his wife's alleged affair, he was out of luck, at least tonight. I wondered how he'd react to news of her visit to the warehouse. Unless he knew more about the place than I did, he'd probably be angry that I couldn't explain the reason for her trip.

Deciding to stay a while longer to make sure Suzanna was in for the night, I pulled into the space I'd occupied earlier.

She climbed out of the Saab slinging a purse over her shoulder. I felt pretty confident she didn't know she'd been followed and decided to take one more picture to prove to our overbearing client his wife got in before ten o'clock.

I turned down my radio and lowered the power window. Frogs and crickets sang their usual nighttime melody. Young voices drifted toward me on the breeze along with the sound of a bouncing basketball. Glancing up and down the street, I saw no one except Suzanna.

Through the camera, I watched her close her car door. Lights approached, a couple of cars heading down the street. After a loud, older model Mustang rattled by, I braced my left arm against the window frame and refocused my telephoto lens on Suzanna.

Before I could snap the picture, her body jerked and she fell face down on the sidewalk.

My heart jumped. I moved the camera away from my face, squinted, then looked through the lens again. She must have tripped. I swapped my camera for the high-powered binoculars and took another look. She wasn't moving.

Had she fainted? Was she having some kind of seizure? The back of her white jacket was splotched with...what?

No. Couldn't be.

Without thinking, I threw the binoculars on the

passenger seat and jumped out. Maybe she'd hit her head on the concrete when she fell. Maybe she had a concussion. She needed help. I stumbled across the grassy median, wondering what I would say if she stood up and faced me.

A noise stopped me in my tracks. A door slamming? I didn't see anyone emerging from a house. A chill raced up my spine. I shrugged it off and ran toward Suzanna, stumbling over a brush and makeup that had spilled from her purse.

My stomach roiled as I got closer, my breath coming in short gasps. The spot on her back was bloody. Oh, my God. She'd been shot. I started to strip off my jacket. Stop the bleeding. Then I saw the head wound. Blood pooled on the sidewalk.

I stifled a scream. Backing away, I tripped on Suzanna's purse and went down hard. My right hand landed on a key ring, the point of one key imbedding itself in my palm. Grimacing, I closed my fist around the keys and jumped to my feet.

How had this happened? I hadn't heard any shots.

Was the killer still out here?

My sense of self-preservation finally kicked in, and I took off running for my truck.

It's been a long time,
Since you went away.
If only I had stopped you
From leaving me that day.

CHAPTER 4

Camera flashes spotted my vision. Why did the police have to take so damn many pictures of the body? That's how I had to think of Suzanna now, as just a body. It was the only way I could remain semi-calm.

Standing in the driveway with the officer in charge, Detective Sergeant Gutierrez, I fought a serious case of the jitters. Too much about this scene reminded me of the day David died. Crime scene officials traipsing across the lawn, roping off the area with yellow tape, talking to neighbors, taking measurements. Police car radios squawking. My head pounded in time with the red and blue lights flashing across the night sky as I tried to concentrate on the detective's questions.

I'd already told my story to his subordinates, but Gutierrez insisted we rehash everything. He didn't like it that I'd been following the dead woman, but there was no law against surveillance. Even so, I sensed the man would have bagged my hands and hauled me downtown if I hadn't mentioned Wade's name. Working for an attorney with a good reputation has its perks.

"If you believe someone in the Mustang shot Mrs. Kemp," Gutierrez said, "then why didn't you get the plate number?"

I met his harsh stare. "At the time, I didn't know *what* had happened. I still don't. The car drove by. *Then* she fell.

The timing wasn't right."

"Someone could have taken a shot from the car window after they passed. How many occupants were in the car?"

"I didn't notice." My arms were wrapped so tightly around myself they might cut off circulation.

"How far away was the car when she went down?"

"At the time, I wasn't paying attention to the car."

"Quite the investigator, aren't you?" Gutierrez' face held no expression as he scratched in his notebook.

I could beat myself up without any help from him. Being an eyewitness to the whole event, I should have been able to recite every detail.

"This is West U," I said. "Not exactly a prime neighborhood for drive-by shootings. That's the last thing I expected to happen. Plus, I didn't hear any shots."

"You ever read the paper?" Gutierrez said. "Criminals don't respect boundaries. Never have."

Biting my lip to keep from saying something I'd regret, I looked up at the Kemps' home. An elderly Hispanic woman stood at a side window, her hand parting the draperies. Must be the live-in. When our eyes met, she stepped back and a layer of sheer fabric fell into place. After a couple of seconds, her silhouette moved away from the window.

Gutierrez was still scribbling. What was he writing, a book? Derogatory comments about me? No matter what he thought, this just didn't feel like a drive-by shooting.

I studied the other houses on the street, noting how they were all heavily veiled behind shrubbery and trees. If someone wanted to hide, watching for Suzanna's return, it wouldn't be difficult.

"You know, it all happened so fast," I said, "like she'd been shot by a sniper."

Gutierrez looked up, smirking. "A sniper. You watch much television, Ms. McKenna?"

"Don't patronize me. Someone could have been inside a house with a full view of this driveway." I pointed across the street at a window, then to Suzanna's car.

"You know anyone with a reason to want Mrs. Kemp dead?"

I clamped my mouth shut. Had someone already reported Ed Kemp's reaction to the divorce papers?

The roar of a car engine saved me from answering.

A red Porsche sped down Sunset and screeched to a stop on the eastbound side. Dr. Kemp jumped out and darted through the spectators who'd gathered along the median strip. An officer warned him not to cross the line, but he'd already seen his wife.

A cry rose from Kemp's throat as he pushed the cop aside. Bursting through the yellow tape, he rushed toward Suzanna's body. Another officer grabbed at Kemp's arm, but he broke free. A few feet from the body, he sank to his knees. Burying his face with his hands, he rocked back and forth.

Gutierrez dismissed me and headed for Kemp. Dreaded memories of David's death flooded my mind. I'd rushed to the scene, too, on that horrible day. Tried to force my way into a building almost leveled by an explosion. A police officer had threatened to handcuff me to the police car if I didn't back off.

If only David's stupid client hadn't been a chain smoker. If only there hadn't been a gas leak at the dinner club. If only David hadn't arrived on time for that meeting. "If onlys" had monopolized my mind for over a year.

Pushing thoughts of David away, I turned to watch Ed Kemp. This didn't look like the cold-hearted husband I'd seen earlier in the day. He would have *wanted* his wife to suffer. True, that didn't mean he wanted her dead. His anger could be attributed to the heat of the moment. He knew a divorce would cost him plenty, more than money and material possessions. He'd been concerned about losing custody.

So, was this an act? I hated being cynical, but my sixth sense had a hard time believing Kemp would grieve for Suzanna the way I grieved for David.

After allowing Kemp a minute of privacy, Gutierrez pulled the doctor to his feet. Kemp turned off his tears, too suddenly I thought, and yanked his arm from the detective's hold. Gutierrez motioned for Kemp to move off the lawn and they stood near the street, talking, the detective recording their conversation in his ever-present notebook.

Hoping to avoid a run-in with Kemp, I backed into the bushy azaleas bordering the flower bed, my head down. A door clicked open behind me, and I turned to see the housekeeper peering in Kemp's direction. Her fingers worked nervously, twisting the sash of her flowered print house dress.

Even though my assignment had ended tragically, I was still curious about Suzanna's visit to the warehouse. Maybe this woman could answer some questions. I checked to make sure Kemp was still occupied before approaching her.

"Hello," I said, "I'm Corie McKenna. You work for the Kemps?"

"*Sí*." Her teary eyes moved furtively. She seemed afraid someone would notice us together.

"I'm sorry about what happened," I said.

"Señora Suzanna—" Her voice cracked in a sob. She looked down, swallowing back her tears. "She very good lady. Who would do this terrible thing?"

"I'd like to talk to you about—"

Kemp's voice rumbled behind me.

"I cannot." The woman's head popped up and she was back inside before I could blink.

Reluctantly, I turned around to face Ed Kemp.

"How could you let this happen?" he said, his face reddening.

"I–"

"Get off my property. Now!"

We stared at each other for a moment. Then I turned, disgusted, and stomped down the driveway. This was not the time for arguing with the jerk.

I managed to leave without speaking my mind, but suddenly I wanted nothing more than to know exactly where Edward Kemp had spent the evening. Why was he in such a hurry to get me off his property? Was he afraid I'd tell the police about his reaction to the divorce? If that obnoxious chauvinist had anything to do with his wife's murder, I wanted to be the one to nail him.

Driving down Sunset, I dialed Wade again, this time at home. He answered with a tired hello.

"Wanted you to be first to know, the Kemps won't be getting divorced."

"Corie? What are you talking about?" Wade sounded wide awake now.

"Suzanna Kemp's dead. Murdered."

"How? Where?"

By the time I'd finished telling him the details, I was home and had pulled the pickup into my garage.

"Well, what do you think?" I said.

Silence filled the line as I listened to the hissing of the truck engine cooling off in the quiet garage.

"Have the police hauled Ed downtown yet?" Wade said.

"Nope. But my gut says it's only a matter of time."

The man is guilty as sin,
Don't think about what might have been,
Not safe to be around, don't let him in,
'Cause he's guilty as sin.

CHAPTER 5

I got the usual seven a.m. wake-up call: a nudge on the arm, a moist nose on my cheek. Midnite, my year-old black Lab, didn't know it was Saturday or what a bad night I'd had. Her tail thumped against the nightstand. No use arguing.

"Okay, I'm up." I dragged myself out of bed and headed for the bathroom. Midnite followed so close her wet nose continually bumped my leg. Usually that annoys me, but today my mind was on Suzanna Kemp. The poor woman wouldn't be rising to greet another day. She'd never feel a dog's clammy nose or silky fur. Worst of all, she wouldn't be around to watch her son grow up. My eyes teared. I knelt beside Midnite and scratched behind her ears, even let her lick my cheek.

"Well, girl," I said, "I saw a woman die last night. Thought maybe the husband killed her, but who knows? God, what a horrible experience." Midnite panted in reply, the usual happy expression on her face. I ruffled her fur before standing.

Carrying on one-sided conversations with the Lab helps keep me sane. I hadn't adjusted easily to the loneliness of widowhood, and she's the only companion I'm interested in, at least for now. I wondered how Ed Kemp was doing this morning, the first day of his life as a widower.

"He's a well-educated man," I said, "a doctor. If he

planned to murder his wife, he'd come up with some elaborate scheme, including a foolproof alibi. He sure wouldn't kill her the same day he got served divorce papers. Or hire me to tail her on the night he planned to do the deed. Know what I mean?" I slipped into a pair of jeans and a sweatshirt. Midnite pranced around me, eager to get outside.

I started some coffee, then we went out back where she instantly scooped up a tennis ball. After making several frisky laps around the yard, she dropped the slimy ball at my feet. I sat on the deck steps, absently tossing the ball for her to fetch, when an unwelcome thought hit.

What if Kemp *wanted* me to witness the shooting? He'd tell the cops nobody would be stupid enough to hire someone for surveillance the night he plans to commit murder. And besides, he had someone who could testify that he was *not* on the scene. My stomach churned.

"I'm not going to help him get away with murder," I said.

Midnite cocked her head, as if she was considering my statement, then nosed my arm. I threw the ball across the yard, and she took off after it. Maybe my dislike for the man was skewing my judgment. After all, Kemp was a doctor, not some redneck tooling around Houston with a gun rack in his pickup. But if he didn't kill his wife, then who did? And why?

Sometimes it's hard to shift my curiosity into neutral, and this was one of those times. I propped my elbows on my knees, supporting my chin with my fists, and thought about Mrs. Kemp. I'd never talked to the woman, knew next to nothing about her character. Why would a doctor's wife go sneaking around a warehouse in the dead of night? Closing my eyes, I pictured her standing at the warehouse door, trying one key after another.

The keys.

My eyes popped open. I turned my hand over,

inspecting the palm where Suzanna's keys had jabbed me. Where were they? I remembered racing to my truck to call 911. I'd thrown them down. The police had looked inside the truck, confiscating my film and the audio tape I'd been recording. They hadn't mentioned any keys.

I rushed inside, stopping to pour dog food into Midnite's bowl before hurrying to the garage. It didn't take long to find the keys lodged between the console and the passenger seat.

Holding up the ring, I inspected seven keys of different shapes and sizes. None of them looked like an ignition key and none were marked "Saab." Technically, they were probably evidence and would have to be turned over to Gutierrez. I traced the jagged key edges with a finger, considering what Suzanna might have seen inside that warehouse. Every scenario I conjured was one that would help to incriminate Dr. Kemp in the murder. I shoved the keys in my jeans pocket and tried to put them out of my mind. After all, there would be no divorce case, so my work was over.

I busied myself with household chores for several hours, all the while wanting to head over to the warehouse and let myself in to satisfy the guessing game I couldn't shake loose. Around noon, the phone rang. It was Wade, the last person I'd tell about my desire to break and enter.

"Corie, glad I caught you." He sounded out of breath. "Can you head downtown, like right now?"

Something about his tone sent up my caution flag. "I guess so," I said slowly. "Why?"

"Cops want Kemp to come down for an interview. Long story short, a nurse called HPD claiming she heard him threaten to kill his wife yesterday afternoon."

"And you're surprised?"

Wade ignored my comment. "Look, he can't go in

there without an attorney. I'm out at the airport. It's my weekend, and the kids are arriving any minute, so I can't leave. Kemp's such a damn hothead, he won't wait."

"I hope you're not suggesting I pick him up."

"Too late for that. He may be on his way to the police station already. You have to intercept him."

"What? How do you expect me to do that?"

"Jump in your car and get down there pronto, that's how."

"Wade, I'm the last person on earth Kemp will want to see, and the feeling is mutual. If the guy's stupid enough to hang himself, it's not our fault."

"Some people might think it is. There's no time to explain. Now get moving. Don't let Kemp get through that front door."

I blew out a breath, reluctantly picking up my purse and car keys. "I'm on my way."

"Make sure he doesn't talk to anyone," Wade said, sounding relieved. "I'll keep trying Joe Garrett. Kemp needs a criminal attorney whether he wants one or not."

"Gotcha." If Wade's old friend from law school took Kemp's criminal case, I'd be back on the job since he usually hired me for his investigations. I was destined to put up with this irritable client.

"And Corie?"

"Yeah?"

"See if you can get Kemp talking. Garrett's going to need your help to prove Kemp's innocent."

"Will do."

We hung up, and I stared at the phone.

Innocent? What happens if I prove he's guilty as sin?

Open up and tell me,
Things I need to know.
You're in a heap of trouble,
Tell me now, before you go.

CHAPTER 6

I made it downtown in record time and nearly wore out the sidewalk patrolling the entrance to the police station. There were plenty of open spaces in the lot directly across the street, but Kemp's red Porsche wasn't in sight, so I felt confident he hadn't arrived yet. Thick gray clouds loomed overhead, and the wind sent dry leaves swirling across the sidewalk. I turned up my jacket collar and stuffed my hands in the pockets.

Getting psyched for another meeting with Kemp wasn't easy, so I kept reminding myself I was here at Wade's request. Our relationship went deeper than the job, and I didn't want that to change. If he needed me to protect Kemp from himself, that's what I'd do. When I spotted the man climbing from his Porsche, I straightened my shoulders, preparing for battle.

The doctor headed across the street, not noticing me posted near the entrance. He looked as though he'd aged ten years since our meeting the day before. Deep lines etched his pale face and perspiration stained the collar of his wrinkled white shirt.

He didn't hurry, and I wondered if a bit of common sense had set in, making him realize the idiocy of showing up without an attorney. I hoped he'd fall for the one and only plan I'd come up with to keep him out of the building. When he reached the sidewalk, I pasted on a harried expression and planted myself between him and the door.

"Finally," I said, checking my watch. "They changed the meeting place. We're supposed to be at the D.A.'s office fifteen minutes ago. Come on."

I grabbed his arm, holding tight as he tried to yank away.

"What's this?" Kemp's face reddened. "What are you doing here?"

"You're not the only one they want to interrogate," I said. "I was there last night. Remember?"

"But they told me 61 Riesner. The police station." He twisted to look back at the building.

"I know, that's what they told me, too. They changed the plan." I kept moving, propelling him back across the street toward my truck where I'd managed to park in a convenient front row spot. "The officer in charge already went over there. Told me to make sure you got the message."

We reached my truck, and I aimed Kemp toward the passenger door. "I know where we're going. Jump in."

"I don't like this," he said.

Dropping my grip on his arm, I placed my hands on my hips. "You're very late. I wouldn't piss them off any more if I were you. They think you're a killer." I unlocked the door, yanked it open, and waved him inside. "C'mon."

He looked across the lot toward his car.

"I'll drop you off at the door. You'd waste another five minutes, easy, trying to find a parking spot."

Kemp's reluctance ebbed, and he slid into my truck.

I slammed the door, stifled a grin, and ran around to the driver's side. Now for the real challenge. I climbed in and hit the automatic locks, hoping the child safety feature worked the way it was supposed to. It wouldn't be long before Kemp realized he'd been duped. Taking a deep breath, I revved the engine and pulled into traffic.

"Now that we have a minute," I said, stealing a sideways glance at my passenger, "you might be interested in hearing where your wife went last night."

"Like that really matters now." He faced straight ahead, one leg jiggling impatiently. "Cops told me you followed her to a warehouse. Doesn't make any sense."

"The warehouse is on Yale. Know anything about it?"

He looked annoyed. "No. I don't even know where Yale is."

"Maybe she had business there. Did she work outside the home? Or have a friend with a business?"

"No and no."

I slowed down purposefully to catch the next red light.

"Do you know anybody who might have had a reason to harm Suzanna?"

"No." Kemp's jaw muscles tightened.

"Had she experienced anything unusual lately? Been approached by a stranger? Maybe been involved in a road rage incident?"

"Not that I know of."

The light changed, and I waited too long to take off. The driver behind me honked his horn. I ignored him.

"Maybe Suzanna told a friend something," I said. "Have you called her girlfriends?"

Kemp gave me a look. "I wouldn't know who to call. You'd have to ask Mrs. Hernandez, our live-in. She knows more about Suzanna's schedule than anyone."

What an impersonal ass. Had he paid any attention to poor Suzanna's schedule? I made a left turn, taking us away from the building that houses the D.A.'s office. The move didn't faze Kemp.

"Aren't you curious why she went to the warehouse?"

"Of course I am," he snapped. "Whatever the hell she was doing ended up getting her killed, for God's sake. And *you* — if you'd kept your eyes open, the cops would have her killer behind bars."

I flinched. Okay, so maybe he was justified for hating me today, but I remembered he was a jerk before his wife was murdered.

"Hard to believe you didn't see the shooter," he went on. "What happened? You fall asleep on the job?"

My grip tightened on the steering wheel. "No. I saw her get hit. The shooter wasn't in sight. If he had been, I could assure the police that it wasn't you."

"What are you insinuating?"

"Not a thing," I said, dripping sarcasm. "I just hope you have a good alibi. Where were you last night while your wife and I were up on Yale Street?"

"That's none of your goddamned business." His frown deepened, the jaw muscles working some more.

"Maybe not," I said, "but your attorney will need to know." Approaching another intersection, I turned on my blinker.

"I don't need any damned attorney. I already told your buddy Alexander that earlier." Kemp's face screwed up and he shifted in his seat, leaning forward to check out street signs. "Shouldn't we be there by now? Where the hell are we?"

The light turned green, and I continued through the intersection. "You really ought to take the advice of professionals, Dr. Kemp. Meeting with the police alone is not a good idea." I dared a glance in his direction.

Realization dawned on Kemp's face, angry red splotches already coloring his cheeks. "You bitch!" He pulled on the door handle, but the lock held. "Let me the hell out of here."

"Sorry," I said, accelerating. "No can do." I gritted my teeth, worrying for a second that Kemp might grab the steering wheel and cause an accident.

He punched the window control, but I'd locked that, too. He pounded a fist on the glass. "You're goddamn kidnapping me. Take me back there right now."

"You're not going back until you have an attorney to represent your interests. Wade should be calling any minute. He's contacting Joe Garrett, one of the best criminal—"

"I know who Joe Garrett is. I don't need him. You're the one who'll need an attorney if you don't let me out of this truck this goddamned minute!"

I felt like belting the guy. "You know, I find your attitude nauseating. Wade's trying to help you."

"Bullshit. The only thing he cares about is keeping those high-dollar malpractice cases Dad refers to his firm."

What? I didn't know anything about Kemp's father. I did know Ed Kemp was the most obnoxious man I'd ever dealt with. Instead of telling him that in so many words, I said, "You keep this up and you'll do one bang-up job of convincing the police you *were* involved in your wife's death."

He collapsed against the seat. "I had nothing to do with it."

"Then where were you last night?"

"I had an appointment."

I tried to calm my breathing. "Okay, an alibi's good. Who were you with?"

"I don't have to tell you that."

Damn him. "Well, you'll have to tell the cops. They'll need name, address, and phone number. You'd better be ready with that information."

"What if I refuse?"

I'd had enough of the jerk. "Hang yourself if you want to," I said. "I won't lose any sleep over it."

We drove around downtown for another ten minutes, giving each other the silent treatment, before Wade called to let me know he'd caught up with Joe Garrett. By the time I dropped Kemp off back at the police station, Garrett was waiting on the front steps. The doctor bolted from the truck like a cat with its tail on fire.

Need to quiz the friends she knew,
So that's why I came to you.
Is there anything you can do,
Help me, please, I need a clue.

CHAPTER 7

Given Kemp's attitude, I expected him to be even more of a suspect after the police interrogation. Garrett would likely come out of the meeting handing me a "to-do" list. Regardless of the outcome, I felt like I owed Suzanna Kemp. Someone had to find out what really happened to her, and if that someone was me, so be it. I wanted a chance to question Mrs. Hernandez, Kemp's housekeeper, and since the doctor was occupied this seemed as good a time as any. I headed for West U.

At Kemp's house, I avoided looking at the roped-off crime scene out front and went around to the back door. Gathering my thoughts to talk to the grandmotherly housekeeper, I was surprised when a middle-aged brunette holding a toddler answered my ring. The boy had blond hair, but his face was a miniature image of Ed Kemp.

The woman frowned slightly. "May I help you?"

"I'm Corie McKenna, an investigator working for Dr. Kemp." I extended a hand, and she wordlessly juggled the child to shake it.

"Nice to meet you. I'm Vivian Coulter, a friend of the family," she said. "Come in, please." She stepped aside, motioning for me to enter. When my eyes had adjusted from the bright sunlight, I got a clear view of her stylish business suit and felt underdressed in my sweats.

"I can't believe they're questioning Edward," she whispered, as if the boy would understand his father was a suspect. "This is a horrible tragedy. So shocking." Her voice had a twinge of an English accent.

"Yes, it's very sad." I wondered if she'd have any information that would help solve the case. "Have you known the Kemps very long?"

"Oh, my family and Edward's go way back. I left work as soon as I heard the awful news." Vivian tucked the little boy's striped shirt in around the straps of his bright blue overalls. "My father has some business associates in from the Middle East," she went on, "and it's quite hectic, but a friend in need is more important than any business."

"It's good of you to help out," I said. Though I didn't know Vivian, I guessed her age at between forty and forty-five and decided she must be one of the four daughters of Winston Coulter, owner of Coulter Oil Company. Growing up in the elite River Oaks section of Houston, I heard a lot about "who's who," even though I never cared and made every attempt to stay away from social events. But Vivian's accent didn't fit. The Coulters I had in mind were native Houstonians.

The little boy started whining, and she stroked his hair. "Poor baby needs his mama," she crooned.

Not wanting to think about the child growing up motherless, I asked another question. "Did you know Suzanna very well?"

Vivian looked up, pursing her lips. "We met from time to time. I hope the police will realize they're on the wrong track."

"Don't worry. Dr. Kemp's attorney is with him. In the meantime, I'd like to learn more about Suzanna's schedule, her activities. Can you help me out?"

"Not really." Vivian grimaced. "My job keeps me occupied. I haven't visited with her in quite some time."

"I see." Looked like Vivian was a dead end as far as getting more personal information about Suzanna. I glanced around the kitchen, decorated in blue and white gingham with a sunflower motif. "Well then, is Mrs. Hernandez here? Dr. Kemp suggested I talk to her."

"She went to the market," Vivian said, "but you're welcome to wait. Why don't we make ourselves more comfortable?" I turned down her offer of iced tea, then followed her into the adjoining family room, sinking into the thick rose-colored cushion on an oversized rocking chair.

"I don't have much time," I said, checking my watch. I didn't want to hang around long enough to run into the doctor when he returned home.

"She won't be much longer." Vivian took a seat on an L-shaped sofa that was covered with a mauve and cream patterned fabric and nestled Eddie on the cushion next to her. He yawned and his eyelids fluttered sleepily.

I looked around the room, at a toy box in one corner opposite a sewing machine draped with blue flannel fabric, to child-care magazines lining the coffee table top. I couldn't imagine Ed Kemp setting foot in the cozy room.

Vivian studied me for a moment, smoothing her chic upswept hair with a manicured hand. "Are you the investigator who witnessed the shooting?"

"Unfortunately, yes."

"I'm so glad you're staying on top of the case," she said. "They *must* find out who did this. The police can't seriously believe Edward was involved." Vivian tapped out a rhythmic beat on the parquet floor.

I shrugged. "Questioning the spouse isn't unusual in this sort of case."

Vivian looked outraged. "But you were there. You

would have seen Edward. Did you see anyone?"

"No, I didn't."

"Well, it wasn't him," she said, her foot tapping faster. "He's a good man from a good family. They're wasting time. You're going to set the police straight, aren't you?"

I didn't like her telling me what to do. "Believe me, if I'd seen anything important, I would have reported it."

"But you must have seen *something*," Vivian said, crossing her arms over her chest. "Treating an innocent man like a criminal after he's lost his wife—why, it's simply heartless!"

Her sharp tone must have scared the baby. He started to cry, and Vivian looked like she might do the same. She picked up Eddie and cradled him against her shoulder, patting his back.

"I'm really out of time," I said, standing. "Try not to worry. Dr. Kemp has a great lawyer."

Vivian didn't attempt to stop me as I left the house the way I'd come. Outside, I met up with Mrs. Hernandez as she approached the back door, carrying two grocery sacks.

Her dark eyes fixed on me. "You."

In spite of her uninviting expression, I forged ahead. "I hate to intrude at this sad time, but I have a few questions to ask you."

A look of disgust washed over her face. "You work for *him*." Her emphasis equated Ed Kemp with some disgusting creature. Maybe a snake or a rat.

"So do you," I said, then chastised myself for acting petty when the woman was obviously grieving. I didn't like being on Kemp's team, but I had a job to do.

"I'm sorry," I said. "That was out of line."

"Is okay," said Mrs. Hernandez, a half-smile curving her lips. "I see you no like him either."

"I'm not on anyone's side," I said. "The truth is what

matters. Can we sit down here for a minute?" I indicated the redwood patio furniture, not wanting to go back inside with Vivian Coulter there.

"*Sí*." She placed the groceries on the patio table. The temperature was cold enough that she wouldn't have to worry about anything spoiling.

"I was here for the *señora*," she said. "Now, I am here for little Eddie. *Never* for Mr. Ed." She stuck out her chin.

"Dr. Kemp didn't know much about his wife's friends or places she went," I said. "He thought you might."

Mrs. Hernandez nodded, but said nothing. I'd have to phrase my questions carefully to get her talking.

"Did Mrs. Kemp go out often?"

"No." The housekeeper's gaze focused on the shrubbery surrounding the porch.

"When she did, do you know where she went?" I tried to keep a light and friendly tone. The woman's expression softened slightly.

"She go shopping. Señora Suzanna, she like to shop." Her left hand fluttered as she spoke. "Even the groceries. I say I will do food shopping, but the *señora* say no, that she do it herself. She take little Eddie with her. Such a nice lady, Señora Suzanna."

I sighed. "Did she ever have friends over when Dr. Kemp was at work?"

"No." Mrs. Hernandez frowned.

"What about family?"

"No. She always say little Eddie is her only family."

I made a mental note to ask Dr. Kemp about Suzanna's relatives. "Where else did she go?"

"To the gym," Mrs. Hernandez replied. "Almost every day."

Finally, some concrete information. "Do you know which gym?"

"Of course," she replied with confidence. "Is called Total Fitness. It is on Kirby. Whenever Señora Suzanna leave little Eddie with me, she write a phone number on blackboard next to telephone. She always tell me, in case of emergency."

My ears perked up as I jotted down the name of the gym. "What about last night? Where did she go last night?" The housekeeper's face scrunched up. Looking like she might burst into tears, she lowered her head, putting her face in her hands. Her shoulders heaved.

I walked over to stand beside her. "Please, if you know something, tell me." I caught a glimpse of the blue checked kitchen curtain moving and wondered if Vivian Coulter were watching us.

After a few seconds, the housekeeper looked up. "It is that woman's fault," she said, dark eyes flickering. "She calls Señora Suzanna."

"Vivian Coulter?"

"No." The old woman shook her head.

"Then who?"

"*No sé.* She no tell me. She only ask for the *señora.* If only she had not called. The *señora* is too nice, wanting to help always. The woman, she has some kind of trouble. I hear the Señora talking. She only want to help. Then she start going out at night."

"Are you sure the caller was a woman?" I wouldn't blame Suzanna if she had another man waiting in the wings. Maybe someone with a little compassion.

Anger filled the housekeeper's eyes. "*Sí.* Señora Suzanna not with another man. She is good person, not like *him*," she said, using that emphasis of loathing again.

I went back to my chair, leaning against the green-striped cushions. Who was the mystery caller, and why did her calls take Suzanna away from home in the evenings? Was it a call from her that took Suzanna to the warehouse on Yale

Street?

"How long has this been going on?"

Mrs. Hernandez put a finger to her brow, deep in thought. Finally, she answered. "She start calling two weeks ago. Señora Suzanna was baking little Eddie's first birthday cake, is how I remember. A few nights later she go out. She stay away for hours. I start to worry."

"Do you have *any* idea where she was going?"

Mrs. Hernandez shook her head. "No, *no sé.*"

"When was the last time she called?"

"Yesterday. In the afternoon." Mrs. Hernandez wiped at her eyes with the back of a hand.

"You're sure Vivian Coulter doesn't have anything to do with this? She said she's a friend of the family."

Mrs. Hernandez stood abruptly. "No. She Mr. Ed's *friend*, not Señora Suzanna's. She know nothing."

"You don't mean she's the doctor's girlfriend?" Surely a lover wouldn't come over like this, so soon after the wife's death.

"One of Mr. Ed's girlfriends," Mrs. Hernandez sneered.

I felt as disgusted as she sounded. I wondered if the housekeeper called Kemp "Mr. Ed" because it reminded her of the talking horse on television. Maybe the rear quarters of the horse in particular. It worked for me.

Let's check it out;
C'mon, let's go and see.
What's this all about?
Makes no sense to me.

CHAPTER 8

Around five, Joe Garrett called me at home to say Kemp hadn't been arrested. Yet. The police hadn't dismissed him as a suspect either. Since all Garrett's time was going to be eaten up by a complex racketeering trial come Monday, he asked me to check into the Kemp case. If the doctor was charged with murder, Garrett wanted to be ready. Best-case scenario, I'd come up with an alternate suspect.

My muscles had tightened at the thought of working on Kemp's defense, but all clients can't be friendly and personable. I'd have to get over it. After jotting down notes from my conversation with Garrett, I headed outside with Midnite to work off some stress. The dog and I were involved in a rousing game of driveway basketball when a gold Mercedes pulled in and stopped a few yards short of us.

"Uh-oh, it's your Grandma." I laughed at how the very proper Olivia Poole would react if she'd heard me. Though we had finally come to accept the dramatic difference in our personalities, Mother wouldn't think it cute to be called grandmother to a dog.

The passenger door opened, and I realized she wasn't alone. Dad, looking trim in gym shorts and a striped polo shirt, popped out of the car and headed toward us.

"How's my girl?" He enveloped me in a warm hug, then pulled the ever-present lollipop from his mouth to give me a sticky, strawberry-scented kiss on the cheek. Midnite sat at attention, looking for either her share of affection or a chance at the candy.

"Fine, Dad. What's going on?" I motioned toward the car, where Mother had stayed behind the wheel. Realizing she wouldn't get out with Midnite around, I opened the gate and let the dog into the backyard.

Dad leaned close. "Your mother kidnapped me from a racquetball tournament," he said. "She's dragging me to a party at Muriel's tonight. Ugh."

I started to laugh, then stopped short. I hoped she didn't plan on taking me, too. The combined matchmaking efforts of Mother and her best friend, Muriel, were double trouble, and were to be avoided at all costs. Their latest target was Jon Longenbotham, and I couldn't take another evening listening to him brag about his new hotel chain.

"What fun," I said, frowning. "Too bad I'm working tonight."

Dad grabbed my shoulder. "Take me with you. Please."

"What are you two cooking up?" Mother stood behind us, wearing a purple Armani suit and gobs of jewelry. Her auburn hair turned under perfectly at chin length, as if ordered to do so. I tugged on the scraggly ends of my ponytail, tightening the elastic band holding the hair in place.

"Nothing, dear." Dad planted a sticky kiss on her mouth.

She made a face. "Frank, please." She turned to me, licking her lips. "Hello, Corinne darling. We stopped by to make sure you're all right."

"I'm great. You look nice. All dressed up for Muriel's party, I see."

"Oh, this old thing." She brushed at her jacket lapel. "It's much too informal for the party. I've come from a committee meeting. We're finishing last-minute plans for the gala on Thursday. You haven't forgotten, have you?"

"How could I?" I smiled, trying to figure out what she was talking about. She has so many parties, dinners, and extravaganzas I never can keep them straight.

Dad touched my arm. "We actually came over because your mother heard you witnessed the Kemp shooting."

I leaned against the fence, surprised. "How did you find out?"

"*Everyone* at the meeting knew what happened," she said, "except for me. Why didn't you call?"

I shrugged. "My cases are confidential." Not to mention I didn't want to fuel the gossip mill.

She scrutinized my face. "Are you sure you're okay?"

"Positive."

"You look a little peaked." She brushed a stray hair from my forehead, a ruse for checking my temperature.

"Just busy, that's all," I said.

Mother grimaced. "I don't understand why you won't get out of this dangerous line of work."

"I wasn't in danger, Mother."

"Well, any time my daughter's in the vicinity of a criminal is too dangerous in my opinion."

"I'm not quitting my job, so we don't need to have this conversation." Again.

Mother rolled her eyes. "Of course you won't quit. Why do I even bother?"

"Good question," said Dad.

She gave him a look that spoke volumes, then turned back to me. "Well, I find it appalling the authorities would suspect Edward Kemp. There's no telling what that little fortune hunter he married was involved in."

"What?" Dad and I said in unison.

"Frank, you remember meeting Suzanna Kemp. Last year at the hospital foundation dinner." She raised a perfectly groomed eyebrow.

Dad rolled his eyes. "Maybe, but I didn't *know* her, and I don't believe you did either." For nearly forty years, he'd been trying to take the edge off Mother's prejudices and preconceived attitudes, with little success.

"I have good sense when it comes to people, Frank." She sniffed. "As far as I'm concerned, the woman manipulated herself into a life she wasn't cut out for. She may have been beautiful, but she had no class. Anyone could see that."

"Anyone who is anyone," Dad muttered.

"What was that?" Mom said.

"Never mind. It's a long uphill road, and I'm losing ground." He and I exchanged a look. "We're glad you're okay, honey."

"I think Dad stopped in to get the scoop from an eyewitness to murder," I joked, hoping to lighten Mother's mood. "You know how he is."

Dad owns the *Houston Globe* newspaper, but he leaves management duties to my cousin Bradley, preferring the role of roving reporter.

"Yes, and you're exactly like him." She smiled and pecked my cheek, then turned to Dad, taking his arm. "We must run, Frank. We can't be late."

When they drove away, I couldn't believe my luck. She hadn't begged me to come along. Maybe she thought I'd been through enough stress for one weekend. True enough. I retrieved the basketball, dribbled it in a circle, and took a few practice shots as I considered what she'd said about Suzanna.

Mother clearly had an attitude about the woman. More often than not her views are in direct proportion to people's rung on the social ladder, a tendency I hated. I would probably never completely forgive her for laying that trip on David and his "common" family from Louisiana. Yet she traveled in the same social circles as the Kemps and could have heard something to justify slandering Suzanna. If she'd seen Suzanna visiting that seedy warehouse it would have certainly skewed her view of the woman. Which brought me back to wondering exactly what Suzanna had been up to before she died.

I tried a long shot, missed, and let the ball bounce into the side yard. That's it! Enough of this guessing game. Odds were high that one of the keys on Suzanna's ring would fit the door to that warehouse, and I wanted to check the place out. I hurried inside to change from my light grey sweats into dark, sneaking-around clothes.

***

Dusk had fallen when I turned onto the 610 Loop entrance ramp. A light rain pattered the windshield. I had brought Midnite along, partly because she loved going for rides, mostly because she'd alert me if anyone else was in the warehouse vicinity. The dog turned in circles on the passenger seat and finally settled herself in a sitting position, her nose almost touching the windshield. Her breath fogged a circle on the glass, so I turned the heater down and cranked up the blower.

When I pulled into the warehouse parking lot, Midnite jerked in her seat and moved restlessly next to me. Everything looked the same as it had the night before. Dingy, quiet, and deserted. Except tonight the pavement was wet.

"Here we go, girl," I said, attaching a leash to her collar. "Let's see if anybody's around." Despite the rain and chilly temperature, I started to sweat as we circled the parking area on foot. Probably nerves. After convincing myself we were alone, I stopped back at the truck, picked up my flashlight, and headed for the door Suzanna had entered. With the gloomy weather, darkness had descended more rapidly than usual. Midnite panted beside me on the front step, rain water dripping off her jet-black fur.

Shining the light through the dirty pane in the door, I saw a small empty office area. Nobody would have an alarm on a run-down space like this, would they? I started trying keys. There were only four on the ring and the second one slid into the lock, easily turning back the deadbolt.

My heart thudded as I stepped across the threshold into the vacant room and held my breath, waiting for an alarm to blare. Nothing. The place smelled stale and dusty. The only sound was Midnite's nails clicking on the linoleum floor as she paced in a semi-circle in front of me. We went through an archway into a short hall with three doors. The first two led to empty windowless rooms. Nothing to see except spider webs and a collection of dead roaches.

I opened the third door slowly, peering into the blackness beyond. I lifted the flashlight, shining it across the enormous room. The place looked about the size of a grocery store, half of it containing long rows of heavy metal warehouse shelving. The unshelved portion looked like a furniture store with row after row of furniture lining the space. The odors of lemon oil and dust mingled into that musty old smell I remembered from David's grandparents' house.

I walked down the first row of furniture, checking out tables of all sizes—coffee tables, end tables, an enormous, ornate Mediterranean dining table with at least twenty-four matching chairs lined up like soldiers, several buffets, and a large china cabinet. The stuff was good quality, but none of it looked new. Not that it was easy to tell through the thick layer of dust coating each piece. Why hadn't the furniture been crated or at least covered up?

The second row contained bedroom furniture—beds, dressers, antique armoires. Midnite especially enjoyed sniffing the stacked mattresses and box springs. We passed a huge desk, leather chairs, half a dozen sofas, and a collection of bookcases. So far nothing to give me even the teensiest clue why Suzanna would have come here.

Turning to the shelving, I looked over a section containing hundreds of stacked boxes. Many of them were labeled "books." There were at least thirty marked either "crystal" or "china." I opened a few of the boxes to confirm that they held what was indicated and found Waterford crystal and Wedgewood china delicately packed.

Suddenly, Midnite was in a frenzy, yanking me around a corner. When I got my footing I raised the flashlight and the beam glared off yellowish eyes. I screamed, jumping back before daring another look. The devilish eyes belonged to a stuffed monkey, its teeth bared. What on earth? I shined the flashlight along the row, past stuffed heads of deer and elk, then jumped again when I saw the full stuffed body of a lioness. Midnite began barking, alternately lunging at the wild animal and backing up as if she expected it to attack us.

"Hush, baby," I said, patting the dog's head, "they're dead. They can't hurt us."

After a few minutes, I was able to coax her away from the animals, and we moved on to a row that held dozens of flat packages wrapped in brown paper. From the size, I guessed art work or mirrors. I flashed my light upward to a row of immense brightly-painted pottery urns that occupied the top shelf. There sure was a ton of furniture in this place, probably enough to fill my parents' thirty-room house. Where on earth had all this stuff come from?

I was about to move on when I heard a shuffling noise. I froze, my heart hammering. What if Midnite's barking had drawn the attention of a security guard? I hadn't seen any sign of a guard, but that didn't mean there wasn't one. I held my breath as Midnite whimpered, pulling on the leash. The noise moved closer. Squeaking noises came from the direction of the shelves. The dog hauled me down the aisle, running so fast I had to let her go or risk losing an arm trying to hold her back. When I released the leash, she took off toward the far wall.

Then something ran across my foot. I screamed again. Rats! Damn!

I ran toward the front door as if my life depended on it. "Midnite, come! Come!" I repeated the command, waving the beam of light back and forth across the warehouse floor, looking for her. I debated going after her and taking another look around. There had to be some clue about why Suzanna had come here. But there wasn't, I told myself.

Finally, Midnite trotted up to me, tail wagging at a fast clip. When she got closer, I grabbed at the end of her leash, but stopped in mid-reach when she dropped something at my feet. I shined the light from Midnite's proud face to the dead rat on the floor.

Granted, the thing looked like it'd been dead for some time, but that didn't make me feel any better. I shuddered and dragged her out of the building as fast as I could. After locking the door behind us, we ran across the parking lot and jumped into the truck. Midnite, really excited now, cooperated, although I think she would have preferred bringing along her prize. I hit the door locks and started up the engine.

"Damned rats. One ran over my foot, you know that? Gross."

Midnite drooled happily on the passenger seat, watching buildings fly by as I sped away.

After a few minutes, I had calmed down enough to be thankful no one had seen my childish performance. It wasn't the first rodent I'd come in contact with since working on this case. There was Ed Kemp, too. But why would anyone in their right mind store such expensive belongings in a place infested with rats?

Heard she liked to work out,
So I'm gonna go and see.
Find out what she was about
Would you like to help me?

CHAPTER 9

"Rats? Yuk!" Kit Thompson jabbed her fork into a stack of pancakes and pulled off a large bite, swishing it around in the maple syrup pool on her plate. She popped the soggy dough into her mouth. About six months ago, the twelve-year-old had moved in next door to me with her mother, and Midnite and I have enjoyed her company ever since. Though I've never had kids of my own, I can't help being critical of Kit's mother, who goes out partying after work more nights than not, leaving the girl home alone. Jean Thompson was currently sleeping off an all-nighter, so Kit joined me and Reba for a Sunday-morning IHOP breakfast. I'd filled them in on my visit to the warehouse.

"You should have seen Midnite," I said, laughing. "She looked so proud." I could joke now, the next morning, after the sensation of little feet running across my shoe had faded.

"Good lord," Reba said, "what were you doin' out there on a Saturday night in the first place? Your social life needs serious help."

Kit giggled, her eyes sparkling. She reminded me of myself at that age, tall and gangly. With her long, naturally wavy brown hair, people might mistake us for mother and daughter, but Reba was the one Kit idolized. Every time I bring the two of them together, I hope the world will forgive me for contributing to the development of a Reba clone.

But then everyone in the restaurant was aware of Reba. Her jeans fit like pantyhose, and she had the attention of every male in the place. She wore a hot pink, western-cut shirt that matched her one-of-a-kind boots. Gold dangling earrings jingled with every move, almost brushing her shoulders.

"And I suppose you'll be fixing up my social calendar," I said to Reba, "beginning with a trip to Nashville? What's the story?"

Reba took her time swallowing a mouthful of biscuit and gravy. "We have great songs," she said, "and I think we're ready for Music Row. We'll be the hottest new act around—Hofstetler & McKenna. You know, like Brooks & Dunn. Whaddya think?"

"Are you nuts?" I shook my head.

"All right, McKenna & Hofstetler. Makes no difference to me. You call it."

"You're crazy. The songwriting is fun, but we're strictly amateurs." And I'm not going anywhere, I added to myself. She must have heard my silent comment, because the Reba-sweet-talk expression formed on her face.

"Corie, honey," Reba drawled. "You have more talent than any ol' body in Nashville. I feel it. I heard 'bout a songwriter's club over there, and they have big connections. I mean big, important connections. We meet with them. Once they hear you sing, we're in."

"In?" What was she thinking?

Kit's head ping-ponged between us. She was entranced in our conversation, her pancakes forgotten. Reba took a bite of sausage.

"I'm too busy to consider a trip," I said. "My mind's preoccupied with the Kemp case."

I didn't want to talk about Nashville and gave Reba a

look that said so. She opened her mouth, then grinned and snapped it shut. I knew she'd bring the subject up again.

"I suppose the furniture in that warehouse was somehow important to Suzanna Kemp, but why eludes me." I twirled my glass in a wet circle on the table. "Our client claims to know nothing about the place."

"Maybe she has friends who are moving," Reba said, "and it's their stuff in the warehouse. Temporary storage between houses."

"I thought about that, but you should see the dust. It's been there a long time." I took the last bite of my ham-and-cheese omelette, chasing it with a swallow of Coke. "One thing's for sure. The cops let Kemp go home yesterday, but he's not clear yet. If they conclude he's guilty, their investigation ends and the D.A.'s office takes over. So Garrett's looking to me for some answers."

"This is so cool," Kit said, unsuccessfully trying to wipe syrup off her mouth with a paper napkin. She loved listening to me talk about work.

"I wouldn't call it cool," I said. "It's tragic."

"But it's so exciting," Kit said, her eyes wide. "Did he do it?"

"I don't know."

Kit tried to rid her hands of the sticky napkin. "You're supposed to say 'no.' The client is always innocent until proven guilty beyond a reasonable doubt." The law fascinated Kit, and she frequently talked about becoming a famous trial lawyer.

Reba laughed. "You're right about that, kid."

"So, I guess y'all think I should check out his alibi," I said.

"Of course," said Kit.

Reba nibbled on a cinnamon bun. "You have to consider the possibility the jerk *was* involved. Not the smartest way to get rid of a wife, but smarts don't come naturally to men, you know?"

"Criminals aren't known for making intelligent decisions," I said. I tried not to encourage Reba's disparaging remarks about men, even when she was right. Especially not in front of Kit, who already had too much negative personal experience when it came to the male gender. Her divorced mother entertained a steady stream of boyfriends.

Finishing my Coke, I remembered Brenda Johnson, a less-than-intelligent former client of Wade's whose husband had been killed while their divorce case was pending. She was charged with hiring someone to murder him. Wade told her not to speak with anyone about the case. A few days later, the hired gun made a deal with the prosecutor and called Brenda, asking for the money she'd promised him. Did she say "what money?" No, she said "I told you, I can't get the money until the insurance company pays me." The tape-recorded phone conversation convicted her. Surely Ed Kemp was smarter than Brenda Johnson.

By the time Kit and I got home, I had decided my next course of action should be to visit Suzanna's gym, Total Fitness, and see what I could learn there. After the fat-filled breakfast I'd eaten, the idea of going to a gym seemed ridiculous.

Not having any fashionable work-out attire, I changed into an old pair of basketball shorts and a sweatshirt. When I came downstairs, I found Kit and Midnite in the kitchen, snacking on Fig Newtons. I took the package away so they wouldn't both overdose on sugar. I knew Kit would want to go with me and wasn't sure how to handle the situation. I felt sorry for her, having to spend so much time alone. She deserved better. The phone rang, solving my dilemma.

"Do I have to?" Kit moaned into the phone, sounding disappointed. "All right." She hung up without saying goodbye.

"Mothers can be a real pain." She headed for the back door, feet dragging. "Thanks for the breakfast. Mom finally woke up. She says we're going to The Galleria. Shopping. Whoop-dee-do."

"Maybe she'll buy you something nice." I tried to sound enthusiastic, knowing Kit felt the same way I did about shopping. Give me a mail order catalog any day.

"Oh, we don't buy anything." Kit rolled her eyes. "It's the usual first, third, and fifth weekend routine. Time to hit on divorced dads. If the mall doesn't work, she might try a movie, maybe a pizza place. Give me a break."

On the way to Total Fitness, I thought about Jean Thompson and her relentless man-hunting. I sure hoped the woman never ran into Wade and his kids. Then I wondered what kind of visitation agreement she had with her ex. In the three months since the Thompsons had moved in next door, I'd never heard a word about Kit's father. Worried that he didn't care enough to ever visit his daughter, I made a mental note to spend more time with her.

***

The gym was easy to find, occupying the end of a strip shopping center that housed a variety of stores and restaurants. I sat in the truck for a minute, reluctant to go inside. Sports are fun, but regular exercise of any shape or form is not my idea of a good time. The parking lot was crowded. Impossible to imagine so many people would go to work out voluntarily. Mother regularly offers me the services of her personal trainer, warning how I'm approaching "that age." Personal trainer or no, it would still be exercise. I declined every time she brought up the subject.

Greeting the muscular young man behind the front desk, I decided to start by telling the truth.

"I've never worked out in a gym," I said. "Could you

show me around—explain some of this stuff to me?" I pointed a thumb toward a floor filled with complicated-looking equipment. Then I added a lie. "I'm thinking about joining."

My clothes made my story about never working out in a gym very believable, especially when compared with the fashionable outfits on the women I saw jumping around in the glass-walled aerobics room.

"No prob," said the guy, coming from behind the counter. "My name's Nick. Follow me."

No prob, I thought, watching his shapely rear view in skimpy knit shorts. I hadn't taken much of an interest in men since losing David, but I didn't mind looking. Maybe I *could* understand how a gym would hold a woman's interest. Men of various shapes and levels of muscular tone turned to look as I followed Nick across the floor. Feeling their eyes on me, I thought about Jean Thompson. No doubt she'd already figured out gyms are the perfect hunting ground for an eager and willing female.

Total Fitness was a moderately sized establishment, nothing like the huge conglomerates that lure new members through bargain prices and advertising done on television or by movie stars. Nick stopped at a contraption labeled *Leg Press*. He proceeded to show me how to adjust the machine for my height and set the weight to my level of fitness. I must have looked more fit than I was, because I could hardly move my legs at the weight he'd chosen. As he adjusted it again, I started asking questions.

"You work out much?" I asked, admiring his muscles.

"Every day," he answered with a wink, motioning to the machine. "Try twelve reps."

I grimaced and started pushing. My angel pendant slid down, hanging across my armpit. I grabbed the chain and stuffed the necklace under my shirt.

"We have a special going on right now," Nick said. "Great time to join."

"That's good news," I said, cutting off his sales pitch. "One of my friends works out here. Maybe you know her." I grunted, straightening my legs to lift the weight.

"Oh yeah? Who?"

"Suzanna Kemp." I started to breathe heavy on the sixth rep.

Nick looked thoughtful, then shook his head. "No, don't think I do."

"I have a picture." I pulled my legs in too fast, letting the weight fall. Loud clanging turned all heads in my direction.

"Sorry." I stood and reached into my pocket, pulling out the picture Ed Kemp had given me, and shoved it under Nick's nose.

He hesitated before looking at the picture, no doubt wondering why I had a friend's picture stuffed into my gym shorts. But he didn't question me, grinning instead. "Oh, yeah! Suzie Q."

"Suzie Q?"

"Yeah, that's what we call her."

I returned to the bench, not in position to continue lifting. Nick's grin told me he hadn't heard about Suzanna's death yet.

"Who calls her that?"

"Oh, everybody," Nick said. He pointed to the weights. "You're not finished."

I reluctantly continued the exercise.

"Now, about our special," Nick said. "The basic membership fee is only fifty bucks, if you join today or tomorrow." He noticed I'd finished twelve repetitions and told me to do another set.

"Sounds reasonable," I said, before inhaling deeply

and starting over. "Suzie comes here a lot?"

"Yeah," Nick said, filling in something on my enrollment card. "Every weekday."

That's why he hadn't missed her yet. "She always wanted me to come work out with her, but I never did," I said. "She probably found some other friends to work out with, huh?" I finished, breathing heavily, and he led me to the next machine.

"Yeah." He wisely set the weight to only ten pounds for leg curls, marked that on my card, and told me to do twelve reps again.

When I didn't begin immediately, he looked up.

"Who does Suzie hang out with here?" I said. "Anyone special?"

The grin returned. It was pretty easy to get him off his subject. "Yeah. Matter of fact, her friend is one hot babe." He pulled at the neck of his T-shirt as though just thinking about her was making him suffocate.

"Who's that?"

"Mitzi Martin." He raised his eyebrows.

"I don't think I know her." I lay face down on the bench and started the curls. "Does Suzie hang out with any guys?" My thighs already ached on the second rep.

"Not really," said Nick. "But some jerk named Larry hangs around her. Seems to bug her. He's not a member, so we kick him out when he shows."

I quietly allowed Nick to explain the other machines to me and listened to the rest of his sales pitch. Before he left me to work out alone, he told me to stop by the front desk to sign up when I finished. I squeezed in one more question. "Has Mitzi been here today?"

He scratched his head. "No, and she usually comes in every morning around eleven. Didn't see her yesterday either."

Not since Suzanna's murder, I thought.

"I'd like to talk to her," I said, making up a story as I went. "I'm having a surprise party for Suzie and I'd like to invite Mitzi. But I don't know where she lives. Can you help me out?"

"Why don'tcha ask Clay, the owner," said Nick. "He has all that junk on the computer." He pointed to a hallway. "First door on the left."

I pretended to concentrate on tricep extensions. As soon as Nick's attention turned to someone else, I went to find the owner. Walking into an office with the name Clayton Mitchell on the door, I gave up all hopes of learning Mitzi Martin's address from him.

Dozens of computer parts lined a Formica-topped table. The cover of the CPU lay on the floor. A man in an aqua shirt with Total Fitness printed on the back leaned over the pieces holding a small screwdriver. When I knocked he stood, unfolding his tall frame from behind the table.

"Hi, Clay Mitchell," he said in a deep voice. "What can I do for you?" The shirt aptly described him.

I was momentarily speechless as we shook hands. It's not often I have to look up to men. This one put a strain on my neck. He had to be at least six foot five. His blond hair was cut neatly around tanned ears, and he sported a trimmed beard and mustache with reddish highlights. He removed his wire-rimmed glasses and placed them on the table. I found myself admiring his warm smile a little too long, almost forgetting why I'd come.

Looking down at the computer parts, I said, "I may be too late. I was hoping for some information you keep on the computer."

Clay laughed, a deep contagious chuckle. I liked him immediately. He turned, pointing to a desk along another wall. "That's the one you're interested in." A fully-assembled computer stood on the desk, the monitor's blue screen emitting a healthy glow.

"Oh, good! I thought you were in real trouble here."

"All is well." He motioned to a side chair. "Have a seat, Miss—"

"Corie McKenna. Your computer had me worried."

"I'll have it back together in no time." Clay chuckled again. "Guess I'm a computer nerd."

I grinned. This guy was definitely no nerd.

"I enjoy fiddling with the blasted things," he said. "Finding out what makes them tick, or not tick, as the case may be. But that's not what you came in here for."

I straightened in the chair, suddenly feeling dowdy in my old clothes. "No, it isn't. I need information on one of your members. Mitzi Martin."

Clay's expression sobered. "This have anything to do with Suzanna Kemp's death?"

So, not everyone here was oblivious to the city's current events. "Yes."

He swiveled his chair from side to side. "I don't pay too much attention to the news, but the name jumped out at me. Mrs. Kemp and her friend were hard to miss. One blonde, one brunette, both very beautiful." Clay stopped swiveling. He stretched his long legs out across the carpet, and they nearly reached the center of the room. "You with the police?"

"No, I'm working on Edward Kemp's case." I reached into my pocket to pull out a business card.

"Oh no, a lawyer?" He feigned a look of horror, then smiled, his hazel eyes crinkling in the corners.

I laughed, shaking my head, and handed him a card. "Not a lawyer. An investigator. Suzanna's husband is our client, but he doesn't know much about her activities. I'm trying to find some friends to talk to."

Clay reached for his glasses and studied my card.

"Corinne. Pretty name."

A blush threatened, and I glanced around the room to ward it off. "I prefer Corie— a little less prim and proper than what my mother had in mind."

He didn't comment further, but turned to the working computer. "Mitzi and Suzanna were certainly friends. Suzanna Kemp was a nice person—the kind that'd do anything for you. I'm sure Mitzi is broken up about her death." He printed out an address and handed me the sheet of paper. "I don't usually give out information this freely, but I'd like to see justice done. Good luck with your case."

"Thanks. I appreciate the help."

His eyes met mine. "Call me if there's anything else I can do, or if you ever have computer problems." Clay's warm handshake lingered longer than necessary, but I didn't mind.

On my way to Mitzi's place, I found myself wishing I could get to know Clayton Mitchell a little better. One way to do that would be to join his gym, but then I'd have to exercise. Might be worth it. Maybe I'd even let him call me Corinne.

Thirty minutes later, I stood at the door of apartment 12F of Bayou Glen Apartments, wondering if I should give up after knocking several times with no answer. A strong breeze blew leaves across the small concrete entry porch. Though the apartment complex was located in an upscale area, the landscaping looked neglected. I turned, wondering which of the covered parking spaces belonged to Mitzi Martin. About half of them were empty.

A man wearing a Houston Texans sweatshirt headed up the sidewalk toward me, holding two bags of groceries balanced on a case of beer. He walked up to the door of 12G.

"Nobody's home," he said, his back to me as he struggled to unlock the door without dropping anything.

He didn't offer anything else and almost closed his

door in my face. I put out a hand to stop it.

"Wait!"

His groceries nearly fell, and he cursed under his breath.

"Excuse me," I said. "Does Mitzi Martin live next door?"

"Yeah," he said. "But she ain't home. You ain't the first person come lookin' for her today either, and I ain't her secretary."

He tried again to close the door, but I blocked it with my shoulder. "Give me a minute, buddy. Who else was here?"

"Some dude in a limo. Sent his driver to the door." The man gave me a disgusted once-over. "Look, she ain't been here since yesterday morning. I saw her take off in the Beamer." He checked his watch. "I'm missin' a ball game here, you know?"

"One more question," I said. "Any idea where I might find her?"

"How the hell do I know, lady? Like I said, I ain't her secretary." He hesitated, then said, "I guess you've been to Whispers."

"What's Whispers?"

"The tittie bar at Westheimer and Seldon," he said. "She dances there." The man muttered "dumb broad" under his breath as he slammed the door in my face.

You didn't know her very well,
Were you truly man and wife?
Say you haven't much to tell,
Did you live a separate life?

CHAPTER 10

Back at my truck, I called information to get a listing for Whispers. So, Suzanna's friend worked at a topless club. I couldn't have been more surprised if Mitzi's neighbor had told me she drove a garbage truck for a living. I wondered if Ed Kemp knew Suzanna's topless-dancing friend. A jerk like him might patronize "men's clubs," but I doubted he'd approve of his wife socializing with their employees.

Humming Garth Brooks' tune about friends in low places, I dialed the club. A recording announced they opened at six on Sunday evenings. Over two hours from now. I decided to drive over anyway, in case Mitzi or any of her coworkers were already there.

I hadn't expected the pristine gray brick building with its ornate leaded glass windows. Huge potted philodendrons lined the circular cobblestone driveway. A sign announced valet parking. If a "tittie bar" could look classy, this one sure did. I pulled up under a black awning that had "Whispers" scrolled across it in hot pink letters, got out, and found the front door locked.

I wondered whether a club patron had been the person looking for Mitzi at home. If she was the hot number I'd been led to believe she was, Mitzi might have jetted off to a tropical island with a sugar daddy for the weekend. I walked around back, but the rear lot was empty. I'd have to call later to see whether Mitzi had reported for work. In the meantime, my stomach complained loudly about missing lunch.

At the James Coney Island down the street, I ordered three of their famous hot dogs all the way, with chili, cheese, and onions. So much for that workout. As I scarfed down the fat-filled meal, I tried to come up with other methods of learning details about Suzanna's life. When I couldn't conjure a more appealing way to move the case forward, I prepared myself for another encounter with Kemp. I thought he'd be a little more agreeable since I was on his side, working to clear his name.

I was wrong.

"What are you doing here?" growled Kemp when he opened his front door. He wore an orange University of Texas sweatshirt over black sweatpants and held a cocktail glass. His wiry hair was either wet or slicked back with some sort of gel.

"Nice to see you, too," I said with a forced smile, exhaling my onion breath in his face. "I have some more questions about Suzanna. May I come in?"

Garrett must have warned him I'd continue working on the case, because he opened the door wider. "Suit yourself."

I entered, noticing his eyes were awfully bloodshot. The strong scent of gin clung to the man. He seemed unsteady as he showed me to the living room where Vivian Coulter sat on a blue plaid sofa, holding the sleeping baby Eddie.

"This is a friend of mine," Kemp said. "Vivian—"

"We've met," Vivian interrupted with a patronizing smile. "Connie, isn't it?"

"Corie," I answered.

My frumpy exercise clothes contrasted sharply with her matching silk tunic and slacks. Diamond studs sparkled on her earlobes. She had a big wet spot on the shoulder of her emerald green top. I grinned. Little Eddie must have gotten her good. I turned to Kemp.

"Vivian and I met yesterday, when I came to speak with Mrs. Hernandez."

"Oh," said Kemp, motioning for me to have a seat. "She's been helping out with my boy." He drained his glass and set it down on the coffee table.

"How thoughtful." I wondered whether Vivian lived close by or had moved in. "Where's Mrs. Hernandez today?"

"She visits her daughter every Sunday," Kemp said, sagging into a navy blue leather recliner. "What do you need this time?"

Drinking obviously didn't improve the man's attitude.

"For starters, I went into the warehouse last night," I said.

Kemp's scowl turned inquisitive. "What did you find?"

"Furniture. Lots of expensive furniture. You know anything about it? Did Suzanna have furniture when you met her? I'm talking enough to fill a mansion."

"No way." The scowl hardened. "She had a few garage sale pieces. We gave them to charity. Why the hell would she go to a warehouse to look at furniture?"

"I was hoping you could answer that," I said.

"Then you're out of luck."

Helpful, as usual. "Today I went to Suzanna's gym," I said, "and was told she usually worked out with her friend Mitzi Martin. Do you know her?"

Kemp shook his head.

"Ever hear Suzanna talk about her?" I had decided not to mention Whispers if he didn't.

Another shake of the head.

"How about a man named Larry?"

Kemp looked more alert. "Who's he?"

"Someone who bothered Suzanna at the gym. I was told they'd thrown him out more than once for harassing her."

"She never said anything about him." Kemp sat up,

perching on the edge of his seat. "What's his last name?"

"I don't know. I was hoping to get that from Mitzi, but she wasn't home."

Vivian, who had been sitting and contentedly patting the baby's diapered bottom, stood suddenly. "He's probably the one who did this," she said, clutching the baby to her chest. "Have you told the officials?"

"The homicide detectives prefer to do their own investigation," I told her.

"You should call them, Edward," she said, turning to Kemp. "He can't get away with this."

"Hold on," I said. "Dr. Kemp isn't calling anyone. First, we don't even know this guy's last name yet. Second, any results of my investigation will be reported to Dr. Kemp's attorney. He makes the decisions."

Vivian's chin jutted defiantly, and I expected a comeback, but she sat down. "I suppose that's right."

I turned to the doctor.

"What about Suzanna's relatives?" I said, remembering Suzanna's comment to the housekeeper that the baby was her only family. "Maybe they know something about this furniture."

Kemp shrugged. "I'm not going to be much help there either. Her parents are dead. I believe her brother is somewhere in Pennsylvania, but I never met him."

"You haven't notified him? I mean, the funeral—"

Kemp shook his head. "I would, but I don't know where to find him. She wouldn't talk about family. Closed up tight whenever I asked any questions, so I stopped asking."

"Who did she talk to? Girlfriends? Coworkers?" Surely the woman had someone to confide in.

"Beats me," Kemp said.

I shook my head. This guy might be the least compassionate husband in history. And what was up between him and Vivian? He didn't seem to be paying much attention to the woman, and she seemed more interested in the baby. Then again, this babysitter thing could all be an act for my benefit.

Grabbing his empty glass, Kemp headed for the wet bar and poured himself a refill. Straight gin. So far, this visit had produced zilch, and if he kept up the drinking he'd be even more useless.

"How about Suzanna's personal things?" I said. "If you don't mind me looking through them, I might be able to find some information useful to your case."

"Help yourself," Kemp said, motioning with his glass. "Up the stairs, second door on the left. Suzanna's study." He gulped the gin, and I turned away, glad to leave him behind.

Upstairs, I ran my hand up the wall to find the light switch and flicked it on. The room was arranged with a desk, chair and a two-drawer file cabinet on one side of the room; on the other was an entertainment center holding a miniature stereo system and a small portable TV. An exercise bike stood in another corner with a basket of wooden alphabet blocks next to it.

Pulling the chair up to the desk, I started going through the drawers and found all the ordinary desk stuff—checks, bills, a box of envelopes, pens, and a roll of postage stamps. Under the phone was a thin address book. I flipped through the pages. There were only a few entries—doctors' offices, drugstores, the gym—no personal numbers.

In the cabinet, everything from bank statements to water bills was meticulously organized in file folders. A quick pass through the canceled checks told me the Kemps weren't paying anyone for rental of the warehouse space I'd seen last night. At least not out of this account.

I moved on to the walk-in closet. Instead of rods for

clothes, three sides were lined with shelves. On a high shelf, I found a fireproof box. Inside it was a smaller box marked "negatives." Suzanna had labeled each folder with the date and a summary of the negatives it held. I removed the top folder marked "Eddie's first birthday." Holding the plastic sleeves encasing strips of negatives up to the light, I could make out pictures of the little boy sitting in a high chair, his hands stuck in the cake.

On the same roll were pictures of what looked like an office. One shot looked like a desk, the next a line-up of tall file cabinets. How odd. Another negative featured a single chair against a wall with a picture hanging above it. Did the woman have a furniture fetish or what? First the warehouse, now this. I quickly glanced through several other sets of negatives, but they were all of little Eddie. Stuffing the first set in my purse, I replaced the others in the box and returned it to the closet.

I had to stretch to reach three larger boxes on the top closet shelf. The first two held an assortment of high-school memorabilia, everything from a dried corsage to silver-and-red pom poms that matched a picture of cheerleader Suzanna Rose Zimmerman in the 1986 yearbook of Quakertown Senior High School.

Riffling the pages of the yearbook, I wondered what had brought Suzanna from Quakertown, Pennsylvania, to Houston, Texas. Suzanna's picture was the last one of the alphabetized graduating class. The comments under her name said "Known for her beautiful hair . . . is a good friend . . . favorite pastimes are driving her Camaro, dancing, and spending time with Larry. . .future undecided."

I stared at the picture of young Suzanna, her pretty eyes gleaming. Could the Larry she'd spent time with in high school be the same one who'd bothered her at the gym in Houston? I scanned the pictures of graduating young men, and found two Larrys. None of the comments about them included Suzanna. I made another pass through the book, on the chance Suzanna had any classmates named Mitzi. She hadn't.

I set the yearbook aside and moved on to the third box, which contained more file folders. I thumbed through bank statements and bills that appeared to be from Suzanna's single days. I pulled out a folder marked "pay stubs." Interesting. Suzanna had worked at Methodist Hospital, which was probably where she'd met her husband.

Before Methodist, she'd worked at a company called Othello Corporation which I'd never heard of. The address on the stub was a post office box, but I might be able to track down the company and find someone who kept in touch with Suzanna. I stuck one Othello stub in the yearbook and replaced the boxes in the closet.

As I left the room, the house was so quiet I wondered whether everyone had decided to join the baby in a nap. Halfway down the stairs, I heard Kemp and Vivian talking, their voices growing louder as they approached the front door. I scooted back upstairs and waited, just out of sight.

"I appreciate your help, honestly Viv, but I need to spend time with my son now. Alone."

"But Edward—"

"No buts." Kemp's voice was firm. "You'd better leave."

Did he really want to spend time with his son, I wondered, or was he worried about how he'd look spending too much time with Vivian so soon after his wife's death?

Vivian gave up her argument. "You be a good boy for Daddy," she said in a baby-talk voice. Then, to Kemp, "Take care, Edward. Call me." The door closed softly behind her.

I'd been so intent on their conversation, I didn't realize at first that footsteps were heading up the stairs. I raced back to the study, flipping the lights on, and threw Suzanna's yearbook open on the desk. Kemp stuck his head in the door ten seconds behind me. He was holding Eddie, the boy's head resting on his father's shoulder. The baby's sleepy eyes opened, not focusing, then drifted shut again.

"This is pretty much a waste of time," Kemp said. "Hope I'm not paying you by the hour."

I gritted my teeth, counting to five before answering. "What's the matter, Dr. Kemp? Is it time for a different girlfriend's shift to begin?"

"Girlfriend?" Kemp said. "What are you talking about?" He hesitated, looking toward the stairs, then back to me. "You mean Vivian?"

"If the shoe fits," I said.

"You're out of line. Viv's an old friend. We dated some when we were kids. Damn nice of her to help out with Eddie, too."

"Whatever." I decided to let it go for now.

"Don't waste my time with some trumped-up bullshit."

I blew out a breath. "For the life of me, I don't know why my mother has always had such good things to say about you."

"Your mother?" Kemp's brows drew together. "Who's your mother?"

"Olivia Poole." With all the benefit work Mother did for the hospital, Kemp would know her even if she hadn't been his patient.

His face reddened. "She's your *mother*?"

"You didn't know? She's terribly upset about your predicament and one of your staunchest supporters. One hundred percent convinced of your innocence. I only wish I felt the same." I smiled sweetly.

Kemp's flush deepened. "Now wait a minute. You can't really believe I had something to do with Suzanna's death."

The baby stirred. I spoke quietly to keep from waking him. "Frankly, Dr. Kemp, you don't sound or act like a man whose wife was just murdered. You've been arrogant, uncooperative, impolite. Your behavior tends to make you look guilty. What do you expect me to think?"

Kemp tensed. "You want cooperation, fine. I'm fucking cooperating. But Suzanna never opened up to me. I don't know what she was doing. I don't know about the warehouse. I don't know her friends. I don't know her family. And I had nothing to do with her death. Period."

The baby woke with a start and began crying.

"Calm down," I said. "You're upsetting Eddie."

"It doesn't take a fucking investigator to see what's going on here," he said, ignoring his son. "I am one pissed-off son of a bitch. First my wife files for divorce, then someone kills her before we even had a chance to talk about it. Oh, and don't forget, the damn cops are trying to pin the murder on me." He turned sharply, walking toward the door, then turned around.

"I need to put Eddie to bed," he said. "Are you finished yet?"

"I think I've had enough for one night," I said through gritted teeth.

Kemp said he didn't mind if I kept Suzanna's yearbook, and I showed myself out. The dash clock read six o'clock when I pulled out of Kemp's driveway, and I suddenly remembered that I had planned to go back to Whispers tonight. After the exhausting session with Kemp, I wasn't up to visiting a topless bar. Instead, I dialed the club on my cellular phone.

A man with a radio announcer's voice answered. "Good evening, you've reached Whispers."

I had expected to hear a female on the other end. "Uh,

hello," I said. "Mitzi Martin, please."

"The girls are working," said the smooth voice. "Is there something I can help you with?"

"I'd like to speak with Mitzi. Is she there?"

"Who wants to know?" The voice was more abrupt now.

"A friend." Either she's there or she's not, I wanted to say.

"Hang on."

I heard a click before a different man picked up the line. "Mr. Atkins tells me you're looking for Miss Martin."

"That's right."

"What's your name?"

"Samantha Shaw." The conversation had me feeling uneasy.

"Miss Shaw, Mitzi's not here tonight, though she should be. I've been trying to find her. Maybe you could help *me*. How do you know my Mitzi?"

His Mitzi? I hesitated. "We're old friends."

"Really? I know all of Mitzi's friends. Have we ever met?"

"How would I know? You haven't told me your name."

"If you were really a friend of Mitzi's, you'd know my name." He spoke with frightening assurance.

"I'm sorry, I don't."

"Tell me where she's staying," he ordered.

"I don't know," I said, louder. I'd had enough of rude men for one day.

"I'll find her," he said. "If you're crossing me, I'll find you, too."

"Just try it," I said, before hanging up.

My first impulse was to drive over to Whispers and talk to this guy, but he'd sounded downright nasty. Showing up there alone wasn't such a good idea. I had to remind myself Mitzi's relationship with him was *not* my business. I needed to stay focused on Suzanna. So, I went home, dialed information for Mitzi's phone number and left a message on her answering machine that I was investigating her friend's death, and asked her to call me as soon as possible.

Later that night, though, I was still thinking about Mitzi and the sticky situations an exotic dancer might face on a daily basis. She may have called Suzanna for help with an annoying customer. And what about that nasty man on the phone? Was he Mitzi's boss? He'd acted more like he owned her. Something about the whole episode just didn't sit right.

One question kept running through my mind. Did Whispers hold such a tight rein on all its employees or just Mitzi Martin?

Wonderin' what the future holds,
And wishin' I could see.
Don't have to be alone I'm told,
There's a chance for you and me.

CHAPTER 11

I had just reached my office Monday morning and was spreading out my assortment of clues from Kemp's house when Reba poked her head in.

"Hey, girl. How's my favorite singin' partner?" Her bubble gum cracked a fast rhythm, and the neon green of her shirt glared across the room.

"So-so." I unfolded the plastic-encased negatives and held them up to the light, hoping Reba wasn't going to start brainstorming about a trip to Nashville again.

"What's this?" She crossed the office and sat on my desk, twisting to get a look at the negatives herself.

"Don't know exactly, but I'm going to have reprints made and find out," I said. "They're Suzanna Kemp's."

"Ah." Reba squinted at the negatives. "Looks pretty boring. An office or somethin'."

"I know, but I'm curious why she'd take them. Could be important."

Reba straightened. "What a case! It's not every day a client comes in for a divorce and ends up charged with murder. More I think about it, more I wonder why we didn't see that doctor was about to go off like a firecracker."

"He's not charged yet," I reminded her. "And last night I settled on reasonable doubt where he's concerned, so don't change my mind."

"You don't think he did it?" Reba's face puckered.

"I have a few other leads to follow up on," I said, skirting the question.

"I could have these made for you," Reba said, taking the negatives and sliding off the desk. "Save you some time."

She was usually swamped with her own duties, especially on Mondays. "You don't have to do that."

"No big deal. You're busy," she said. "That's what friends are for. Always there when you need them."

Huh? I looked up, but she was already gone in a flash of neon. I noticed a pile of pamphlets on the corner of my desk. A bright pink Post-it note on top said "Check these out" in Reba's handwriting. What a con artist.

The pamphlets described hotels and attractions in Nashville. The one on the bottom was a Gray-Line Tours itinerary for a bus trip from Houston to Nashville during the second week of December. A bus trip? She had to be kidding. I tossed the pamphlets into my top desk drawer, shaking my head at Reba's persistence.

Then I turned to Suzanna's yearbook and slipped out her paycheck stub. I planned on making a visit to the hospital to talk with Ed Kemp's co-workers and also to check on former co-workers of Suzanna's. For now, I pulled out the business pages and looked up Othello Corporation. No listing. I called information. They had no record of a company by that name.

A faint noise turned my attention from the project at hand. Maggie Robbins, my former college-mate, stood in the doorway. Not one of my favorite people.

She looked ready to go on the air at a moment's notice, even though she didn't usually appear until the evening news broadcast when she reported on social events around the city. A fuschia blouse with a ruffled neckline brightened her gray tweed suit. She might have worn the cheery color to try and attract attention away from the dark circles under her eyes—the ploy didn't work any better than me trying to mask my surprise at her visit.

"Maggie, what brings you here?" I said, trying to sound hospitable.

Her smile wasn't as wide as usual, but she shook my hand with a firm grasp. "Good to see you, Corinne. We don't keep in touch like we should."

I personally didn't think we should, even preferred not to. In college, we had barely tolerated each other.

"Sorry to barge in without an appointment," said Maggie, "but this is urgent."

Her version of urgent was probably picking up tidbits about my mother or one of the holiday season's events. Might as well ask, and get it over with. "What's the problem?"

She draped herself over a chair, crossed her legs, and smoothed back a strand of her bottle-blonde hair with an unsteady hand. "Is it true you were following Suzanna Kemp the night she was killed?" The question didn't come out with Maggie's usual aplomb. Her voice quivered.

It took a few seconds for her question to sink in, not being what I expected from her.

"You reassigned to the homicide beat?" I said.

"No." Maggie nibbled her lower lip, an uncharacteristic habit.

"Then why do you ask?" I got up and went to the door to see if she had brought her accomplice cameraman with her. The hallway was empty. I shut the door firmly and sat in a chair beside her. "Are you recording this conversation?"

"I wouldn't do that." Her full lips pouted.

Right. "I'm sure you have reliable sources, being in the business, so you already know I was an eyewitness. Why are you here?"

"Because I need to know what happened that night."
She twisted her purse strap into a tight coil, let it loose, and twisted again.

"Is this a professional question or a personal one?"

"Professional, of course." Maggie jiggled her foot. "I heard Joe Garrett's representing Kemp."

"And?"

She watched me, as if deciding whether to go on or not.

"Spit it out, Maggie."

She exhaled a whoosh of air. "Okay. I was with Ed Kemp on Friday night."

Oh, great. "You're *dating* him?"

"Don't put words in my mouth. He's a married man. It was *not* a date."

"Then what was it?"

"I needed a contact. The station wants a historical piece on doctors who were instrumental in the development of the Medical Center. They're hoping to run it in conjunction with the annual gala. I'm to interview all the doctors who were around when the original Thomansen research wing opened."

She twisted her handbag strap so tight I thought the leather might tear.

"Only two are still living," she went on, "and Arthur Kemp is refusing to give interviews. I needed a foot in the door."

"And you wanted the interview badly enough to date Ed Kemp?" My nose wrinkled in distaste. "Exactly how far will you go to get a story?"

"It wasn't like that," she said. "At least that's not what I had in mind. When I invited him to dinner I told him it was about a piece I'm doing. He didn't think twice before accepting. I thought he was just being helpful."

"Did Joe Garrett contact you about Kemp's alibi?"

"Not yet."

"You sound like you think Kemp will be charged."

"I didn't say that, but if he is—" Maggie's voice trailed off.

"What's the real issue here, Maggie? We don't ever meet for chit-chat. Something's up."

She looked at the floor for a second, before facing me. "I guess I want you to tell me he didn't do it – that you have some evidence to clear him. Exactly what did you see on Friday night?" Her foot jiggled faster.

I normally would have enjoyed watching her squirm, but this time it made me uneasy. "You first. Tell me what's bothering you. Worried about your reputation?"

"That's not it." Maggie dropped the purse strap and began turning one of her large gold earrings round and round. "He showed up at seven, like we'd planned, but he'd been drinking. It was awful."

"Go on," I said.

"He tried to call me yesterday. I wouldn't answer the phone. I didn't know what I'd say to him."

I raised my eyebrows. Maggie Robbins at a loss for words?

"The police haven't called me yet," she explained. "I know they will, but I wanted to talk to you first. Edward Kemp has a good reputation as a doctor, and I don't want to be the one to ruin it. Please tell me you have something to support his defense."

I was beginning to get the gist of where our conversation was heading. "But I don't have anything," I said. "What time did you last see him on Friday night?"

Maggie looked like she might start crying, and the words finally spilled out. "He wanted to come home with me. Said if Suzanna was out doing it, then he would, too. He was so antagonistic. He grabbed me. I pushed him away. Then he started calling me names. Right there in the restaurant parking lot. Thank God no one witnessed it. I'd die of embarrassment. He drove away about nine o'clock."

"You'll be telling this to the police?"

Maggie nodded slowly. "I had a panic attack when I heard about his wife. He was absolutely irate that night. And very drunk. I'd feel a lot better if I knew he didn't kill her."

I couldn't say anything to dispel Maggie's concerns. My reasonable doubt had grown thinner with every word she'd said.

***

Before lunch, I went by Wade's office to fill him in on my progress.

"I may be the only one who believes Ed is innocent," he said. "Didn't get a read on what Garrett really thinks, but then he's accustomed to defending people whether or not they're guilty."

I had told him about Maggie's visit and the details of my weekend's investigation, relieved that he hadn't questioned how I'd gotten access to the warehouse.

"I haven't given up on Kemp yet," I said, stretching the truth. "This is what I'm planning. Number one—keep looking for Mitzi Martin. I'm not positive she's the mystery woman who'd been calling Suzanna, but chances are good that she is. I'll talk to other friends and find the guy who pestered her at the gym. Check out his alibi for Friday night." I paused to scribble a checklist.

"Reba said she's having pictures developed for you," said Wade. "What do you expect to learn there?"

"Maybe pinpoint where they were taken. You think your buddy Charlie would tell you anything about the pictures from Suzanna's camera? They bagged it as evidence at the scene." Wade's friend at the Houston Police Department often did him favors.

Wade picked up a pen and made his own notes. "Can't hurt to ask."

"The only thing I saw in that warehouse was furniture," I said. "If she took pictures of it, I'll try to figure out why. I'll find out who's leasing the warehouse, too." I added to my list.

Wade sat back in his chair. "You know, Corie, Garrett and I don't expect you to devote your life to the case. It doesn't sound like you took any time off over the weekend. And you accuse *me* of being a workaholic."

"I don't mind, really." I avoided looking at him. He knew I purposely focused on work, not allowing anything else to fill the void left by David's death.

"You need to take time out for fun," Wade said. "We both do."

If I didn't know him better, it almost sounded like there was a message between the lines there.

"I'm planning on some fun tonight," I said. Unless Mitzi called me, I'd go to Whispers looking for her.

"Great!" Wade's eyebrows lifted. "Doing what?"

"I'll be out clubbing. Want to join me?"

He looked pleased and surprised at the invitation. "Unfortunately, I have a response due to a motion for summary judgment tomorrow. If I don't read these cases tonight, there's no way I'll get it done." He patted a stack of *Southwestern Reporters* on the desk corner.

"I'd like a rain check, though," he said. "As soon as I get caught up."

"Sure." That would never happen.

The phone buzzed, putting an end to our meeting. I left his office without explaining I planned on visiting a men's club.

On the way back to my desk I thought about how nice

it would be to go out and do something fun with Wade again. David and I had spent a lot of time with Wade and his ex-wife before their divorce. Now David was gone and Laura had moved to Austin. Wade worked as hard and as long as I did. It was about time we enjoyed ourselves again. I plopped into my desk chair, my heart feeling a little lighter.

Reba had already left the envelope of reprints on my desk. I thumbed through them, then laid them out to do a more thorough inspection. They looked like ordinary pictures of someone's office. Three of the photos focused on a wall with a portrait. If the guy in the picture was someone famous, I didn't recognize him. After studying the prints for a while, I couldn't find anything significant. Pulling out my to-do list, I jotted down a note to try and identify the man. What a long shot.

On to the next task—find out if the Larry that Suzanna graduated with was the guy from the gym. I pushed the reprints aside and grabbed her yearbook. Thirty minutes later, I caught up with Clay Mitchell in the weight room where he was pressing over two hundred pounds. Before he noticed me, I had an opportunity to admire his long legs straddling the bench and the sheen of sweat on his muscles as he held the barbell. One of the gym's employees was spotting him and nodded hello when I walked over to them.

Clay's face lit up when he saw me.

"Don't let me interrupt," I said, as he got up from the bench.

"You're not an interruption. I've been thinking about you all morning."

My cheeks suddenly felt hot. "Oh, why? Have you seen Mitzi?"

"Uh-uh. I had a personal question for you." He leaned against the wall, grinning. "I wondered if you're seeing anyone special."

I felt a blush creep up my neck. "Not really."

"How about dinner sometime?"

"How about lunch now?" I said, surprising myself.

Clay agreed and we went next door to the salad and juice bar. Quite different from my usual Kentucky Fried Chicken or Whataburger lunches but I enjoyed the company. I forced down a salad complete with sprouts and seeds, wondering if this stuff really filled him up.

It turned out that Larry Rogers in the yearbook *was* the same guy who'd been seen talking to Suzanna at Total Fitness. Since Larry wasn't a member, Clay couldn't give me any help with an address. I assured him I could handle that on my own. We made plans for dinner Tuesday night before I headed back to the office in an afterglow, singing one of my songs about new beginnings.

When I'd finally gotten my mind back on business, I returned to Suzanna's pay stub. I dialed the Assumed Name Division of the County Clerk's office. After listening to an on-hold recording at least five times through, a woman came on the line.

"I'm looking for any assumed names used by Othello Corporation," I said. "Are you the correct person to ask?"

"Yes, ma'am," she said. "Hold please."

I heard one more round of the recording before she came back on the line.

"Othello Corporation does business as Whispers Nightclub," she said.

I was speechless.

"Ma'am," said the woman on the phone. "Is there anything else?"

"No, thanks." I shook myself to make sure I'd heard her correctly, but it was no mistake. I had only assumed Suzanna and Mitzi met at the gym. Replacing the receiver, I wondered what Suzanna's position at Whispers had been. She might have been a cashier. Maybe she worked in the kitchen or behind the bar. She could have been their bookkeeper. But probably, someone as pretty as Suzanna Zimmerman Kemp had danced topless on the stage next to her good friend Mitzi.

Yes, honey, she's gone,
And nothing's gonna change it.
Time to move on,
And I can help arrange it.

CHAPTER 12

"You want me to *what*?" Dad snickered.

"You heard right," I said, changing the phone to my other ear. "You don't want me going into a topless club by myself, do you?" Aside from Wade, Dad was the only man I'd ask to accompany me on the trip to Whispers.

"Of course not, but shouldn't you be telling the police about this woman?" Newsroom chatter echoed in the background. Dad preferred working amidst the crowd at *The Houston Globe* to his spacious private office.

"Right now there's nothing to tell," I said. "All I want to do is ask her some questions. She may be able to help me, she may not. I need an escort."

He sighed. "Okay, count me in. I can play a believable sugar daddy."

"Just don't tell Mother." She doesn't like Dad helping me on cases and she'd never approve of where we were going.

"Don't worry. There's some committee meeting at the house tonight. She won't even notice I'm gone."

"Good. I might raid her closet while she's busy. I don't have a thing to wear for a night out with a gigolo like you."

He laughed, and I heard another phone ring. "Gotta run, sweetie. I say we show up when the after-work crowd has petered out and the regulars have put away half a night's drinks."

"Perfect. I'll come by the house around nine."

After we hung up, I doodled on a tablet, noting what

I knew about the case so far. Suzanna and Mitzi used to work together. I should have figured that out sooner. What else was I missing? Maybe Suzanna's old friend Larry could add some pieces to my puzzle.

The Houston residential pages listed six Larry Rogers, so I logged on to a computer database that steered me in the right direction within minutes. Only one of the men listed in the database was the right age to be the Larry Rogers in Suzanna's yearbook, and the middle initials matched.

By late afternoon I had reached Rogers' run-down apartment complex in southwest Houston and parked my truck next to a faded blue Thunderbird with tape holding its cracked windshield together.

Knocking on the door of Rogers' apartment, I checked out the empty beer cans littering the concrete patio. Two shriveled hot dogs lay on the rack of a grimy outdoor grill. When the door behind me opened, I jumped. I'd half expected Rogers wouldn't be home from work yet.

The man at the door wore black and red striped boxer shorts. Nothing else. Larry Rogers had lost some wavy blonde hair since his graduation picture had been taken. The guy was still attractive, but a cutback in beer consumption would've improved his physique.

He squinted into the bright light, then staggered backward, appearing half asleep. "Whatcha need?"

I checked my watch, wondering whether he collected unemployment or worked a night shift. "I'm looking for Larry Rogers," I said, handing him one of my business cards.

Rogers opened his right eye a little wider, inspecting the card, then me. "Why?"

"We have a mutual friend, Larry," I said. "May I come in?"

"Whatever." Rogers stumbled into the room and dropped into a worn recliner.

I followed and sat down on the edge of a brown chair with a spring sticking out of the seat cushion. Empty pizza boxes and McDonald's wrappers cluttered the coffee table. The room stank of rancid grease.

"Who's the friend?" Rogers asked, eyeing me suspiciously.

"Suzanna Kemp."

"Ah!" Rogers threw a hand in the air. "I should've known. This is freakin' great. If this is a warning to lay off, Suzie should have sent someone tougher." He smirked.

He didn't know about Suzanna's death. Ignoring his comment, I phrased a question to test his honesty. "How'd you meet her?"

Rogers' eyes narrowed. "Went to high school together. Why do you care?"

I crossed my legs, trying to look casual. "Just curious how well you knew her." Larry didn't notice my use of the past tense.

"Pretty damn well, I'd say. We were supposed to get married 'til she decided she's too good for me."

"Really? I'm sorry to hear that." I shifted positions, avoiding a pointy spring aimed at my thigh. "It's sad when you're committed to a relationship and the other person throws it away," I said, trying to keep him talking.

"You're damn right," said Rogers. "Moved here with a good job offer, a wedding date set and everything. Then she up and left, and it's been downhill ever since." He paused. "Shit, why am I spillin' my guts to you?"

"Because I'm here? I'm a good listener?" I shrugged. "How long ago did she leave?"

"Going on two years already," Rogers said. "Seems like forever. If I wasn't such a loser, we'd still be together. Can't seem to do a damn thing right."

Where to go from here? It seemed to me like he

should have gotten over being jilted two years ago. But I had to admit I hadn't gotten over David's death either. Broken hearts don't mend on command.

"You gonna tell me what you want?" Rogers folded his arms over his pudgy stomach.

I shifted, not eager to break the bad news. "Yes. I understand you've been in contact with Suzanna recently."

He blew the air out of his cheeks. "Don't worry, I'm not gonna bother her again. You'd think she'd help out a friend, but no! She's too good for that."

"Help out?"

Rogers stomped to the sofa and grabbed a pair of gray sweat pants that lay across the arm. He put them on. I wondered what had caused the sudden modesty.

"I lost my job," he blurted. "I'm workin' as a freakin' waiter for Christ's sake, tryin' to make ends meet. Not exactly what I went to college for. I'm broke and she's loaded. I asked her for a loan."

"And she said no?"

"That's right," he said, looking like a petulant child.

Time to switch gears. "When you and Suzanna were together, did she own any furniture?" I still wondered if the furniture in the Yale Street warehouse could have been Suzanna's prior to her marrying Kemp.

Larry waved an arm across the room. "You're lookin' at it. We were gonna live with used stuff until we could afford a house. If she wants it back now, it's all hers!"

"No, that's not it," I said, changing the subject again. "Do you know Mitzi Martin?"

His eyes turned curious. "Sure. They were roommates for a while after Suzie left me. What's going on?"

"Have you seen Mitzi in the past few days?"

"No. Every time I get near either one of those women, that hulk throws me out of the gym." He walked over to stand directly in front of me. "What's happened? Something's wrong."

"Larry, I think you better sit down."

Twenty minutes later I was heading toward home on Highway 59. I'd left Rogers dry-eyed, but guzzling beer like a man who was dying inside. Or hiding something. I'd questioned him about his whereabouts the night of Suzanna's death. He didn't say much, only that he worked nights, waiting tables at Emilio's Restaurant. He'd had a hard time finding a job after being laid off from Kelley Oil.

Sitting in rush hour traffic, I wondered how Rogers had reacted when Suzanna wouldn't lend him any money. I could hardly picture the man flying into a murderous rage over her refusal, but he had showed up at the gym more than once to harass her. Did he give up after the second or third time, or did his anger at her refusal get out of hand?

***

The aroma of mesquite-grilled beef coming from Kit's yard hit me as soon as my feet touched the driveway at home. I lifted my nose, sniffing like a bloodhound. The salad I'd eaten for lunch hadn't done a thing to satisfy my appetite.

I heard Kit's distinctive two-note whistle before her head popped up over the fence connecting our yards. Midnite used to look into the trees whenever Kit whistled, but she finally figured out the noise was coming from the girl, not a bird.

"You hungry?" Kit said.

Midnite paced, drooling, on my side of the fence. "You talking to me or the dog?" I asked, before accepting her dinner invitation.

Over rib-eye steaks, huge baked potatoes, and chocolate cream pie, Kit bribed me to help her write a paper due the next day about South American mammals. Her mother, as usual, claimed to be working late. She'd called and told Kit not to wait up. Kit seemed to take it in stride, even though she'd prepared the special dinner for her Mom, but it made me angry.

For the next couple of hours, I concentrated on helping the girl. By eight-thirty she had a completed outline for the paper, and I agreed she could use my computer to type it. We forwarded Kit's phone to my place on the off chance her mother might actually call to check up on her.

I would have felt better taking Kit over to Mother and Dad's for the evening, but didn't know how Jean Thompson would react if I started making decisions regarding her daughter. Better to leave her in my den with Midnite for company and where she could hear if her mother came home before she finished the paper. After reviewing the workings of my alarm system with Kit, I left for my rendezvous with Dad.

***

At Whispers, the whole building seemed to vibrate with pulsating rock music. I tapped my foot with the beat, trying to get into my role. My wavy hair hung unrestrained over my shoulders, and I'd overdone the makeup. Wearing a pair of snug-fitting black slacks from Mother's closet with a skimpy sequined top meant to be worn under a jacket, I hoped I looked slutty enough to hang out in a tittie bar with an older man.

Dad had a casual arm slung across my shoulders. He seemed so comfortable I wondered if he'd been here before, then decided I didn't really want to know.

"Close your mouth," he said, shouting to be heard over the music. "And stop looking like such a prude."

I couldn't help myself. The employees strutted around nearly nude, looking as carefree as they would in the privacy of their own bedrooms. The hostess who'd showed us to our table was barely dressed. She wore something similar to a black push-up bra with dangling beaded strands bouncing off her midriff with each step. The bottom piece of her ensemble wasn't much bigger than a dollar bill held on by strings circling her body.

I'd have preferred sitting with my back to the action, but that would have defeated my purpose. I had chosen the chair that afforded me the best view of the club, with Dad right next to me so we could keep up our touchy-feely pretense.

One chesty woman gyrated on top of a grand piano as another more statuesque performer strutted along the stage. Men leered from the stage-side tables, and I expected they'd start drooling any second. The heavy mix of cigarette smoke and strong perfume didn't seem to bother anyone else, but it was burning my eyes.

"I can't believe grown men would waste an evening sitting in this place," I said, taking a sip of the white wine I was drinking for appearances. "This is sick."

Dad hugged my shoulders. "It's no big deal," he said. "Remember, this is business. Finish the drink. When the waitress comes over to take your order, get her talking. Find out what she knows. I'm going to see what I can dig up."

He was right. This was business.

As he approached the bar, I took a deep breath, another swig of wine and turned toward the entrance. A stocky man in a tuxedo stood near the door, watching everyone who came and went. Every so often he'd survey the crowd inside. I saw him put his left hand to his ear and tilt his head. Then he turned to face the corner. The bouncer, I decided, communicating with other security personnel.

The wine, combined with the roaring music, didn't help my equilibrium, but I drained the glass and flagged down a red-haired waitress wearing a tank top.

When she reached for my empty glass, I put a hand

out and touched hers. "Is Mitzi here tonight?"

"Who?" She leaned toward me, trying to hear, and almost dumped the contents of her tray on my lap.

I raised my voice. "Mitzi Martin. She still works here, doesn't she?"

"Yeah, I guess so, but I haven't seen her." The girl shrugged. "You want another Zinfandel?"

I nodded.

"Ask one of the girls over there," she said, motioning to a table behind me. "They know Mitzi a lot better."

She walked away, and I twisted in my chair to get a better view of the corner she'd indicated. A bunch of women in exotic get-ups sat together with one man who was focused on the current performance, leaning back in his chair as he watched the dancer who seemed to be performing only for him. The girl sitting to his right ran her hand down his straight black hair, caressing his neck, but he paid no attention.

I scanned the room, looking for Dad, and saw him talking with two female employees. He laughed and touched one woman's arm as though he did this every day. God, I hoped he didn't. I couldn't watch any more. Sitting here wasn't doing me any good anyway. When my glass of wine arrived, I picked it up and headed toward the bouncer.

He watched me approach. I leaned against the wall, casually sipping my drink. "Hi. May I bother you for a second?" I tried for a brilliant smile.

He grinned, looking toward Dad and the girls. "What's wrong? Your friend desert you?" He was a burly man, the kind who must have his sports jackets specially tailored to fit over bulging biceps.

My heart skipped a beat when I realized he was the guy with the radio announcer voice. I made a face. "Oh, well. Easy come, easy go."

"If you want me to call a cab, give me the word," he said.

The front door opened partially and a man yelled, "Hey, Atkins. Somebody out here wants to say hello."

"Be right back," he said, turning his palms up in a shrug before going outside.

I inched toward the door and stretched to peer through the high window to see if I could get a better look at him in the entrance lights. A black, older-model Cadillac had pulled up out front, and a stocky man stood by the driver's door.

Atkins suddenly landed a hard punch in the man's gut, and the guy doubled over with a grunt loud enough for me to hear inside. I ducked into the shadows. What was this all about?

"Vince doesn't want your business," Atkins yelled. "Stay away from him."

"Screw you, Leo. I'll be back."

A car door slammed and I hurriedly backed away from the door. Atkins came in, brushing off the front of his jacket. He smiled at me as if nothing had happened. "You were saying?"

My heart rate had jumped considerably, but I tried to look calm, hoping my story would sound authentic. "A couple of my friends used to work here," I began, "but I don't see 'em tonight." I glanced around, pretending to scan the room for familiar faces.

"Yeah? Who?" Atkins closed the space between us. He seemed even more huge now.

Sweat trickled down my neck.

"Suzie Zimmerman for one."

Strobe lights sparkled across Atkins' dark eyes. His bushy eyebrows crawled together. "Ya wouldn't believe the turnover we got here," he said, "but I remember Suzie Q—that babe hasn't danced here in a while. Who else?"

I was hesitant to bring up Mitzi's name right after witnessing his attack on the man outside. "I didn't know Suzie left. No big deal. Is Mitzi still around?"

Atkins shook his head. "She isn't here. Have *you* seen her lately?"

"Not for six months or so. Last I heard, she still worked here, that's all."

"Oh," he said, not looking convinced.

"I'd better check on my date," I said, anxious to get away. "If you see Mitzi, tell her to give me a call." I realized too late the foolishness of that message.

"Will do. What's your name?"

I flipped my hair back, trying to look nonchalant. "Judy. But never mind. I'll check back another time." Turning, I headed for Dad who was deep in conversation with a petite brunette wearing sparkly gold shorts with a black halter top. She balanced a tray with several empty glasses and some new drinks on it.

"Sweetheart," he said, putting an arm across my shoulders, "this is Babs. We've been having a nice chat. Babs, my *friend* Corinne."

Babs shook my hand, then put a finger to her chin. "Nice to meetcha," she said. "I just love that name, Corinne. Heard it years ago and made up my mind when I have a daughter, that's what I'm gonna name her."

"That's nice," I said.

She took Dad's empty highball glass and placed a new drink down on the nearest table.

"I know you're probably wonderin' why a broad workin' in a joint like this is thinkin' about havin' kids," Babs said. "But the money's good, you know. It's not like I'm gonna spend the rest of my life here. I got plans."

"Makes sense to me," Dad said, handing her a twenty.

"This guy I used to know had a wife named Corinne,"

Babs said, fishing around for change. "Talked about her a lot. Nicest guy you ever wanna meet."

I'd been tuning her out, watching the bouncer, but her statement caught my attention. "Really?" I said, turning to look at her. Babs didn't seem like the type to work in this place. Her face held a bittersweet expression.

"Yeah. He used to come in here." She stuffed Dad's twenty into her pocket. "It was the saddest thing. Poor guy got killed in an explosion. I couldn't believe it."

My heart seemed to stop. She couldn't possibly be talking about David. I felt Dad's cautioning hand on my arm.

"He was real cute, too," Babs said. "Tall, blond." She looked at me with innocent eyes.

"What's the matter? Oh, God, you're not *his* Corinne, are you? I'm such a dimwit sometimes."

Now I've found a secret
One I'd rather not know.
Something that you kept from me
So long ago.

CHAPTER 13

"It wasn't David," I said firmly, staring at Dad. "He didn't come here."

Babs slapped a five-dollar bill and some change down next to Dad's drink and backed away. "I'm so sorry. You'd think I'd learn to keep my mouth shut. Should have never brought it up."

I reached out, grabbing her forearm. "Tell me his name wasn't David."

"Corie," Dad said. "Let's get out of here."

Babs gaped at us in stunned silence, her lips quivering.

"Tell me," I insisted, keeping one eye on her and one on Atkins. No doubt the establishment frowned on patrons grabbing its girls.

"Corie." Dad unclasped my hand from Babs' arm. "What was the man's name?" he asked her.

"It *was* David," said Babs. "David McKenna." I couldn't help but notice her breasts bouncing in sync with her nodding head.

"Thanks, dear," Dad said. "Sorry for the scene."

Then he took my arm and dragged me from the building, obviously expecting me to either explode or burst into tears any second. I felt on the verge of doing both.

Outside, he tipped the valet and retrieved his keys. I

hugged myself, trying to ward off the chilly night air as Dad towed me across the parking lot toward his Land Cruiser.

"David wouldn't come to this place," I said, once we were out of earshot. "He wasn't like those men."

Dad wrapped an arm around me. "I'm sure there's an explanation."

"But she's lying. Why would she say he was here?" My hands curled into tight balls. "She's making this whole thing up." But how did she know his name?

Dad dropped his arms abruptly, opening the passenger door. "Get in," he ordered, "and stop being irrational. You're acting like your mother."

He knew that would shut me up. I kept quiet for a few minutes, trying to calm myself by counting street lights as we drove east on Richmond Avenue.

"Okay, maybe he was there," I finally said.

At a stop light, Dad turned to me. "Corie, I know it's been a hard couple of years for you. But most husbands aren't saints. Frankly, I'm surprised this bothers you so much. Those women at the club are doing a job, making a living." He hesitated, clearing his throat. "I know how you hate it when your mother judges people she doesn't know."

I cringed, unwilling to admit my behavior mirrored hers.

"You and David were close," Dad continued. "You spent a lot of time together. Babs didn't say he was a regular. Who knows? Maybe he met clients there." He patted my knee before taking off at the green light.

A single tear slipped from the corner of my eye. When would I get over missing David so much? People lose loved ones every day. How did they cope? I took a deep breath and blew it out, trying to clear my head of the depressing thoughts.

"You're right as usual," I admitted.

"That's better," said Dad. "Now, I got some useful info from Babs. Want to hear what I found out?"

I forced a smile. "You know I do."

"Good," he said with a self-satisfied grin. "Mitzi Martin has worked at Whispers ever since their opening night two years ago. She and the owner have dated steadily for at least a year. His name is Vincent Ochoa." Dad leaned forward to turn up the heat. After adjusting the vents, he continued his report.

"Babs seemed to think Mitzi spent more time at Vincent's place than at her own. That would explain why you didn't find her at the apartment. Babs doesn't think much of Ochoa. Said he treats the girls like they're his property as much as the building is. Most of them play along because it's their job, but Mitzi is in love with him."

"Really? Where can we find this guy?" It would be best if I could get my mind back on the case. *Find Mitzi and solve Suzanna's murder*, I thought.

"He was there. The guy at the table in the corner surrounded by women. That's Ochoa."

I sat up, excited about the lead. "I saw him. Let's go back."

Dad shook his head. "That's not such a good idea."

It took me a minute to realize what he meant. "He's probably the guy who threatened me on the phone last night," I said. "The one who called her 'my Mitzi.'"

"Exactly. But since we know he's occupied, let's find out where he lives and see if she's there. Maybe she came home since last night."

"My questions about Mitzi sure perked up the bouncer's interest," I said. "Maybe he and Ochoa have known where she's been all along, and they're protecting her from somebody else. We have to consider every possibility."

Dad smiled and gave me a light punch to the shoulder.

"That's my girl. Let's go."

Information had a listing for a Vincent Alberto Ochoa and a Vincent Ochoa. The River Oaks address given for Vincent Alberto was closer, so we checked it first. The Land Cruiser wound down the drive of a mansion hidden behind a veil of shrubs and trees on a quiet River Oaks street.

"I'd have guessed the guy at the club to be in his early thirties," I said, "unless the dim lighting threw me off. Wonder if the place pulls in enough for him to afford this address?"

"Good point," said Dad. "Anyway, the house looks deserted."

Only the truck's headlights lit the area surrounding the sprawling, Spanish-style home. The lamps on the posts lining the driveway weren't on. The house was dark. The lawn looked straggly, as if the gardener had gone on an extended vacation. Dad pulled up in the circular driveway near the front door and took a flashlight from the glove compartment.

"Don't think anyone's living here, but I'll go take a closer look," he said, pulling a red lollipop from his stash in the console. "You stay here. Have a pop."

"No way. I'm going with you." I jumped out and followed. Dad knew better than to try and change my mind.

An owl hooted through the silence as we walked to the main entrance. A few circulars about community meetings, a pile of new telephone books, and a cardboard box lay on the covered porch near the front door.

Dad rang the bell, sucking on his candy. No one answered. He shined the flashlight across the leaded glass beside the door, then noticed the padlock attached to the doorknob.

"This house must be for sale," he said, indicating the contraption used to store entry keys and make homes accessible for realtors and potential buyers. He leaned forward, putting his nose on the glass, and shined the light through the pane. "It looks vacant."

"Oh, well, we had a fifty-fifty chance of picking the right place," I said.

Dad checked his watch. "Bet there's time for us to hit the other address before Ochoa goes home for the night."

I agreed, remembering the image of Ochoa leering at his dancers.

Within minutes, we'd reached the sleek, modern Montrose condos that more aptly fit my image of the Ochoa at the club. But we couldn't get past the high fence and security guard to discover whether or not Mitzi Martin was inside.

"I'm sorry, I can't give out any information about our residents," replied the stern man when we asked if Vincent Ochoa lived there. "Would you like to leave a message?"

The guy may as well have answered our question. If we left a message, who else would he give it to but Vincent Ochoa?

"No, thanks," said Dad. "We'll catch him at the office tomorrow."

As we drove away, I saw the guard standing in the drive copying down the Land Cruiser's plate number.

"Where to now?" Dad asked.

"Home, I guess. We've done enough for one night, even though it didn't get us anywhere." I rubbed my throbbing temples. All I'd accomplished was hearing something I wish I hadn't.

A little after midnight we pulled up beside my truck at Dad's house. "You coming in for a snack? Ruby made some double-fudge brownies today." He licked sticky lollipop remains from his lips.

"Not this time." Ruby, their live-in housekeeper, was like my second mother, but even her treats couldn't improve my mood tonight.

"Promise me you won't worry about what Babs said," Dad told me. "It doesn't mean anything."

I nodded, but got out of there without actually making a promise. Driving home, I couldn't keep from thinking about David. Maybe I had unconsciously adopted Mother's bias about some subjects. The thought of my husband being enticed by topless dancers was not a welcome one.

I wondered if anyone had ever done a poll about why husbands feel the urge to patronize clubs like Whispers. Was it because their needs weren't being met at home? And how many of them went even further, picking up strangers, checking into motels for a few hours? I punched the accelerator. This line of thinking wasn't healthy. David would never have had an affair. Would he? But then I wouldn't have thought he'd ever step foot in Whispers either.

A tune locked in my head and I started fitting in lyrics—*Thought I really knew you; Tell me, was it all a dream*? I hummed a little more, trying to fit words into the rhythm. *Things aren't always what they seem.* My composing session was cut short when a West University police car pulled out a block ahead, bringing me back to my senses. I tapped the brakes.

"Stop being stupid," I said aloud. "He's gone, and none of this should matter." But it did matter.

By the time I pulled into my driveway, I had decided to talk to Wade about my discovery in the morning. He had known David's habits as well as he knew his own. I shouldn't assume things based on a conversation with a waitress. The views of David's best friend would carry more weight with me than Babs' comments, assuming he'd tell me the truth.

Trudging across the sidewalk from the garage to the house, I heard Midnite's collar jangling on the other side of the back door. Why hadn't Kit put her out in the yard as usual when she left? I'd had one of those underground electric pet protection systems installed so Midnite couldn't dig a hole and escape underneath the fence.

From Midnite's agitation, it didn't seem like Kit had even remembered to let the dog out for a potty break. I hoped she'd at least finished her paper for school the next day.

I held the door wide for Midnite, but she stubbornly stayed inside, bouncing around the kitchen. The sound of a car coming down the street caught my attention. It turned into the driveway next door, and I heard a garage door opening. Jean Thompson was just now getting home. I went inside, shutting the door behind me.

"Okay," I said, patting Midnite's head. "Have it your way." If the dog needed to go out, she'd let me know. I bent to scratch behind her ear, a gesture she normally luxuriates in, but tonight she moved away, trotting down the dimly-lit hall. Kit must have left a lamp burning in the den.

I moved toward the refrigerator, doubtful I'd be able to fall asleep without some help. Another glass of wine maybe. That should do the trick. If I drank myself into a stupor, I'd pass out eventually. Maybe I wouldn't even remember I'd ever had a husband, much less worry about his activities before his death. I filled a large wine glass with Chablis and carried it into the hallway.

The red light of the answering machine on the foyer table blinked several times. I stopped, watching the light, but I was interested in escaping reality, not immersing myself in it. The messages could wait until morning.

Maybe I need a change of pace. I could move to a ranch somewhere. Montana. Wyoming. I'd always hated classmates referring to me as a rich spoiled brat, but there were advantages to being a trust-fund baby. I could afford to pick up and leave Houston whenever I wanted to.

I stood, leaning against the table, considering the

possibility. Midnite had sneaked up on me and her nose nudged my leg. More than once. I looked down. The dog was trying to get my attention.

I knelt, tipping up her large head with my free hand. "What is it, baby?"

She pulled away from me and trotted down the hallway, turning a couple times to see if I was following her. My heartbeat quickened. What could it be? The security alarm had been set when I came in. Maybe Kit had fallen asleep while working on her paper. I hurried into the den behind Midnite.

The computer was still on, Kit's work still up on the screen. Some papers had fallen from the top of my desk onto the floor. I scanned the room. A lamp had toppled from a table near the window and broken. Large chunks of pottery dotted the carpet. In a panic, I looked under the desk and checked the closet. No Kit.

"Oh, God," I said. "Where is she?" Kit wasn't the type of kid to leave the house without turning off the computer. I hoped for a simple answer. Had she gone to bed? Maybe she was in the bathroom. I checked the downstairs powder room, with no luck, then took the stairs three at a time.

"Kit," I yelled, praying there wasn't any reason to worry. No one answered. I ran through the upstairs, checked the two beds, all the closets, the bathroom, even looked behind the shower curtain. Kit wasn't there.

I knew her well enough to know she wouldn't have left my house this way without a good reason or without leaving me a note. I wondered whether Jean Thompson looked in on Kit when she came home late, or whether she'd go on to her own room without checking.

The answering machine! I flew down the stairs to see if any of the messages might be from Kit. Pounding on the back door startled me. I jumped, then saw that the visitor was

Jean. She had a hysterical look in her eyes.

"Where's Kit?" she demanded when I opened the door. "Is she here?"

"She was," I said. "But no, she's not here now. Are you sure she's not at home?"

My own alarm seemed to heighten Jean's panic. She grabbed my arm. "What do you mean she *was*? What happened to her?"

I bit back a retort. I'd save my lecture for later, after we knew Kit was safe. She had to be safe.

"Are you sure she's not at home?" I asked again, waiting for my recorder to rewind. "Did you look everywhere?"

"Of course I did," Jean cried. "What if something terrible happened?"

"Don't worry," I said. "She'll be all right."

I willed myself to act composed, more to calm her than anything. Hysteria wouldn't help anyone. We stared at the machine, listened to a message from Reba about a client, one telephone solicitation, then had our answer.

"Mrs. McKenna, this here is Officer Dewitt. I'm with the West University police. There's been some trouble at your house tonight. Kit Thompson called it in, and we investigated. If you're in contact with her mother, please tell her we have Kit down at the station on University Boulevard."

I didn't want to waste a moment calling to inquire about Kit's welfare. The station was only a two-minute drive away. Jean must have felt the same, because when I jumped into the Ranger, she was right beside me.

Someone is checking me out,
What could that be all about?
Maybe I'm getting too close,
And that's what worries him most.

CHAPTER 14

We found Kit sitting in the police officer's lounge watching *The Late Show* on television. Several Hershey wrappers, a near-empty bag of Cheetos, and a Coke can occupied the table next to her. At first glance, the girl looked unaffected by the evening's events. Then she saw Jean and flew into her mother's arms. I turned to Officer Dewitt.

"I'm glad she's okay," I said, after introducing myself. "What happened?"

He adjusted wire-rimmed glasses that sat low on his thin nose.

"She called 911 and reported a prowler. Said the dog started barking, and she saw a man outside the window. We arrived within minutes, but didn't see anyone." He lowered his voice. "May have been an overactive imagination."

Dewitt approached Kit and her mother. "Mrs. Thompson?"

Jean freed herself from Kit's hold to shake his hand. "Thank you for taking care of my daughter," she said.

The officer nodded. "Curious youngster. She kept us pretty busy answering questions at first. Wanted a tour of the station. You may have a little policewoman on your hands."

Kit grinned. Jean looked horrified.

"You're lucky nothing serious happened," Dewitt went on. "We didn't see a prowler this time, but it's not a good idea to leave young ladies like Kit home alone."

Jean pointed at me. "She's actually the one who left her alone."

I counted to three and took a deep breath before responding.

"She has a paper due in school tomorrow," I said, staring at Jean. "I helped her with it, and she used my computer to type it up. Were you working late? Again?" My own guilty feelings about leaving Kit kept me from saying more.

Kit grabbed one of her mother's hands and one of mine. "Guys, it's cool. Don't worry about me."

"Now ladies," Dewitt said, "just remember, better safe than sorry. You never know when a random act of violence will— "

"But it's not," interrupted Kit.

"Not what?" said Dewitt.

"Random. The man came to Corie's house on purpose." Kit put her hands on her hips. "He looked in her mailbox, in the windows, and around the back yard. I think he was checking Corie out, because he didn't try to break in."

＊

After Kit's revelation at the police station, I didn't have much time to think about what I'd learned about David that night. Instead, I lay awake wondering whom Kit had watched prowling around my house. Alerted by Midnite's barking at the back door, the girl had turned off the lights and looked out the window. When she saw a man on the back porch with a flashlight, she turned quickly to hide, knocking the lamp off the table. Hoping the man would think the dog had made the noise, Kit ran upstairs and called for help.

From my bedroom window, she'd seen a red vehicle parked in the driveway. "I wanted to write down a license number," Kit had told me. "But I was too scared to go back downstairs where I could see better. It was some kind of big truck, not quite as big as Reba's Suburban."

I reviewed my day, trying to figure out if my actions could have precipitated the guy nosing around. Had I aggravated Larry Rogers, Suzanna's ex-fiancé, by asking one question too many? He didn't fit Kit's description of a "tall fat man with brown hair," and I couldn't envision him having the wherewithal to hire an investigator. The guard at Vincent Ochoa's condominium complex had taken down Dad's license plate number, but even if he'd had it traced, the number wouldn't have led to my house. Besides, he'd just taken it down as a security precaution. Could be this was a case of mistaken identity, and the prowler wasn't interested in me specifically. Right.

I shifted positions fitfully. Midnite whimpered on the floor beside me. I turned my thoughts back to Friday's meeting with Edward Kemp and his obnoxious behavior. If he acted the same way at work as he had at our office, no wonder someone at the hospital believed he would kill his wife.

Maybe he's checking me out, I thought. What if I'm getting too close? Maybe Kemp's afraid I'll prove his guilt instead of his innocence.

Neither Wade nor Joe Garrett would appreciate my line of thinking. Before spending any more time trying to make a case against someone else, I needed to believe in my client. To do that, I'd have to learn a lot more about the man. His workplace would be a good place to start. Having made that decision, I finally fell asleep.

***

I arrived at the office early Tuesday, hoping to catch Wade before he left for court.

"He's at breakfast with a client, reviewing testimony for a hearing," Reba told me, a concerned expression on her face. "You feel all right, girl?" She raised a hand to my forehead. "You look feverish."

"I had a horrible night," I said without explanation. "Tell Wade we need to talk. Soon." I had to ask him some questions about David before my imagination drove me crazy.

"Tell me what's goin' on." Reba sat down behind her desk and dunked a blueberry cake doughnut into her coffee.

"I wouldn't even know where to begin." I turned to leave her office. "Some other time."

"Don't keep me hangin'," Reba said. The soggy doughnut barely made it from the cup to her mouth. Then her phone started ringing. Good time for a getaway. We could talk later, after I sorted things out.

I checked my phone messages, forced myself to return a few calls, and turned to the computer to record the time I'd spent working on Kemp's case. Then I typed up a progress report, even though there hadn't been much. My questions seemed to be multiplying. Frustrated when Wade didn't show up after a couple of hours, I printed out a to-do list, stuffed it into my jeans pocket, and pulled on a navy blue blazer. Maybe interviewing witnesses would get my mind off David.

At Methodist Hospital, I learned Suzanna had worked in the accounting department, but struck out on finding any current employees who had known her. Next, a receptionist at the information desk directed me to Dr. Kemp's appointment secretary, Sallie McMillan. I assumed Sallie could answer questions about Kemp's schedule and his relationships with co-workers.

Sallie sat behind a long counter in a waiting room that served a group of five orthopedic surgeons. The phone rang steadily, giving her little time to think, much less talk to me. During a brief lull in the calls, I told her my business. Sallie motioned for one of the other girls to cover the phones. I followed her, curious what the attractive thirty-ish woman thought of Dr. Edward Kemp.

In a break room down the hall, Sallie poured us each a cup of coffee. We sat in blue chairs around a small white Formica-topped table. Three nurses huddled at an identical table in the far corner, absorbed in their own conversation. Sallie fingered a dark blonde ringlet nervously and examined her split ends for a few seconds before beginning to talk.

"I've been expecting to hear from the police," she said softly.

"Are you the one who told them about Dr. Kemp threatening to kill his wife?"

Sallie's eyes widened. She shook her head. "No. That was Bella, one of the nurses. But I heard him, too."

"You heard the threat?"

She nodded. "The day he got the divorce papers he started screaming that she wouldn't get away with it, that he'd kill her first. You know how crude men can be, especially when they're angry. They say really stupid things without thinking. He's one of the worst, but I never took him seriously."

"What about now? You think he killed her?" I sipped the too-hot coffee, burning my tongue.

Sallie picked at her chipped red nail polish. "I *want* to say no. He really *is* a good doctor." She hesitated, looking up at me.

"What about his schedule? He left my office about two o'clock Friday afternoon. Did he come back here for any appointments?"

"No," said Sallie. "The last appointment on Fridays is usually at one."

"Is there anyone here who spends time with Dr. Kemp away from the office? Friends, golf buddies?"

"He plays golf sometimes, with other doctors. Nothing regular." Sallie shifted in her chair.

I suspected she had more to say. "Who else?"

"I shouldn't be talking about this," she said, her face flushed. "My job—"

"We're defending the doctor," I reminded her. "The prosecutor will find out everything. We need to know, too."

"Okay." She eyed the nurses and lowered her voice. "Lydia Jones, Kemp's private secretary. She's sleeping with him," Sallie said. "Not that she's the first one, or the only one. I think her life's goal is to become a doctor's wife. She's been working on it full time."

"You think the doctor sees their relationship the same way she does?"

Sallie shook her head vigorously. "Not at all."

"Let me back up a minute," I said. "You didn't answer me earlier. Do you think Dr. Kemp was involved in his wife's death?"

"Well, I can't help thinking about the baby," Sallie said. "Dr. Kemp's son is the most important thing in the world to him. Everyone here knows that. He's like a different person when he's talking about his son. I don't know how far he would have gone to keep her from taking the boy away."

"That's a good point," I said.

Sallie blew on her coffee to cool it. "The other thing that bothers me is the rumor about the insurance policy."

I set my cup down so abruptly coffee splashed onto the table. "What policy?"

"Everybody's talking about the extra million-dollar life insurance policy he took out on his wife. Through our group insurance."

Sallie gave me the name of the employee benefits person who could verify the rumor. I knew they wouldn't hand any information over to me, and I believed Kemp would know better than to kill his wife shortly after buying such a policy. If he did have the insurance, he'd better have bought it long ago.

Sallie had to get back to the phones, and I headed for Kemp's private office. The young woman stationed outside balanced herself on the edge of her chair behind a bouquet of long-stemmed red roses. She had the telephone lodged between her ear and shoulder. Her potent cologne overwhelmed any fragrance from the flowers. A nameplate on the desk identified her as Lydia.

As I approached, the woman whispered something into the phone and giggled. Her long red curls concealed more of her cleavage than the sheer blouse did. Although there were papers on the desk next to the computer, I doubted she had to do much typing to keep her job.

Since she didn't make a move to hang up, I walked toward the open door to Kemp's inner office. A private look around might prove interesting—give me a better insight into the man. Sallie had told me he was in surgery this morning. Fine cherry bookcases lined the wall behind Kemp's desk. An ornate cabinet, its doors slightly ajar, occupied one corner. A cut glass decanter half filled with an amber liquid sat on the desk beside a pile of medical reference books. The leather desk blotter was nearly hidden by papers. I would have thumbed through them if I hadn't noticed Vivian Coulter sitting on the forest green leather sofa, holding Eddie Kemp.

Before I could say anything, the secretary rushed into the room. "Miss Coulter, sorry for the interruption," she said, though I didn't see a smidgen of remorse in her expression. Her dark brown eyes glared at the older woman, then focused on me. "Dr. Kemp isn't in, Miss—"

"Corie McKenna. I'm working for the doctor. You must be Lydia." The girl's half-dozen rings scraped my fingers as we shook hands. I nodded hello to Vivian.

"Is the doctor in?" I asked, innocently, not wanting Vivian to tell Kemp I'd come to interview his secretary.

"He's in surgery." Lydia glanced at the desk, then

walked around to the other side. Her gaze scurried around the room as though she were searching for something. I stepped closer, watching her nervously straighten the papers on the blotter. Then she backed up to the corner cabinet. I managed to catch a glimpse of the wet bar inside before she closed the doors. It was the perfect setting for a busy doctor's after-work tête-à-tête with his secretary.

"I'm sure he won't have time to see you today," Lydia said firmly. I wondered if she had a habit of saving Kemp's last appointment of the day for herself. Her frantic behavior was curious.

"I'll take my chances. Ms. Coulter and I can chat while we wait." I'd pry some more information out of Vivian since interrogating Lydia now was out of the question. I hadn't decided whether or not to believe Kemp when he said Vivian was just a friend. Two pairs of eyes assessed me. Lydia's angry dark brown ones and Vivian's cool grey ones, accented by her violet silk dress.

Vivian glanced at a wall clock. "Miss Jones, have you told Dr. Kemp that Eddie and I are here? We've already been waiting for some time. He should be out of surgery by now." She spoke with a superior tone, and the animosity between the two women crackled in the air.

"I left the message," Lydia snapped on her way back to her desk.

Vivian stood and paced, bouncing Eddie on her hip. I wondered why she wanted to see Kemp. Looked like the babysitting she'd taken on had dominated her schedule. Maybe she was here to demand he hire a nanny so she could get back to her real job. Or maybe she and Kemp were both hiding the extent of their relationship.

"How is the case going?" Vivian asked after Lydia was gone.

"We're making some progress," I said, "though I have

a long list of questions and not enough answers."

"Maybe I could help," she said.

"Possibly, but I'm not sure Dr. Kemp would want me to discuss his case with you."

Vivian smiled. "Don't be silly. Edward won't mind at all." Eddie yanked on a tendril of her hair, but she didn't seem to notice. Then he started writhing around in her arms.

"Excuse me, just for a moment," she said. She put the child down on the carpeted floor and shuffled through the navy blue diaper bag at her feet.

I sat in a tweed wingback chair and waited until Vivian slid back into an upright position. She folded her hands in her lap.

"Now, what do you need to find out?" She had given Eddie a couple of vinyl baby books, but he'd discarded them and was crawling away from her.

"The two of you seem to spend a lot of time together," I said. "You and Dr. Kemp, that is."

Her pleasant expression evaporated. "Edward told me about your insinuations, and I think you misunderstand the situation. I'm doing my best for Eddie, bringing him over here to have lunch with his Daddy because they don't see each other enough, trying to make a dreadful situation a little more tolerable." Vivian's eyes teared.

"I'm sorry," I said, "but it's my job to ask questions. You and Dr. Kemp seem pretty close, perhaps more than friends."

"You have an overactive imagination," Vivian said. "Why don't you focus on Edward's case? Of course, it won't be a very big job. He will be exonerated, I'm sure."

I leaned back in the chair. "Really? What makes you so certain?"

"First of all, the police will see Suzanna was involved in something disreputable." Vivian scowled. "God knows what! Going to that part of town, at night, into a warehouse."

She made it sound disgusting, as if she'd never consider setting foot in one. Vivian looked like the type who'd be found only in country clubs, River Oaks mansions, beauty salons, or elite vacation spots. I doubted she knew about Suzanna's former profession. That would have really set her off.

"You sound as if you didn't like Suzanna."

"That's not true," Vivian said. "She could be very sweet, but we didn't know the real Suzanna, did we? Edward's parents never approved of his marriage, and perhaps with good reason."

"What reason?"

"Suzanna never fit in, bless her heart," said Vivian, without further explanation. She turned to gaze at the boy crawling on the floor around his father's desk.

I didn't see much use in discussing Suzanna's stint as an exotic dancer with Vivian, so I changed the subject. "She may have had a good reason for going to that warehouse," I said. "Maybe the Kemps leased it."

"I doubt it." Vivian shook her head.

"Why?"

"If Edward needed to lease space, he'd do so somewhere closer. There are some very nice buildings just south of here. No, I don't think her visit to that warehouse had anything to do with Edward."

She had a point. Kemp probably wouldn't stoop to being seen in the part of town where the warehouse was located.

"We won't have much luck convincing the D.A. to quit investigating Dr. Kemp until we get some concrete information to help," I said. "Is there anything else you can tell me?"

"What more do you need to convince them he's not

guilty?" Vivian's eyebrows drew together. "Being in emergency surgery is as air-tight an alibi as I've ever heard."

Now it was my turn to look confused. I hesitated before deciding to tell her what I knew. Maybe a confrontation between Vivian and her old buddy Edward would bring out the truth about that night.

"He wasn't in surgery," I said. "He was out to dinner with Maggie Robbins. But he left her in time to get back home before the murder."

Vivian quickly looked away, but not before I saw the shock in her eyes. Kemp had lied to her. Why?

Loud voices from the outer office caught our attention, saving Vivian from responding to my statement. In a second, the door was flung open and a red-faced Edward Kemp stormed in.

"What the hell are you two doing here?"

"I tried to tell them you were busy," Lydia said, smugly.

He ignored the secretary.

"I have work to do, and I don't need interruptions." He slapped the corner of his desk. "God, you women drive me crazy. I have patients to tend to, and neither of you has an appointment." I guessed he hadn't planned on a lunch date with Vivian and Eddie.

Then he saw his son, who had grasped the leg of an end table and was trying to stand. Kemp went over and picked him up, gaving him a brief hug. When he turned toward me, fury still creased his face.

"What *are* you doing here, anyway?" he asked in a lowered tone of voice.

Vivian stood. "We were talking about your case, Edward."

I was surprised she'd taken my side.

"And what, pray tell, could you say to help my case?"

Kemp asked, turning his attention to Vivian.

"We were talking about the warehouse." Vivian pouted. "I assured her you had no connection to the place."

Kemp whirled toward me. "I've already told you I know nothing about that damned warehouse. Instead of wasting your time and my money asking stupid questions, why don't you find out who really killed my wife?"

He stood about two feet from me, and his face looked as red as mine felt. Several choice phrases flitted through my head, but I was afraid I'd spit at him if I opened my mouth.

"I don't have time for either of you right now," he said. "I'm a busy man."

I didn't wait around to take any more abuse.

Coincidences happen, don't you agree?
But I don't like it when they happen to me.
Somethin' doesn't feel right, I wanna know why,
Follow my advice, girl, don't trust that guy.

CHAPTER 15

On the way to my truck I thought about resigning from Kemp's case. Garrett had other investigators he could hire. But if I gave up now, someone might get away with murder, maybe Edward Kemp, and there was no way I'd want him to get off if he were guilty.

Muttering every expletive I knew, I stomped across the parking garage. I had no hope of getting information out of Lydia now. After hearing how her boss had yelled at me, the woman wouldn't tell me a thing.

Was the guy really a major jerk, or was he turning up his obnoxious quotient to get me off the case? But he hadn't treated Vivian any better, and they were supposed to be friends. It could be that the stress had finally sent him over the edge. If I were Vivian, I'd forget about lunch, take Eddie home, and avoid his father whenever possible, friend or no friend.

Waiting to pay the garage attendant, I realized the only thing that would convince me of Kemp's innocence was finding the real murderer. Just because the guy's a creep, I reminded myself reluctantly, doesn't mean he's a killer. I had learned one important clue, though, while at the hospital—Kemp allegedly had a large insurance policy on his wife's life. That looked very bad for the case, but Garrett would know how to handle that problem. In the meantime, figuring out why Suzanna had visited the warehouse seemed to be the next logical step. I turned toward the 610 Loop, heading for Yale Street.

Delivery trucks and vans lined the parking area of the business complex near what I'd come to think of as Suzanna's warehouse. Workers on the dock next door were loading a truck with cardboard cartons. Across the lot, men wheeled huge rolls of carpeting into a warehouse. The place I was interested in was all quiet out front.

Rather than using the key to get back inside, I opted to ask questions next door. A simple black and white sign read "Gadgets, Inc." Inside, I found a lone woman at a desk surrounded by a hodgepodge of boxes. An ancient printer on a stand behind her clattered so loudly I wondered how she could work in the same room. Metal shelving loaded with more boxes lined the back wall.

The middle-aged woman looked up from her paperwork, a grin on her rosy face. She removed her glasses and let them dangle from a chain around her neck. "Howdy. I'm Ethel Stein. Watcha need, honey?"

Skipping over introductions, I said "Do you know if the space next door is vacant?"

Ethel pushed back her chair and stood. Her lime-green sweatsuit clung to an overweight frame. "You mean right over here?" She motioned toward Suzanna's warehouse.

I nodded.

"Far as I know some furniture's in there. Got moved in 'bout a year ago," she said, "and I never seen it leave."

"You know who owns the furniture?"

"Can't say as I do." Ethel walked to the window and looked out on the parking lot. "I'm here 'most every day, but I never seen nobody come or go." She scratched her head with the eraser end of a pencil, then turned around. "Why you askin'?"

Ethel seemed like a nice enough woman, but I didn't want to spend time telling her the whole story. "A friend and I are looking for some space to lease and she sent me over to check it out. Maybe I got the wrong address."

"Maybe not. Heard they're gettin' the boot 'cause the rent's not paid. We could become neighbors."

"That'd be nice," I said.

"Seen some might-fine pieces go in there," she said, looking out the window again. "They're havin' an auction to sell everything off. First Saturday of the month. Had a flyer stuck under my wipers. Bet there's some deals in there." She beamed. "I won't miss it."

"Sounds interesting. In the meantime, who do I contact about leasing the place?"

Ethel dug around in her desk drawer, finally producing a business card from a leasing agent. "You're not gonna buy stuff early, are you?" she said, before letting go of the card. "To be fair, you ought to come to the auction."

I assured Ethel she'd have first picks as far as I was concerned.

I stopped to talk with a few more people at neighboring businesses. Nobody had seen activity around Suzanna's warehouse. Then I went back to my truck and called the number on the card Ethel had given me.

The leasing agent had a tinny little voice. "We have a very nice property just a wee bit farther north," he said. "It's bigger, and I do believe we might negotiate for the same rent."

"I'm not interested in any other place. My business works *very* closely with Gadgets. I understood the space next to them would be vacant soon. Perhaps if I talk directly with the tenant, we can work something out. If you'll just give me a name, I'll make contact."

"I'd rather call myself," the man said. "Can't promise

I'll get him today 'cause I'm lone man on the totem pole, if you know what I mean, but I don't mind, not at all." His laugh sounded like a schoolgirl's twitter.

I put on my best no-nonsense voice. "I hear your tenant's behind on the rent, and I need to do business right away. We're interested in signing a five-year lease with six months down. More if you like. But we're in a hurry. In fact, I need to wrap this up today."

The phone clattered as though he'd dropped it. Papers rustled in the background. "I'll locate the tenant, I will, but he's hard to catch sometimes."

Like most people being contacted about collections, I thought.

It didn't sound like I'd get anywhere without upping the stakes. "Look, I need a name and number. If you can't help me, I'll find space somewhere else."

"No, no, please. I understand the pressures of running a business. Yes, I do. I'll have the information for you in just a sec." More paper rustling. "Here he is. Leo Atkins." He recited an address and phone number.

I mumbled thanks and hung up, staring at my notepad. Could he mean the same Leo Atkins who was the bouncer at Whispers? Could a bouncer own all that expensive furniture? I supposed it was possible. The guy could have inherited from a wealthy relative, or he could have leased the warehouse on behalf of someone else.

But what did this have to do with Suzanna? Atkins had sounded like he knew her from when she worked at the club. They might have kept in touch. Maybe even met at the warehouse on Friday night. But why?

The instrumental portion of a John Michael Montgomery tune on the radio started my left foot tapping. I sang my way up to the nearest Jack In The Box drive-through window. Thinking about Atkins, his boss, Suzanna, and Mitzi had caused a kind of nervous hunger. I sat in the parking lot, stuffing myself with french fries and a huge cheeseburger. My thoughts drifted to David and his alleged visits to Whispers. Hoping to talk to Wade, I dialed the office between bites.

"Wade's not here," Erin, the receptionist, told me, "But I sure am glad to hear your voice. An old woman called, rambling. Some Spanish, some English. Mrs. Hernandez. Do you know her?"

"Yes, Ed Kemp's housekeeper. What did she say?"

"She was hard to understand, but I got what I could. *La dama mala. Ella llama otra mas tiempo.* Something about the bad lady calling her again?"

The bad lady. In Mrs. Hernandez' mind, the caller had caused Suzanna's death. My heartbeat quickened. "Did she leave a number?"

She had and I hurriedly dialed the number Erin had recited. Mrs. Hernandez answered and started spouting off Spanish as soon as she realized it was me.

"Slow down" I said. "*Despacio, despacio.* Speak English, please." My rusty interpreting could never keep up with her.

"She call me today," Mrs. Hernandez said, forcing her words. "Is same lady who call Señora Suzanna and ask for help."

"Did she tell you her name?" I said, crossing my fingers. I needed a break on this case.

"Martinez. She so upset about Señora Suzanna. She say her name Mitzi Martinez."

Martinez? She had to be Mitzi Martin, the woman I was looking for. I grabbed a pencil.

"Where is she? Did she leave a phone number?"

"No. I do not know. She say be careful. She sorry for causing trouble."

"Is that why she called you? To warn you about

something?" I slumped back in my chair.

"She hear the news, but did not want to believe. When I tell her what happened, she cry and cry. Say she is afraid. Then she hang up."

"What is she afraid of?" I wanted answers, and Mrs. Hernandez' revelations only created more questions.

"I do not know." Mrs. Hernandez' voice was barely audible.

Sighing, I ran a hand through my hair. My forehead felt damp despite the cool day. I shouldn't have gotten my hopes up. "Thanks for telling me, Mrs. Hernandez. If she calls you again, please try to find out where she is. I need to talk to her."

"Sí."

After hanging up, I threw the rest of my burger into the paper sack and crumpled it. My appetite had disappeared. Damn! I had about as good a chance of finding this woman as I had of winning the Texas lottery.

Was Mitzi afraid that whoever had killed Suzanna would try to kill her, too? Or did her fear stem from her involvement with Suzanna's murder? If I knew why Vincent Ochoa and Leo Atkins were so eager to find Mitzi, I might have the answer.

Anyone in Houston who listened to the radio or watched television news would have heard about Suzanna's murder every hour on the hour. Yet Mitzi had called Mrs. Hernandez to verify what had happened. Wondering if Mitzi had left town, I decided to swing by her place again.

At Bayou Glen Apartments, most of the parking spaces were empty. I took inventory—one black BMW, a gray Honda Accord, and an old red Bronco. The space I thought was Mitzi's stood empty. There was no sign of the impolite neighbor I'd run into the other day. I strode up to Mitzi's door and lifted my fist to knock, but sensed something was wrong.

I leaned toward the door, listening. Loud bumping and crashing noises came from inside. I doubted Mitzi was making all the racket. People didn't usually trash their own place.

Digging in my shoulder bag, I grabbed the canister of pepper spray I carry for protection. Then I checked the doorknob. Unlocked. I opened it a crack and waited. It was quiet now.

A draft from the opening carried a pungent odor I didn't recognize. I turned my head away, holding a hand over my nose. The next thing I knew, a huge man flung open the the door and knocked me down. Good thing, or the explosion that followed might have killed me.

Tell me, is she on my side,
Or does she have something to hide?
Why then would she run away,
Though I'm beggin' her to stay?

CHAPTER 16

I lay on the sidewalk, the wind knocked out of me. Pain blossomed across my back. My shoulder felt like bone had chipped off when it had collided with the concrete. I tried to move, but my limbs wouldn't oblige. The heat was so unbearable, it seemed like I was being baked alive. Sirens screamed in the distance.

A car door slammed, and I heard running footsteps. Then someone picked me up by the armpits and dragged me across the lawn. From my new vantage point, I had a clear view of the fire engulfing the apartment unit.

"Oh, geez," said a man's rough voice. "Why's this happening to me?" I managed to prop myself on one elbow and turn to see his face. It was Mitzi's neighbor—the one who'd been annoyed when I'd questioned him. He hadn't seemed like the heroic type, but I was grateful he'd pulled me to safety. His navy blue uniform shirt had the name "Kevin" embroidered across the pocket.

He touched my forehead. "Are ya okay?"

I nodded weakly, rubbing the back of my head where a lump was already forming. From the smell of scorched hair, I had a feeling my eyebrows wouldn't need plucking anytime soon. Kevin stood and approached the building. He danced back and forth near his apartment door, probably trying to figure out how to save his things. Heat from the flames drove him back.

Two fire engines rounded the corner, careening to a stop at the curb. As I pulled myself to a sitting position, another pain shot across my shoulder blades. Firefighters leaped from the vehicles and hustled into action. One went door to door, ringing bells and knocking to rouse anyone left inside. Others unreeled hoses. They fought the blaze and watered down parts of the building that hadn't caught fire yet.

Kevin approached one man who was wetting down the surrounding grounds. I couldn't hear what he said, but the fireman put out an arm to keep him away and shouted, "Stay back, sir. We'll handle it."

"But my apartment. My stereo," Kevin yelled. He moved toward the fire. The man motioned him again to keep his distance.

"You can't let it burn up," Kevin wailed. "I owe a thousand bucks on that thing."

Feeling woozy, I managed to stand and stumbled toward them. "Stop worrying about your stereo," I said. "What about people?" I turned to the fireman. "There might be a woman in there," I said, pointing toward Mitzi's door. "I was here when the fire started. You *have* to look for her."

The man shook his head. "Sorry, ma'am. Nobody's going in there now." He looked at the flames, already shooting through the second-story roof.

"Have you seen Mitzi lately?" I asked Kevin.

He shook his head. "Don't think she's been home since last time you were here."

"If she is in there, this could be homicide," I said, loud enough for the fireman to hear.

"What?" Kevin said.

"A man was in her apartment when I got here. He ran out, just before the building exploded. Bulldozed me in the process." The fireman didn't look like he believed me.

"Did you see him, Kevin?" I said.

"Nope." Sweat rolled down his round face.

The fireman adjusted his red hat. "Folks, move back. Let me do my job. Ma'am, Investigator Rollins will want to talk to you. He'll be here soon."

I backed away, wiping at my eyes, trying not to break down. My arms trembled uncontrollably as I watched flames licking at the building. This must be how it was the day David died, except the blast that killed him had been much bigger than the one I had just witnessed. I shuddered, praying Mitzi wasn't inside her apartment.

About two dozen residents huddled on the lawn across the driveway. One woman was on her knees, her hands clasped in prayer. Another stared from behind dark sunglasses, hands at her throat, twisting the ends of the blue paisley scarf covering her head.

"Excuse me, ma'am," said a voice behind me. "I understand you saw a man running from the scene." The man approaching me wore a gray suit with a loud red tie and black cowboy boots. Despite the grim circumstances, he smiled, deepening the lines around his graying mustache.

I nodded, brushing stray hairs from my face. "Yes, sir. I'm Corie McKenna."

"Jeb Rollins, arson investigator. Tell me what happened."

I told him the details, ending with the explosion that had knocked me down.

"Explosion?" he said.

I shrugged. "That's what it sounded like."

He scribbled in his notebook. "What brought you here?"

"Mitzi Martin lives in 12F. A friend of hers was murdered Friday night. I'm investigating the murder."

"You're with the police?"

"No. I'm working with Joe Garrett."

"Ah." He made another notation. "And you thought Ms. Martin knew about the murder?"

"I don't know what she knows. I haven't been able to track her down yet." I kneaded the small of my back.

"Interesting," Rollins said. "Have any idea why someone would torch her apartment?"

"Not even a guess."

Rollins stroked his mustache. "What about the man? Can you describe him?"

"No. He had his head down, like a battering ram. Hit me about here." I put a hand to my shoulder, judging height. "I'd say he must be nearly six feet tall. But he wore a cap. I couldn't see his hair or his face."

"That's all?" Rollins didn't sound impressed with my investigative abilities.

"Dress shoes. He was wearing black wingtips. And he was husky," I said, rubbing a sore thigh and wondering how big a bruise I'd have.

My gaze swept the parking lot. There were a couple more vehicles parked there now. One would belong to Rollins, one to Kevin. The red Bronco was gone. I hadn't seen or heard it drive away, but then I might have blacked out when I fell.

"Ms. McKenna?" Rollins said.

"Just a second." I spotted Kevin, who'd joined the group across the driveway. Firemen had ousted several more people from the burning building and the crowd had grown to about thirty. Paramedics were busy treating everyone who needed medical attention. The woman in sunglasses was sobbing. I wondered if she'd had a pet inside. God, how awful that would be.

I looked back to the vehicles in the lot. "There was a red Bronco parked right here," I told Rollins. "Mitzi's neighbor was one of the first people I saw after the fire started. Maybe he saw it leave."

I was thinking about the red truck Kit had seen at my house. If it was the same one, I wanted to know who the owner was, what he wanted, and why it had turned him into an arsonist. Since my concern was mere speculation, I didn't mention the incident to Rollins. Instead, I pointed out Kevin and Rollins said he'd make sure and question him.

After the investigator had finished with me, he went to talk to one of the firefighters, and I headed across the lawn, toward where Kevin stood talking with a couple of guys.

A dark-haired boy, about four years old, stepped in my path. "Are you a fire woman?"

I smiled. "Afraid not." The child appeared to be alone. I wondered whether he belonged to the crying woman. The scarf covered most of her head, but I'd caught a glimpse of brunette hair. Scanning the crowd, I saw she was hurrying in the other direction, approaching a tan car parked on the driveway's shoulder. If the kid were hers, she wouldn't be leaving him. Then a pregnant woman with a little girl in tow rushed over and grabbed the boy by the arm.

"I told you to stay by me," she said. "You scared me to death." She let go of his arm long enough to swat his behind, then looked at me, embarrassed.

I pretended not to notice and turned to join Kevin's conversation. "Those speakers, man, they were fine," he said, hands waving. "I can't believe this. If I didn't have bad luck, I'd have no luck at all." He looked at me, his hands stopping mid-conversation. "What?"

"There was a red Bronco in the lot near your apartment earlier. Did you see it leave?"

Kevin pursed his lips. "I, uh, maybe."

"The driver might have set the fire. He could be responsible for you losing your stereo system, so if you know something, spill it." I paused to let that sink in.

"You serious? Man, some red truck's all I remember. Could have been a Blazer, a pickup, who knows? All I know's he zoomed past me. Rattled the windows in my Chevy."

"Concentrate, Kevin. Could you describe the driver?"

"Look, you ain't the police. Whaddaya want from me?"

I let out a whoosh of impatience.

"At least it wasn't homicide," Kevin said, turning back to his buddies.

I grabbed his arm. "What did you say?"

"There's no homicide. The broad from next door is right over—" He pointed, then turned his head and stopped. "Where'd she go?"

I made the connection too late. Spinning around, I saw the tan car driving away. Ignoring the stabbing pain in my back, I jogged toward my truck, only to realize the Ranger was blocked in by a fire engine. Movie characters always knock someone from a motorcycle and take off after their prey, but I didn't see any motorcycles around. Instead, I ran down the driveway and watched the car round the corner.

I sprinted all the way to the gate. After confirming she was gone, I sank into an exhausted heap on the grass. My head was experiencing its own explosions. At least I didn't have to worry about Mitzi being burned to death. Instead, I wondered whether she had something to do with the fire. Mitzi Martin could be desperate and on the run, needing help. Or she could be one of the bad guys.

Sometimes the truth is hard to take,
It makes you feel your heart might break.
When you're filled with worry and strife,
Release it and go on with life.

CHAPTER 17

"My hearing must be failing," Wade said, raising his eyebrows. "Run that by me again."

"Did David ever go to topless bars?" I said, enunciating each word. "I have to know."

Wade scratched his head. "What led up to this? Are you feeling okay?"

"Sure. Fine." I didn't want to tell him about being knocked down and almost blown up. Wade already worried about me too much. On my way back to the office, I'd replayed the day of David's death, then my talk with Babs. By now I was too emotional to have a decent conversation and was fighting to appear calm.

"Tell me what's happening." Wade came around his desk to sit beside me on the sofa. He brushed back my bangs to examine the bruise on my forehead.

"What happened? If it's the Kemp case, I'll tell Garrett to hire someone else."

I pushed his hand away. "Stop. We're not talking about the case. My question is about David and what he did with his personal time."

Seconds ticked by, our eyes locked. Finally he said, "No, David didn't hang out in topless bars. Can't say he never went to one, but he wasn't the type, generally. Why are you asking this now?"

"Did *you* ever go to a topless bar with him?" As best

friends, they'd spent a lot of time together.

His blue eyes didn't waver. "No." He put his hand on my forearm. "Level with me. What's going on? I haven't seen you this upset in a long time."

My story came out in a rush. How I discovered Suzanna Kemp had worked at Whispers with the elusive Mitzi Martin. About our visit to the club and Babs telling us of a nice man named David McKenna who used to frequent the place until he died in a horrible accident. When I finished, tears were streaming down my face. Wade put his arms around me, and I let my weight rest against him.

"Good God, Corie, lighten up. You're taking the word of some waitress in a topless joint."

I lifted my head from Wade's shoulder and gave him a harsh look.

"Okay," he said. "So she did seem to know a lot about him. I guarantee there's an explanation. Maybe she met him *once* and he made a big impression."

"Is that supposed to make me feel better?"

"She could have heard about the accident and that made the name stick in her memory," he said. "It's possible she met someone else, then heard about the accident and only thought it was the same guy."

"Someone else with a wife named Corinne?"

"So it's a long shot." Wade sighed. "Maybe he was there once. I don't know. But I *do* know what kind of man he was. So do you." Wade patted my back.

I wiped my wet cheeks, tasted salt on my lips. "I guess you're right."

"Good," he said, as if that settled the whole matter. "You're usually such a level-headed woman."

The remark rankled my raw nerves. "Ed Kemp started this whole mess," I said. "Let me tell you a little about what *he's* been up to." I couldn't keep the sarcastic edge off my voice.

"Go ahead," said Wade, moving back to the chair behind his desk.

I stood and began pacing. "Looks like Kemp has girlfriends all over town. First, there's Maggie Robbins. Even though she says it's business, *he's* out for a good time. A woman named Vivian Coulter is *always* hanging around him. He's got a sex goddess in see-through clothes for a secretary." I stopped and gave Wade a pointed look. He didn't say anything.

"Word has it he took out a million-dollar life insurance policy on Suzanna," I continued. "And some say the man would do *anything* to keep his son." I struck a pose with my hands on my hips. "Garrett has his work cut out for him."

The sympathy I'd seen on Wade's face earlier disappeared. "I don't know what's gotten into you," he said softly, "or why you don't want to believe what I've told you about David. But you're supposed to be investigating the Kemp murder fully, not spouting off allegations and taking your own frustrations out on a client."

"The client is a first-class creep," I said, "and I don't trust him." I regretted the comment instantly. Wade's expression turned stony. He stood.

"Until you have facts on the alleged insurance policy, don't assume anything. Why don't you put down what you have so far on paper, and I'll give it an unbiased review. Facts, Corie. That's what Garrett's looking for, not a bunch of emotional b.s. Have it on my desk in the morning."

He stood, grabbed his briefcase, and yanked his jacket off the hanger behind the office door. "Make sure you include the details about how you got that knot on your head," he added, before slamming the door. The room was quiet, except for the echo of the metal hanger clanging back and forth.

I sank back down onto the sofa and punched the

padded arm. "Good job, McKenna," I said aloud. "Now you've alienated your best friend."

After my temper tantrum subsided, I went to my office and began work on the report Wade had demanded. Reading it, he'd realize I wasn't exaggerating about how bad Kemp's case looked. My fingers moved over the keyboard, outlining what I'd learned so far, but my mind wasn't on the job.

I felt guilty for unloading on Wade, but why didn't he understand? If Babs knew David, I wanted more details. And someone else to back up her story that David had visited the club.

Mitzi might know, but how would I ever track her down if Vincent Ochoa, her own boss and alleged boyfriend, couldn't even find her? I called Clay Mitchell to compare his verbal description of Mitzi to the woman at the fire scene, just in case her neighbor had been mistaken. It seemed to match, but Clay said he could do even better. The gym's membership records included computerized photographs. He promised to print Mitzi's picture and bring it to dinner. I had almost forgotten about our date.

Checking my watch, I decided there wasn't time to go back to Whispers first. On my next trip to the club, I'd ask which employees had worked there two years ago and see if any of them knew David. I leaned back in the chair, drumming my fingernails on the desk. Suddenly, I felt like crying. What difference did it make whether he'd gone to Whispers or not? What good would knowing do me?

Absolutely none. I had better sense than I'd shown lately. What was wrong with me? Part of the problem, I knew, was that I was living my life like a sad country music song. Part of me wouldn't acknowledge that David was gone. At times, I'd pull into our driveway expecting to see his car parked there or reach out to touch his side of the bed, surprised to find it cold. For God's sake, his clothes were still hanging in the closet. His home office looked the way he'd left it.

All the therapist appointments Mother had arranged for me hadn't helped me accept the truth. Logic told me he was gone, but emotion waited for him to miraculously reappear so our lives could go on as if nothing had happened. I needed to get a grip on reality. Straightening in the chair, I felt a new resolve.

Before leaving the office, I tossed my report on Wade's desk. So there! I didn't need a therapist to explain that action. He'd hurt my feelings, and throwing the report gave me a childish sense of satisfaction.

At home, Midnite greeted me at the back door. Her tail thumped my leg as I scratched her head. She was always glad to see me, and I didn't have to worry about us getting into an argument. Pets are a lot easier to deal with than people. Which reminded me of my date. Butterflies danced the tango in my stomach just thinking about it. I glanced at the clock and decided I had time to take Midnite for a walk.

Outside, traffic noises carried through the evening breeze. I shivered and zipped up my jacket. With a jerk, Midnite pulled toward the gate. I tripped on my own feet, catching myself before colliding with concrete for the second time that day. The muscles in my legs had tightened from my earlier fall. My back ached. The leash slipped from my hand and Midnite pulled away, just as I heard footsteps shuffling on the sidewalk.

Heart racing, I yelled "Who's there?" All I could think of was the man in the red Bronco.

"It's me. What's going on?"

"Kit!" I blinked and she came into focus. A street light cast a dim glow through the trees and across the driveway. The girl was kneeling, allowing the dog to lick her in the face. Ugh.

"You shouldn't be out here in the dark alone," I said, "especially not after that prowler last night."

"Hey, it's not totally dark. Why are you so nervous?" she asked.

"I'm worried about you. Is your mother home?"

"Not yet, but she's on her way. She's even cooking tonight," Kit said. Our heads turned at the sound of a car coming down the street. "There she is now. Want to come over?"

"Can't. I have a date." I retrieved the end of Midnite's leash.

"Wow, cool!" Kit looked at my dirty jacket and ripped slacks. "I hope you're changing. How'd you get so messed up?"

"I think I ran into your buddy this afternoon. I should say he ran into me."

Kit knew exactly whom I meant. "Did you call the police?" She stood, an expectant look on her face.

"No, he didn't stick around long enough to be caught."

"You know what he looks like, though." Kit jiggled with excitement.

I sighed. "Didn't even see his face."

"Oh, well," Kit said matter of factly. "We'll get him next time."

I cringed at the thought of a next time. "Don't you worry about it," I said. "This is my problem."

***

I contemplated canceling right up to the moment Clay arrived, promptly at seven-thirty. I had a bad case of the first-date jitters, which I attributed to my emotionally-charged day. Peeking through the dining room curtains, I felt like a teenager as I watched him climb out of an old Charger. The street light wasn't bright enough for me to tell the year, but the car had to be a classic.

For a second I thought I'd been transported back in time. One of my friends in high school had driven a car like that. I stopped to check a mirror on my way to the door. Same thirty-four-year-old me. A little rounder and more wrinkled, but wiser, I hoped.

One look at Clay's sincere smile made me glad I hadn't called off the date.

"It's great to see you," he said, bending his tall frame to give me a friendly hug.

"You, too."

His cologne was light and masculine. Or maybe the muscles I felt in our brief contact were what made me acutely aware of his maleness. His arms were like rock. Clay reached into the inner pocket of his sport jacket and produced a manila envelope.

"Here's the picture you wanted."

"Great!" I took it from him. "Come on in."

I fixed drinks, mineral water for Clay and a Coke for me, and we sat in the living room, studying the print.

"So, this is Mitzi," I said. As expected, it was the woman I'd seen at the apartment complex. In the picture, she wore a sweatband that held dark wavy hair away from her face, just as the scarf had. Although her eyes had hidden behind sunglasses when I'd seen her, the woman's pouty red lips were very distinctive.

"Is she the woman you saw?" Clay said.

"Unless she has a twin, it was her."

"Good." Clay looked relieved. "I was concerned. It's unusual for her to miss one work-out, much less days in a row. I imagined the worst."

I wondered, was his worry more than a passing interest? "What else do you know about Mitzi? Why would she disappear?" I hesitated. "Unless she had something to do with Suzanna's death."

A groove formed between Clay's eyebrows. "They were good friends. Mitzi wouldn't hurt Suzanna." I could tell he didn't approve of me bringing up the possibility.

"Did you spend much time with them? Talk much?"

"No, just hello, good-bye, answered questions about their workouts. That sort of thing." Clay leaned against the sofa arm, frowning.

"Ever go to the men's club where Mitzi worked?" I half expected Clay to get up and leave to avoid my interrogation.

He made a face. "Never. Those places turn me off."

I wondered how David would have answered the same question. My thoughts must have drifted, because Clay touched my shoulder to get my attention.

"I'd love to hear more about your work," he said. "But let's do it over dinner. Where would you like to eat?"

I smiled, suddenly realizing how hungry I was.

***

After a second glass of white Zinfandel at Pappas Seafood, I began to relax.

"I apologize for involving you in the investigation," I said. "Sometimes it's hard to separate work and pleasure."

"I don't mind," said Clay, raising his glass. Something about the angle of his jaw reminded me of David. Mentally chastising myself for making the comparison, I sipped my drink.

"Speaking of work," I said, "it looks like your gym is doing well." I sounded like a babbling idiot. I'd relaxed enough to take down the fence I usually put up between myself and any man, but wasn't sure that was such a good thing.

"Thanks," Clay said. "Where do you work out?"

"Here and there," I said, sucking in my flabby abs. The arrival of our shrimp cocktails kept me from having to elaborate.

We small-talked our way through the main course, nothing too personal. College years, vacation spots, a smattering of politics. I avoided bringing up family, but did find myself wondering what Mother would think of Clay. His small business wouldn't impress her at all. If they ever met, he'd have to win her on charm alone.

The restaurant was starting to empty when I excused myself to make a trip to the ladies' room and almost knocked Maggie Robbins down with the swinging door.

"Hey, watch it." Maggie jumped backward into the room before she saw it was me. "Oh, hello Corinne."

I eyed her slinky royal blue dress and giggled, a result of the wine. "Hi. What're you doing here?"

"Just having dinner." Maggie looked at her shoes, avoiding eye contact. "Good seeing you. Have to run." She darted out the door before I could comment.

Despite my giddiness, I recognized her behavior as suspicious and followed her into the restaurant, just in time to see her rushing Edward Kemp toward the door.

I'd never had a high opinion of Maggie's judgment, and this time she'd gone way too far. Although she'd told me about wanting an interview with Kemp's father, I didn't think the goal warranted having dinner with Ed Kemp. Again. No matter what kind of story she wanted. Especially not if she suspected Ed of killing his wife.

Back at the table, I didn't mention running into her. Thinking too much about Kemp and the case would ruin my light-hearted mood for sure. To help me forget, I let Clay talk me into an after-dinner cocktail.

Although the alcohol partially deadened the aches and pains I felt from my fall, I had trouble climbing out of the car when we got back to my house.

"I can help you get some of those kinks out," Clay

said.

"Really?" I said, wary of what he had in mind.

"Don't get me wrong. I'm licensed in physical therapy. How'd you get hurt?"

After I gave him a shorthand version of my afternoon, Clay recommended ice and ibuprofen. "You should probably wait until some of that alcohol wears off before taking the medication, though. In the meantime, I'm serious about working out the kinks. Want me to give it a shot?"

"Okay." I don't know whether I said it because I wanted relief or because I wanted him to touch me. The drinks had lulled me into a sense of security I hadn't felt in a long time.

Clay didn't even suggest going into the bedroom. Or removing any clothes. Instead, he had me lie face down on the living room sofa and knelt on the floor beside me. His hands moved professionally on my sore back and leg muscles. The pressure hurt, but it was a good hurt. An exciting hurt. I tried, unsuccessfully, to repress sexual thoughts.

"How's that feel?" Clay said. "Am I pressing too hard?"

I moaned.

"I guess that's good," he said, chuckling.

"Um-hmm." I wondered if I could get out of this situation without going further than I intended. Trouble was, I didn't know if I wanted out of it.

I forced myself to think about other things, to get my mind off the feeling of Clay's hands on my body. David, of course, readily sprang to mind. It shocked me to realize I could think about him at a time like this without feeling incredible guilt. Here I was, in our own living room, with another man. No, *my* living room. If I didn't stop putting ridiculous restrictions on myself, I'd go crazy. If Clay didn't drive me insane first. I stifled a wild impulse to roll over and pull him down on top of me.

He ran his hand down the center of my back with a lighter touch, then sat back on his heels. "Feel any better?"

"Much." I rolled onto my side.

"Glad I could help," Clay said.

Our eyes met. The mantel clock started to chime eleven. The evening had come to a turning point, and I had mixed feelings about how I wanted it to end. Clay took the lead.

He patted my hip, rolled onto the balls of his feet and stood. "You should ice your shoulder as soon as possible."

When I moved to get up, he took my hands and pulled me to a standing position. Feeling his breath on my forehead, I raised my head to look at him. "Thanks. I feel *much* better."

"Good." He didn't release my hands.

The silence was making me uncomfortable. I wondered if he felt the incredible tension filling the space between us. I sure did.

"How long should I keep the ice on?" I said, my eyes moving over his face, taking in every detail. Were his cheeks flushed, or was it my imagination?

"Twenty minutes on, twenty off," he said. "Alternate as long as you can stand it."

"Okay."

Clay's right hand came up to touch my cheek. "It was a great evening." He moved closer. "And I'd like to do it again. Soon." His hand tipped my chin higher.

For an instant, I was terrified of losing myself, of losing my memories of David. Then I didn't care.

Clay's kiss was tender, but firm. He tasted of wine and wintergreen LifeSavers, the combination delicious. When he moved away, the aftereffects of the kiss rippled to my toes.

My emotions swirled as he reminded me about the ice, talked about going out again on Thursday night, then left after another dizzying kiss. When the door closed behind him, I slumped against it. This was a first. I was actually attracted to another man without feeling like I'd committed a crime. Maybe this was some kind of crossroads in my life.

I walked into the study, my aches and pains lighter. Looking at the papers on top of David's desk, I felt silly for leaving them there all this time. Might as well clean things out now, while you're in a good mood, I told myself. Sitting in David's chair, I opened one of the large bottom desk drawers. I pulled out folders and piles of paper, stacking everything on top of the desk. Then I turned the stereo to a country music station and hummed along with George Strait singing "The Cowboy Rides Away." Before starting to sort, I fixed an ice pack and sat with the bag between my shoulder and the chair.

Within minutes, the waste basket was filled with papers and notes that David had saved for no apparent reason. I made a pile on the floor of things related to the firm. I'd give them to Wade.

Feeling industrious, I moved to the next drawer. David had stored his old calendars there. I paused, then picked up the binder that held his most recent loose-leaf calendar pages and turned to the back. The last month was October, the month before his death. November and December would have been in the leather binder he'd kept with him.

I debated whether to throw all the calendars away, keep them in the drawer, or box them up. Unsure of which route to take, I flipped through the pages, randomly reading scribbled entries.

Maybe I should have stopped with the easy stuff. Reading notes about appointments he'd kept and people he'd called made me feel like he could be upstairs taking a shower before bed. Tears threatened. Twisting my pendant chain, I began reading the client billing notations. David's handwriting had never been too legible, and I had to concentrate.

Then I noticed it. At first I wasn't sure, but holding the book at a different angle I deciphered the word Whispers penned in on a day in early October. I kept reading, moving my index finger across every line of notes on each day. Near the end of the month, I spotted the word Whispers again.

"Find out more about Whispers," it read. Babs had been right.

Oddly enough, the discovery didn't make me jealous. Only curious. David had gone to Whispers for some specific reason. I paged backwards to see if the visits started even earlier. I didn't find anything before October.

Then the name Ochoa popped out at me from an entry on September 15th. The notation said "Ochoa not in Mexico. Then where?"

We need to talk now,
Don't walk away.
I need to hear, yeah,
What you have to say.

CHAPTER 18

I stared at the page. Could David's "Ochoa" be one and the same as Vincent Ochoa, owner of Whispers? I shook my head, clearing the cobwebs. There could be thousands of Ochoas in Houston. But David *had* done corporate legal work and Vincent Ochoa *did* have a corporation. He could have hired Alexander & Glover to handle his legal affairs.

Wade might know, but I hesitated to call him after our little clash. I turned back to the calendar. The only other thing that jumped out at me was a small heart David had drawn at the top of July 8th. "Don't forget Corie," he'd written. It was our anniversary—the sixth and last.

I dropped the calendar back into the drawer and slammed it shut. It was too late for tears, in more ways than one. I needed sleep.

Sometime during my fitful night, I decided to gather all the facts before making another appearance at Whispers. I'd go through all of David's files, both at home and at the office. Reba knew as much or more than Wade did about David's practice. If his visits to the club were work-related and had to do with Vincent Ochoa, she'd help me figure out the connection.

Despite my intention to arrive early enough to avoid Wade the next morning, his Lexus pulled up next to my pickup in the parking lot at seven-fifteen. Why was he so early? I said hello, hoping he'd understand my negative attitude toward Ed Kemp after reading my report. I hoped it made sense and wasn't too badly colored by the angry mood I'd been in when writing it.

To my surprise, Wade greeted me with a heartwarming smile. A light breeze tousled his hair. The sunlight enhanced lines around his blue eyes. The wrinkles didn't age him, only gave him a more distinguished look. This morning, though, the eyes were rimmed with dark circles.

"Sure am glad to see you," he said. We fell in step, heading for the elevator.

My eyebrows raised. "You are?"

"I want to apologize." Wade pushed the elevator call button. "For acting like an ass yesterday."

Short of agreeing with him, or admitting I hadn't acted any better, I didn't know what to say, so I kept quiet.

"Been under the gun lately," he said. "Sorry. Tried to call you last night so I could get a decent night's rest. Were you really out, or just screening your calls?"

I smiled. "I was out, and your apology is accepted."

"Now I'll be able to concentrate on work today." Wade adjusted his suit jacket and straightened his tie. "Good friends are hard to come by, Corie, and I don't want to lose you. Whenever you need to talk, I'll be here."

As the elevator doors slid open, I blurted, "How about now?"

"Sure," Wade said. "Over coffee?"

We settled at the small conference table in his office. "Is this about Kemp?"

"No, but my report's over there on your desk, as you requested." More like ordered, but he'd apologized for that. I sipped my coffee.

Wade looked thoughtful. "Then this is still about David."

I nodded and filled him in on my discovery. "Don't

worry," I said. "I'm not getting all emotional about this. Only curious. I think he went to the club for business reasons. Did the firm represent Othello Corporation or Vincent Ochoa?"

Wade stroked his jaw, as though checking the closeness of his morning's shave. "We did some work for a man named Alberto Ochoa," he said slowly. "He was an elderly gentleman."

"Maybe they're related." Alberto, I remembered, was the name on the listing for that vacant house Dad and I had stopped by the other night.

"It's possible," Wade said, "but Alberto wouldn't be involved with a topless club. He was an old-fashioned, very moral type guy. What does it matter anyway?"

"David personally did some work for Alberto Ochoa, right?"

"Yes." Wade busied himself with adding more sweetener to his coffee.

"Why do you think David was looking for him?"

"Doesn't seem like a big mystery to me. The client was probably on vacation or something." Wade stirred his coffee so fast it sloshed over the sides of the cup. "Maybe David called him, he wasn't in, that's that."

Sometimes close friends can tell when there's something left unsaid. Words lurking under the surface, unspoken, on the other's tongue. Wade's expression seemed suspicious.

"Tell me," I said.

He looked up, trying to avoid my eyes. "Tell you what?"

"About Alberto Ochoa. There's more, isn't there?"

Wade shrugged. "The firm doesn't represent him anymore. We were discharged a couple of years ago. He hired a firm in Brownsville to take over all his business dealings."

"And? What else?" My palms felt sweaty.

Wade pushed back his chair and stood. With long strides, he covered the distance to the window, then back. "Okay. Alberto Ochoa owns Rios Entertainment. Used to be his mother's company. Rios is the parent company of all the Rio-Niño restaurants and the Grandioso dinner clubs."

Wade hesitated. He knew I'd made the connection. My heart seemed to stop.

"Hal Smith worked for Alberto Ochoa as general manager," he added quietly.

I slumped back in my chair. Now I understood why Wade had tried to end the discussion quickly. The Grandioso club. David's early morning meeting with Hal Smith. The explosion. I buried my head in my hands.

If only I had kept my mouth shut and ignored what Babs had said. Asking too many questions had dredged up memories I'd like to wipe out forever.

Wade touched my shoulder. "Are you all right?"

I took a deep breath and lifted my head. "Sure. But explain something. If the firm had already been discharged, why was David meeting with Hal Smith at all?"

"Cases don't end overnight. There's a transition period. You know that." He sat down, pulled his chair closer, and leaned toward me. "I'm sorry we got into this. You shouldn't dwell on the past."

I clenched my coffee cup. "I'm only trying to get answers."

Wade drummed his fingers on the table. "I don't understand. None of this matters now."

It did matter. But I'd never convince him.

He checked his watch, and I took it as an opportunity to end a conversation that wasn't going anywhere.

"You're right," I said, starting toward the door.

Wade turned. "Now what?"

I forced a smile. "Back to work on the Kemp case."

On my way out, I grabbed a small pad from Reba's desk, scribbled a message, and stuck the yellow square on her computer screen. *See me ASAP. Corie.*

My curiosity was on a roll. I wanted to see the Rios Entertainment file right now. David's timesheets, too. I knew the firm didn't store old files on-site. Reba would have to order boxes from archives. The urge to scrutinize David's activities right before he died gnawed at me. I couldn't assume, as Wade could, that Whispers was unrelated to Alberto Ochoa's restaurant and nightclub business. I'd study the files and then schedule a meeting and talk to Alberto Ochoa myself.

The phone rang as I settled into my office chair.

"So glad I caught up with you," Mother gushed.

The last time I'd seen her she'd been defending Ed Kemp. I didn't feel like pursuing that subject.

"Darling, I must apologize for being testy the other night. Your work is none of my business."

Wow! Another apology. My second of the day. She must want something.

"Don't give it another thought," I said. "I haven't." Right! I twisted my head, getting a better angle to chew on a hangnail.

"Oh, and I wanted to make sure you hadn't forgotten the gala tomorrow night. You will be there, won't you?"

Gala? What in the world—

"The Thomansen Gala, at The Ritz-Carlton," she prompted. "It's so exciting, how it's all coming together. I'm delighted we're able to raise so much money for cancer research. Please say you'll come."

I sighed. "Mother, I have other plans."

"You've known about the gala for months, Corinne," she said, her voice choppy. "Don't tell me you have to work."

"No, I have a date." A hint of pride crept into my

voice, knowing the revelation would shock her. If she'd already arranged for another of her stodgy but rich bachelor acquaintances to escort me to the gala, she didn't let on.

"That's wonderful. Then I'll see you both there," she said, her voice hesitant. Was she afraid I'd be dating one of the Hell's Angels or what?

"I don't think so, Mother." I couldn't subject Clay to her scrutiny so soon. I didn't have any idea whether he owned or would even dream of wearing a tuxedo. Enduring one of Mother's high-society evenings might be enough to scare him away, and I didn't want that to happen.

"You could at least mention the gala to your date," she said.

"Okay," I agreed. After hanging up, I marveled at her self-control. She hadn't even asked his name.

I flipped my calendar book open. Sure enough, I'd penciled in Thomansen Gala. I remembered now why the event sounded familiar. Maggie Robbins had said her meetings with Ed Kemp were to arrange an interview with his father during the event. I wondered if she'd had any luck.

I made a mental note to call Clay later and see how he felt about attending. There was the problem about the tux, so I'd tell him black tie up front. If he hesitated, I wouldn't insist. But Clay did seem like the type who'd be glad to support something benefiting medical research. I'd call Dad, too. Although he and I usually try to avoid Mother's functions, the gala might be fun if he'd come. Dad and Clay would definitely hit it off.

Thinking about Clay had put me in a lighter mood. Humming as I pulled out my copy of the report on Kemp's case, I reviewed my list of things to do and wondered what to tackle first.

Now that I knew Mitzi was in town, I had to find a way to locate her. Did she have family in the area? There were probably as many Martinezes in Houston as there were Ochoas. I wondered about her reason for hiding and whether she knew anything about Suzanna's murder. She might have a criminal record. In Harris County you can get that information if you have a person's date of birth, but I didn't know hers.

Clay wouldn't approve of my line of thinking, but viewing Mitzi as a murder suspect gave Ed Kemp's case a new perspective. If only I'd had a chance to approach the woman at the apartment complex. What had she been running from? When and if I did find her, what kind of reception would I get? My mind wandered into its musical mode, and I grabbed a tablet to jot down a few lines. I was sketching a staff and notes to match the tune running through my head when Reba walked in, munching on a giant chocolate chip cookie.

"Sorry I took so long. Finally got Wade off to court. What's up, girl?" Her beaded dangling earrings jingled when she plopped into a side chair. "You ready to plan our trip?"

"Not likely." I pushed the tablet aside.

"Watcha workin' on? Let me see." She took my notes and started humming a tune that sounded remarkably like the one I had in mind.

We could have probably worked up a good song, but that wasn't my morning's goal. I told her about the files I needed from archives.

Reba grimaced. "Wade said you'd been asking questions about David. What do you need the files for?" She crunched off another bite of cookie and crumbs scattered.

"Last night I started cleaning out David's things. Finally. I guess my date prompted that."

"Ooh, a date? That sounds productive." Her brown eyes twinkled. "Tell me more."

"I'll fill you in about Clay later. Anyway, I found

some odd notes about Alberto Ochoa, like David was trying to find the guy or something. And another man named Ochoa turned up on the Kemp case. Maybe I'm reaching here, but I'd like those files as soon as you can get them."

Reba laid the remains of her cookie on the desk corner. She dropped her chin onto a fist, thinking. "I remember Mr. Ochoa. He was a charming old guy."

"That's what Wade said."

"But that son of his." Reba shook her head. "What an S-O-B."

"You knew his son?"

"Yeah. Vincent Ochoa. Old Mr. Ochoa went by Alberto, but he's Vincent Alberto Ochoa, Senior."

Bingo. "What does the son look like?"

"Good lookin' as you can imagine," she said, "but what a snake! Kept wantin' to hire me, for what I'm not sure." Reba pulled at the shoulders of her orange knit top, adjusting the V neckline that showed ample cleavage.

"Then he *is* that guy who owns the topless club."

"He didn't give me a job description, but it wouldn't surprise me a bit," Reba said. "The jerk hit on me every time he showed up here."

"Then David knew Vincent Jr., too?" I was starting to get excited, finally able to piece some things together.

"Uh-huh. Sometimes his Daddy sent him over with papers. Not often." Reba slapped her knee. "Junior was somethin' to look at, but he didn't have what it takes up here." She tapped her head with a forefinger. "I don't think Alberto trusted him."

"From what Wade said about Mr. Ochoa, I doubt he'd approve of his son's nightclub."

Reba nodded. "Bet you're right."

I wondered whether Alberto Ochoa had ever met Mitzi. Vincent, Jr. might not have taken his lovers home to meet the family, but asking him about her was worth a try.

"I need to talk to Alberto, Sr. Do you have a phone number?" Reba had resumed munching on the cookie. I waited for her to swallow.

"We did. But you were right about David trying to find the old man. When we got the letter dismissing the firm, David was shocked. He tried to reach him for days, but nobody was home. Left messages, never got a call back. Then the phone was disconnected—no forwarding number. Our mail to him came back unopened. It bugged David so much, he would have flown to Mexico to try and find Alberto. Talk to him."

"Would have?"

Reba nodded. "Yeah. The Ochoas have a place in Monterrey. David had me book him a flight there."

I sat back in my chair. "He was going to Mexico? When?" Why hadn't he mentioned the trip to me?

Reba looked away for a second. "He planned to leave on November 8th."

The day after the explosion.

Looks like she's got a hold on you,
Before you know it, they'll come to get you.
If you know something you'd better tell me now,
I need to know who, when, where and how.

CHAPTER 19

David wouldn't have left town without telling me, would he? I thought back to the days before the accident. Wade had been in the midst of a complicated custody trial. I worked late every night interviewing witnesses and serving subpoenas for him. David had been busy with a corporate reorganization. Though we both loved our work, thrived on it, we also savored hours spent together. That month, our schedules practically demanded setting appointments to see each other.

How often had I wished we'd spent some quality time together that last night? I vividly remembered tiptoeing into the bedroom at two in the morning and hearing David's soft snore. Crawling gently under the covers, careful not to awaken him. We hadn't really talked in three days. Yes, he might have planned a trip without my knowing.

Reba snapped her fingers an inch from my nose in a flash of red acrylic nails. "Come out of it, girl."

She sat back down in her chair. "You didn't know about the trip?"

"No, I didn't." Shuffling papers on my desk, I couldn't help feeling defensive. "What did he hope to accomplish down there?"

"You know, I wondered about that myself." Reba looked thoughtful. "Remember how hectic it was around here, with that danged Fleming trial? If we hadn't been so busy, I would have questioned it. You know how I am."

"Yes. Kind of like me, more curious than a cat."

She propped her elbows on my desk. "It *is* odd he'd go all that way to talk to a client who'd fired him. What'd be the point?" She whistled a few bars of the tune we'd been composing, then said "I'll bet there's an explanation in the file."

"I hope so." It was silly for me to push the issue, wasting time looking through old files, but maybe the exercise would ease my mind.

"I'll call archives right now." Reba stood, setting her earrings to jingling again. "Might take 'em a couple hours to send the boxes over." She stopped in the doorway. "You say this has somethin' to do with the Kemp case?"

I shrugged. "Don't know yet. I'm grasping at straws."

"That's okay," Reba said. "I'll charge the delivery to the doctor anyway. He can afford it." She disappeared for a second before poking her head in again. "Almost forgot. Wade's friend Charlie called about the pictures Suzanna Kemp took. Wade talked to him about getting copies, but it's too late. The D.A.'s office got hold of 'em, and Charlie says they're about to indict Kemp."

"Because of the pictures?"

"I don't know, but guess who's prosecuting?"

The look on her face said it all. "Oh, great. Jill White?"

"You got it." Reba grinned. "Wade will be all over this case."

So, Wade's infatuation with the Assistant D.A. wasn't only my imagination. For the life of me, I didn't know what he saw in the woman.

"Maybe I'd better see Ms. White and find out what she's got on Kemp," I said. Competition with Jill was likely to result in me working harder for Kemp's side.

I headed downtown.

***

Jillian White had taken the D.A.'s office by surprise a couple years before. A petite girl from a ranch in west Texas, she'd come straight to Houston after law school, clerked for a federal court judge, then moved into her current position of hotshot prosecutor, winning nearly every case that came her way. The good ol' boy attorneys acknowledged her success as "not bad for a woman."

I ran into Jill from time to time, but had never witnessed her performances in the courtroom or in the rodeo arena, where I'd heard she excelled in barrel racing competitions. According to Wade, she was top-notch at both activities. He talked about Jill a lot, and I wondered if he'd gotten around to asking her out yet.

The offices of the district attorney housed nearly two hundred prosecutors on ten floors of a Fannin Street high-rise. Houston depended on these people to help keep criminals off the streets, but the city didn't waste any money on fancy office space. The hallways were lined with small, plain cubicles that gave me claustrophobia just looking at them.

Jill's space failed to reflect her illustrious career. Her "office" wasn't much more than ten feet by ten feet, boxes crammed around a worn wood veneer desk, which made getting in and out of the room nearly impossible. Her blonde head was bent over a file as she scribbled notes on a yellow legal pad. She looked up when my foot scraped against one of the boxes.

"Well, if it isn't McKenna." Jill stood, a full head shorter than me, extending a small hand. I always felt like a giant around her. "Don't tell me ol' Garrett has you out lookin' up excuses for Edward Kemp." Obviously a woman who liked to get to the point.

"That's right."

We shook hands, and I noticed hers were even rougher than mine. Jill's rose-colored suit and strand of pearls contradicted the calloused hands and gruff voice. Though I couldn't detect a trace of makeup, her blue eyes looked vibrant behind tortoise shell glasses. An unruly strand of curly blonde hair had slipped out of the barrette fastened at the nape of her neck.

"Kemp's case is still under investigation," she said, "so if you're lookin' to discuss it, you're out of luck." The woman was playing her little power game and loving it. What did Wade see in her?

"I heard you're going to indict him," I said.

"I'd say that rumor is probably true." Jill smiled, self-righteously, I thought. "Hope the doctor is enjoying his last few days of freedom."

"So, you've already convicted Kemp," I said. Never mind that I'd been doing exactly the same thing in my head. "Isn't it a little early for that?"

"Some cases are simple. Especially those with credible witnesses." Jill balanced herself on the edge of the desk.

I squared my shoulders, my adversarial side coming out. "We've obviously talked to different people."

Jill adjusted her glasses. "Really? Ms. Robbins told me she'd come to see you, too."

Damn. Maggie Robbins would be a *very* good prosecution witness. Everyone in Houston knew her from television. The jurors would see that sincere, cheerful, newswoman's smile and believe anything she said. Maybe Garrett should file a motion for a change of venue.

"As you know, there are two sides to every story," I said.

"True." Jill took off her glasses and tapped one of the arms against her teeth. "And what's your side? Being an eyewitness, I'm sure you have an interesting story to tell about the night of Mrs. Kemp's murder."

"I don't jump to conclusions without all the evidence," I said. "Which reminds me, I'd like to see the photographs Mrs. Kemp took that night."

Jill smirked. "Be my guest. They're useless." She walked around the desk, opened a drawer and withdrew a packet, tossing it to me.

I opened the envelope of prints and flipped through them.

"See what I mean?" Jill said. "The pictures are meaningless."

"Maybe, maybe not," I said. From a cursory inspection, I decided she was right, but wouldn't tell her that. It looked like Suzanna had taken some pictures of the warehouse furniture. There were several shots of cars inside a garage and one out-of-focus picture of a house. I flipped through them a second time, counting. "Only fourteen?"

"Rest of the film was unexposed." Jill tried to slip the escaped tendril of hair back into the barrette.

I handed the pictures back to her and turned to leave. "Keep up the investigation, Jill. You wouldn't want to put an innocent man behind bars. Think about it—he's a doctor. Someone who's dedicated his career to life, not death. He's no murderer." I was trying to convince myself, too.

"Don't you read your Daddy's newspaper?" she said. "*Anyone* can turn to crime." Thin black eyebrows rose above the frame of her glasses. It gave me some pleasure knowing the pretty blonde hair wasn't genuine.

"Just don't forget reasonable doubt," I said.

On my way back to the parking garage, I thought about our debate. Jill was right again. The growing crime rate was a sad commentary about the state of the country. She was also right about Maggie Robbins being an excellent witness.

I'd have to lay it on the line to Kemp. Tell him the bad news. He had to be straight with me. Maybe the man had some information that would help him to save himself, but I'd probably have to drag it out of him.

A woman in a blue Chevy held up the line at the cashier's booth of the parking garage. She jostled around in the front seat, then turned, looking into the back, then opened the glove compartment. I thought about going up and giving her a few bucks just to get the line moving. The man in the black Mazda behind me looked even less patient than I felt. Sunglasses covered his eyes, but I could relate to his scowling expression. I thought he'd lay on the horn any second. Finally, the Chevy moved ahead. I paid for my parking quickly and accelerated out into the street.

I took a right on Fannin, then relaxed and started thinking about Maggie again. What information had she given to convince Jill she'd already won the case? Maybe nothing more than what Maggie had told me. Kemp had left their dinner, giving him enough time to drive home and murder his wife. He was angry because Maggie had refused to spend the night with him. I sure was glad for the confidentiality rules that prevented me from testifying against Kemp. His behavior at the office that same day had been pretty damning.

I slowed for a red light, noticing at the last minute I should be in the far left lane. Normally, I'd shoot across a couple of lanes to make my turn, but the black Mazda was to my left, just behind me. From the look on the driver's face earlier, I didn't want to test his patience any more. It wasn't the first time I'd had to circle a block due to daydreaming.

After what Maggie had experienced Friday night, I still couldn't believe she'd subject herself to Ed Kemp again. Why had she been at Pappas with him last night? Either he would agree to arrange an interview with his father for Maggie, or he wouldn't.

At Louisiana Street, I made a right to get back on track. Thinking about Maggie reminded me of why I'd hated journalism, a profession I'd tried out for a couple of years. Deadlines. Pressures. I had some in my job, but liked to think of them as challenges. It was time to tackle this particular challenge head-on. I'd start right after lunch.

I punched my cell phone on and dialed Dad's office to see if he was free to join me. Cruising down Milam and hitting the green lights just right, I waited for an answer at his office. A casual glance in the rearview mirror told me the black Mazda was still with me, too close to my left rear bumper. What was with the guy? He looked like the type to climb out of his car and start swinging if he got mad. Had I done something to anger him?

I checked the side mirror, then the rearview again. Damn crazy Houston drivers! The stress of dealing with traffic got worse every day. I thought about moving to my Montana "dream ranch." Maybe someday.

"Hello? Is anyone there?"

The voice brought my attention back to the phone. "Hi, Greta. Does Dad have lunch plans today?"

"I'll ask, Corie. Just a sec." She put me on hold, tuned in to a classical radio station. The music sounded familiar. Something I'd once studied for a piano lesson, decades ago. Mozart's Piano Concerto in D Minor, unless my memory failed me. Funny how some things stick with you.

Speaking of sticking with me, the Mazda was still in my rearview. Was it more than coincidence? Making a snap decision, I hung a right on Polk, swerving around the corner as I ran the red light. The Mazda driver didn't hesitate to cut across a lane to follow. My heart rate increased, matching the crescendo of the concerto's closing bars.

No coincidence.

I pressed the gas pedal harder and moved to the far left

lane. The black car stayed a couple of lengths behind me.

"Hi, sweetie. How's my favorite daughter?"

I wasn't in the mood for our normal repartee. "Dad, someone's tailing me."

"Thought you called about lunch?" He chuckled, obviously not catching the seriousness in my tone.

I took another left on a one-way street, darted in front of a bus, and turned right at the next opportunity. "I'm not kidding."

In the mirror, I saw the Mazda swerve around the front of the bus, barely missing it. He was picking up speed, closing the distance between us. What the hell was the nut doing?

"Where are you?"

"Downtown." I took another left turn and stomped on the gas to make it through a yellow light. "Oh, good. Someone pulled in front of him. He had to stop."

"Head for the police station," Dad said.

I thought about it for a second, but even as a child I hadn't followed orders. Dad knew that, too. I calculated my distance from the freeway. Besides, chances of getting a cop's attention in the weekday hustle and bustle around the police station were slim.

"No. I can lose him."

"When did all this start?"

"I only noticed a few minutes ago. I think he waited for me to return to my truck in a parking garage." I checked my mirror. "Oh-oh, here he comes." The light just ahead of me had turned red. I ran it.

"Any idea who he is?"

I squinted, looking for a license number. There was no plate on the front of the car. "Not a clue, but he's gaining on me."

"Turn off, keep turning, zigzag."

"That's what I've been doing," I said.

"You should call 911."

"Maybe." My truck's tires squealed as I took a quick right, swerving around another corner.

"I'm on a side street now, in a neighborhood."

The area didn't look too desirable. Nearly every house sported burglar bars, wood trim with peeling paint, and an unkempt lawn. The streets were deserted, which might be preferable to having gang members hanging around. "I don't see him anymore."

"Good." I could hear Dad talking to Greta in the background. "Corie, I'd feel better if you drove to the nearest substation."

I made another turn, traveling down the narrow street as fast as I safely could. My sweaty palms slid on the steering wheel. Maybe I should take Dad's advice.

I'd heard a lot about carjackings in the city, but if the guy wanted the pickup why hadn't he held me up in the garage and taken it then? I didn't think that was his purpose. Not after Kit's report of the man poking around my house the other night. Maybe this guy also owned a red Bronco.

Deep into the neighborhood, I spotted an open garage door. The one-car building was empty. "Guess what, Dad? I think I found a place to hide."

"Tell me where you are."

"I don't see any street signs." Making a snap decision, I turned into the short driveway, pulled the Ranger into the garage, and flipped off the ignition.

"Dad, hang on, okay? Just a minute." I jumped out of the truck, leaving the door ajar, and ran to the garage door, yanking on the manual cord to close it. I could hear Dad yelling at me over the phone but couldn't tell what he was saying.

"I'm okay," I whispered into the receiver. "Hold on."

As the door came down, I noticed there was no other exit. Not even a window. I stooped down, looked to make sure no cars were in sight, and moved to the outside. Hearing traffic approach, I yanked the door closed, then flattened myself against the garage wall next to a large oleander bush.

My knees wobbled and my heart threatened to beat itself right out of my chest. I put the phone to my ear.

"Dad, you still there?"

A screen door slammed and a man started shouting.

"Who's that?" Dad yelled. "Where are you?"

Speechless for the moment, I watched a stocky Hispanic man rush at me from the small house next door, spouting Spanish that bore little resemblance to what I'd learned of the language.

He spoke so fast, I could only understood two words. You loco. Maybe he was right. Thank God he wasn't armed. At least not that I could tell, so far. The man stood about two feet in front of me, his beer breath hitting me in the face, his left hand waving a cigarette like a baton moving in time with his hollering. Then the sound of a car's engine distracted him.

When the man turned to look, I shrank behind the bush, still clutching the phone.

"Don't worry," I told Dad, with feigned confidence.

The black Mazda rounded the corner. As it passed my hiding spot, I got a good look at the back of the car. No license plate there either. The police noticed every time I forgot to renew my inspection sticker. Why didn't they catch guys like him? At the end of the street, the car took a right turn.

I'd lost one maniac, at least.

As for the Hispanic man, he turned, eyes narrowed. He raised a fist in my face and blew a puff of smoke in my eyes.

What do you want?
Get out of my face.
Why did you follow me
Into this place?

CHAPTER 20

"Thanks for convincing the guy I'm harmless," I told Dad when we reached the restaurant. "The experience gave me an incentive to brush up on my Spanish."

"That's not exactly what I told him," Dad said, laughing. "But he understood perfectly. Said he has his hands full with *three* crazy daughters. Poor guy."

I glared at him across the table. We'd met at Manuel's Cantina, a favorite lunch spot of Dad's. I shifted in my chair, too nervous to sit comfortably.

"Any idea why you're being followed?" Dad picked up a tortilla chip, salted it, and scooped up a generous portion of salsa. Although he's okay with the type of work I do, his approval doesn't exempt him from worrying. Having me for a daughter probably helped form the permanent crease between his brows.

"No. I wonder if he'd been tailing me before, and I never noticed."

"Maybe he's only trying to scare you," Dad said, "but getting so close wasn't a smart move. You'll be able to give the police a good description."

I shook my head. "All I saw was sunglasses, dark hair, black Mazda, tinted windows. Maybe he was out to terrorize whoever got in his way this afternoon."

"Oh, sure," Dad said. "And it just happened to be you."

I didn't believe that either.

Ana, Manuel's wife, had seated us at a corner table.

Unlike more boisterous Mexican eateries, this one played soft Latino music. The place was always crowded and Ana headed toward our table now, squeezing through the narrow aisle while balancing a tray covered with chicken enchilada platters, the day's special. Before she reached us, a man in black jostled by, his elbow nipping her arm. The tray tottered, but she managed to keep control.

"People are too impatient," she said, placing our platters on the table as she turned to frown at the man. Though he appeared to be alone, he sat at a six-person table three away from ours. With the line of people waiting to be seated, I understood Ana's irritation. I thought she might say something to him, but she headed straight back to the kitchen.

"Best enchiladas in Texas," said Dad, cutting into his meal without hesitation.

The food smelled delicious, but steam rose from the plate, and I was in no hurry to burn my tongue.

"Let me fill you in on what's been going on," I said.

"I don't see you for one day and you've been getting into all kinds of trouble, haven't you?" Dad blew on a forkful of food to cool it off.

"And doing a good job of it."

Between spooning salsa over the enchiladas and munching on chips, I told Dad about my latest adventures. From the prowler at my house, to Kit's being taken to the police station, Mitzi's desperate call to Mrs. Hernandez, and the explosion/fire I'd narrowly missed. By the time I'd finished, Dad didn't look too hungry. His plate was still half full, but he let his fork fall to the plate with a clatter.

"Is that all?" He picked up his iced tea and finished the drink in one long gulp.

"I think so." I started eating as Dad told me what he'd heard in the newsroom about the apartment fire.

Leaning over my plate to avoid getting sauce on my

clothes, I sensed someone watching me. I raised my eyes to meet the stare of the rude dark-haired man still sitting by himself. He looked away, fondling the stem of his margarita glass with one hand, a folded newspaper clutched in the other.

"Why do you think the guy torched the place?" Dad said.

"I don't know. To scare Mitzi? If only I'd been able to catch up with her. I've been half suspecting her of being involved in the murder somehow, but now that doesn't make sense." I glanced toward the dark-haired stranger again. Since he wasn't looking my way, I took the opportunity to check him out. White shirt, Wranglers, boots. Something about him looked familiar. He held the newspaper a few inches off the table, but didn't appear interested in reading it. Maybe he was waiting for friends.

"I'm sure Mitzi's good and scared now," Dad said, "but what if he wasn't out to hurt her? Maybe his goal was to destroy something inside the apartment."

"That's possibe." I ate fast, wanting to finish my lunch before the enchilada sauce jelled on the plate. "How would anyone ever determine what that something might be?"

Dad shrugged. "Let's look at the whole picture," he said. "Somebody else wants to find Mitzi. Since our visit to the club, they know we want to find her, too. They're watching her place *and* yours. They think you might lead them to her. Voilà, they have you followed."

I swallowed a big bite, then washed it down with Coke. "Maybe." I didn't like his scenario one bit.

"You find any tie-in to Suzanna's murder yet?"

"I found out the warehouse is being leased by Leo Atkins."

"The man from the club."

I nodded, munching on a chip. "That furniture in the warehouse will be auctioned soon. I'd like to know more about that. Unless I figure out why Suzanna went there and took pictures of it, I'm stalled."

I checked out the man again. His head was bent toward the table and he'd covered one ear with a hand. Reaching for my Coke, I accidentally knocked the spoon out of the salsa bowl. Red sauce splattered across the table. I grabbed for napkins, knocking the dispenser over in the process.

"What's wrong?" Dad said.

"Something's up with that guy," I whispered.

Dad turned slightly, glancing over his shoulder. "You always did attract the tall, dark, and handsome type," he said. "Wink at him."

"Very funny." I pushed my empty plate to the table edge.

"I'll find out about the auction for you," Dad said. "If it isn't advertised in the paper, I'll make a few calls."

"I'm betting both Atkins and Vincent Ochoa have something to do with this whole mess," I said.

"I'll check on them, too, but don't forget my number one rule."

"Never assume."

Dad grinned. "Right. When you focus on only a part of the picture, you overlook the obvious. Keep all the facts working together."

Reviewing my last couple of days in fast forward, I remembered my visit to Larry Rogers' apartment. He'd seemed so harmless I had assumed he wasn't involved. That wouldn't do. I'd have to make a trip to the restaurant where he worked to check out his alibi. I felt sorry for the guy, being jilted for the likes of Ed Kemp, but there were two sides to every story, and Larry may have deserved to get dumped.

We talked for a while about the Thomansen Gala scheduled for the following evening. Dad rolled his eyes, but said he'd promised Mother he would go. After hearing I might show up with a date of my own choosing, he said he'd be there for sure. In the meantime, he'd call when he knew something.

I'd put the prying eyes of the stranger out of my mind until we headed out. When Dad stopped to say goodbye to Ana, I saw the man stand. As he headed for the door, carrying the folded newspaper, he reached up to his ear and I noticed the wire trailing along his neck. When he pulled a pair of black sunglasses from his shirt pocket and put them on, I grabbed Dad's arm.

"It's him," I whispered.

"Who?"

"Shh." I froze, keeping the death grip on my father's arm, my peripheral vision straining until I saw the door swing shut behind the man.

"That guy! He's the one who followed me. He's been sitting here staring at me, and I didn't realize it was him until he put on those sunglasses."

Dad grabbed my hand, yanking me toward the door. "Get in your truck. I'll follow him. We'll stay in touch by phone."

We hit the parking lot, separating immediately.

I pulled into traffic that was heavy for early afternoon. I hoped Dad could keep up with the guy. After driving a mile or two, I saw no sign of the Mazda. My phone chirped, and I grabbed it up in mid-ring.

"Dad?"

"Yes. I'm still in front of the restaurant. The guy vanished. Is he with you?"

I checked my mirrors. "No."

"You're sure it was him?"

"Not a hundred percent." I reminded myself of how many men with dark complexions and hair might eat at a

Mexican restaurant in one day's time. And how could the man have tracked me to Manuel's?

"Nobody's following you now, right?" Dad said.

I checked the rearview mirror again. "Nope. I'm all clear. Could be a false alarm, but I swear the guy was wired. Do you think he was listening to our conversation?"

"Truth to tell, I think you're a little skittish."

"I guess." I hung up after promising to call Dad if my follower showed up again.

Nobody trailed me to Emilio's Italian Restaurant in southwest Houston. The sun had finally broken through the hazy clouds, raising the temperature to the low sixties. I left my jacket in the truck and hiked across the crowded parking lot to the front door.

The lunch crowd hadn't thinned yet. Using the crowd as a cover, I scanned the restaurant for Larry Rogers. After a couple minutes I made my way to the bar. I hadn't seen Larry, and decided it wouldn't matter whether he was here or not—it was his co-workers I needed to talk to.

Three people worked behind the bar, but they needed three more. The bartenders scurried back and forth, taking orders and filling trays with drinks. When the man seated in front of me left his stool, I grabbed it. The only female bartender looked like my best bet for learning more about Rogers. Not too young, maybe about his age, and a serious worker, unlike the other cutesy female employees. Her name tag said Pat. When she looked my way I raised a hand, waving a twenty.

She promptly served me a Coke. When she handed me my change, I handed the ten back to her. "I need to talk to someone about Larry Rogers. Know him?"

Pat laughed. "I thought this only happened in the movies. You serious?"

"Deadly."

Pat's expression sobered. "Yeah, I know him. Works nights, mostly."

"He here today?"

"Nope."

"You ever work nights?"

"Only on weekends."

One of the other bartenders gave Pat a dirty look. "Yo, Pat, take up some slack here," he yelled, pointing to the throng of customers.

She ignored him. "I don't know much about Larry," she said, twisting a strand of hair around her index finger.

"I appreciate your talking to me," I said, hoping sincerity would buy more information. "I know you're busy, but I have to find out if he was here last Friday night."

She looked down at the bar for a few seconds, thinking. "I stayed till about eleven Friday. He was probably working then, but O'Donnell can tell you for sure. He's the owner, and believe me, he keeps track of everything. Go down that hallway." She pointed to her right. "The door at the end. Says employees only. Knock and he'll answer."

O'Donnell wasn't nearly as helpful as Pat had been. I didn't really expect him to invite me into the "employees only" area, but he could have opened the door more than a crack. His squinting brown eyes traveled up and down my body when I asked him about Larry Rogers.

"Rogers doesn't work here any more," he snapped.

I tried to hide my surprise. "Since when?"

"He's fired next time I see him," O'Donnell said.

I nodded. "Oh. Why?"

"Guy's not pulling his weight. Who are you, anyway? Another one of his girlfriends?" O'Donnell glared at me.

Another one? I pulled out a business card and handed it through the crack in the door.

"No, I'm not," I said, giving him a second to examine

the card. "If you could answer some questions, you might avoid a visit from the police later." That remark earned me an invitation into O'Donnell's small office in the back corner of the building. The space was nondescript—white walls, a desk, two chairs, one gray filing cabinet. The place matched O'Donnell's outfit—black slacks, white shirt, solid gray tie. Only a calendar pad filled with pencil notations occupied the desk top.

"That the employees' work schedule?" I said, motioning to the calendar.

His shifty look made me wonder if O'Donnell had a personal reason for fearing the police.

"What exactly do you want to know?" he asked.

"It's simple. Did Larry Rogers work Friday night, and if so, what were his hours?"

O'Donnell glanced at the calendar pad, then removed a thick ledger from a desk drawer and turned to his records for Friday. He studied it for a minute, before looking at me. His gaunt face seemed more pale than it had earlier. "Who are you working for?"

"That's confidential," I said. "I need to confirm Rogers' whereabouts Friday night."

O'Donnell nervously shuffled the pages of his book. "He punched in at three-oh-five in the afternoon," he said. "Was supposed to work 'til eleven. Couldn't find him when I looked for him at eight. Whatever trouble he's in got nothing to do with my restaurant." O'Donnell's hands shook as he replaced the ledger in the drawer.

"Do you think he's in trouble?"

"Sure. Isn't he?" He stared out the window, avoiding my eyes.

I leaned forward. "A woman has been murdered, Mr. O'Donnell. I don't think Larry did it, but I'm trying to find out who did. If you know something, please tell me."

"Murdered?" O'Donnell practically jumped out of his chair. "Someone murdered her?" He paced in the narrow space between the desk and the window. "Jesus! I knew he was in trouble."

I was confused. "Mr. O'Donnell, wait. Who are you talking about?" From what I'd learned so far, I couldn't fathom Suzanna Kemp ever coming to see Larry Rogers at the restaurant.

"The trouble started the day she showed up," O'Donnell said.

"Who? What was her name?"

"I don't know her name," O'Donnell yelled. "She got everybody's attention, though. A real looker."

"Can you describe her?" I asked, picturing Suzanna.

"Black hair. Lots of it. Curly. Short, short skirt." O'Donnell sighed. "Couldn't miss her. She was crying. Makeup running all down her face. She dragged Larry to the back. It looked like they were arguing."

"When?"

O'Donnell looked at the desk calendar pad. "Monday night."

"Then what happened?"

"Rogers left with her. Out the back door." O'Donnell slapped his hand on the desk pad. "He didn't punch out or tell me he was leaving. I don't know who she was, or where they went. I swear."

I edged my chair away from the desk. Why was he so agitated?

On a whim, I dug around in my purse and found the picture of Mitzi Martin that Clay had brought me the night before. I held it out to Mr. O'Donnell.

"Is this the woman you saw?"

He glanced at the picture, not moving to take it from me. I could tell by the flicker in his eyes, Mitzi had been the one who'd come to see Larry.

"What if it is?" O'Donnell said, beads of sweat popping out on his forehead.

"Why are you so upset?"

"Lady, I don't want any more trouble around here. Business is good, and I can't afford to get mixed up in anything."

"What are you talking about?"

"A couple of thugs came over here last night," he said, "looking for her. If I knew anything I'd have told them, but I don't. They scared the crap out of me. You understand? I told them, and I'm tellin' you, I don't know anything."

You might be in danger.
Watch out for that stranger
Lurking near your door.
You can't trust him anymore.

CHAPTER 21

"I'm one of the good guys, Mr. O'Donnell," I said, trying to put what he'd told me into perspective. "I want to find the woman, too. Her name is Mitzi Martin. She's in danger, and we might be able to help her."

O'Donnell slumped against the back of his chair, silent. It didn't look like the beautiful-damsel-in-distress plea would work on him. Anxiety had splotched his pale complexion with red.

"Any idea who the men were?" I said.

"No." O'Donnell sounded weak, frightened. The sag of his cheeks became more pronounced. "They waited in the parking lot, near my car. It was dark. They jumped me."

"You know who sent them?" I asked the question, even though I could hazard a pretty good guess.

"They called him *jefe*. Never said a name." O'Donnell fingered his shirt collar nervously. "They had a black car. I couldn't tell what make."

I didn't believe in coincidence. It could be the same car that had followed me. Dad was right. They thought I'd lead them to Mitzi. Fat chance. I wasn't having any luck catching up with her so far.

"Did they say why this man wanted to find her?"

"No, and I didn't ask. You wouldn't either if they held a knife to your throat." O'Donnell pulled the collar away from his neck, revealing a blood-red slice mark about three-quarters of an inch long. The skin around the wound looked swollen, and I wondered if he should have had stitches. No wonder the man didn't want to talk to me.

"Did you report the attack to the police?" I asked.

"No!" O'Donnell almost came out of his chair with the force of the word. "They said they'd kill me if I went to the police."

"Don't let those guys control you." Easy for me to say.

Looking at the laceration filled me with contempt for Vincent Ochoa. If Mitzi wanted to leave him, why wouldn't he simply let her go? This seemed more than a love affair gone bad. Had Mitzi gotten into some trouble, then dragged Suzanna Kemp in with her?

"Maybe Rogers is hiding her from the men who threatened you," I said. I pulled out my notebook and found Larry's number. "May I use your phone to call him?"

O'Donnell placed his hand on the telephone and pulled it across the desk towards him. "I have work to do. There's a pay phone out in the hallway." He glanced at my notes. "Anyway, he's not there anymore."

"What do you mean? I just went by his apartment days ago."

"He moved out. Manager was glad to see him go since he never paid the rent on time. Didn't leave any forwarding address. If he had, I'd have fired him already."

After leaving the restaurant I made my own call to the apartment complex manager, remembering Dad's motto—never assume. The manager confirmed O'Donnell's story and had not seen a girl matching Mitzi's description. Rogers had left his furniture, and from the sound of it he hadn't cleaned up the trash littering his apartment. Management had already cleared the place out and repainted for a new tenant.

Driving down Chimney Rock, I searched the rearview

and side mirrors, my eyes peeled for a black Mazda. Toyotas and Mitsubishis set off false alarms. I spotted a couple of black Mazdas going in the opposite direction. I didn't seem to have a tail. Now what?

I had planned to go back to Whispers, but I wasn't so eager to make the trip after seeing O'Donnell's injury. At the moment, my best lead was our unyielding client, Ed Kemp. I drummed my fingers on the steering wheel, wondering how to get his undivided attention. Finally, I picked up the phone, adopting an impersonation I'd perfected in high school.

"Of course, Mrs. Poole, we'd be happy to squeeze your friend in. Dr. Kemp can see her at three o'clock," said Sallie, Kemp's appointment secretary. "I'm glad to hear your shoulder is better." I hung up, grinning as I headed for the Medical Center. If Mother found out I'd used her name to deceive her doctor, she'd be furious.

An hour later, I was sitting on the examining room table, flipping through *People* magazines. When Kemp came through the door, fifteen minutes past the appointed time, I had him right where I wanted him. In a confined space, no distractions.

When the doctor looked up from the information sheet I had filled out using an alias, his smile instantly changed to a grimace. "What are you doing here?"

I jumped down from the table, putting myself between him and the door. "Do you greet all your patients this way?"

"You're not a patient," he said. "And I'm busy. *You* don't have an appointment."

"I do now." I folded my arms. "Besides, I didn't notice a room full of people waiting to see you. I suppose your patients have read about you in the newspaper."

"My patients know I'm innocent," he said, "and my time is valuable."

"So is mine, but we need to talk."

Kemp met my glare for a few seconds, then gave in and looked away. He sat on a wheeled stool and rolled it over to where he could lean against the wall.

"Okay, talk." His eyes held no warmth.

"I've been working on your case for several days, generating a lot of questions. I hope you have answers."

"Make it quick," Kemp said, looking at his watch.

"Dr. Kemp, did you know your wife worked at a nightclub called Whispers before she came to Methodist?"

Kemp's head snapped up. "What?"

I suppressed a smile. "You're familiar with Whispers?"

"I know what it is," he said. "Where'd you get that asinine idea?"

"Suzanna worked there as a topless dancer. Mitzi Martin worked with her. They were friends."

Kemp stood. "I already told you, I never heard of that woman. And I don't believe a word you're saying. Suzanna wouldn't have done that."

"The Suzanna you knew probably didn't want you to know about her past. Seems like she did a good job concealing it."

Kemp ran both hands through his kinky hair. "Is this what I'm paying you for? To dig up dirt about my wife? You're supposed to find out who killed her."

I noticed a blood pressure pump hanging on the wall, and was sure mine was rising. "I need your cooperation. You might have seen or heard something that would help me solve the case. Hear me out."

Kemp reluctantly sat back down. I filled him in on Larry Rogers and the people who worked at Whispers. Kemp professed he'd never heard Suzanna mention any of them. If he was telling the truth, Suzanna had done an excellent job keeping her background a secret. If he was lying, he was good at it.

"Do you have any idea why I'm being followed?" I said.

Kemp laughed, a harsh, grating sound in the antiseptic little room. "I don't care who it is or why. I certainly have nothing to do with it."

My hand tensed, itching to slap the doctor's face. I tried to ignore his sarcasm, reminding myself he was a client. From his smirk, I could tell the bozo took a perverse pleasure in aggravating me.

"Then I'll tell you something you *will* care about," I said. "I saw the prosecutor today. She thinks she has an open-and-shut case against you."

Kemp's eyes widened. "You're joking."

"I'm not. Doctor, I know Garrett told you to be careful about what you say and do. You need to pay closer attention to his advice. Your behavior, people you're seen with in public—everything can have an effect on the outcome of your case. The prosecution will drag in witnesses you never dreamed of. No matter what I do, what evidence I turn up—"

Kemp stood again. "I haven't done anything wrong," he shouted, closing in on me. With the rush of his breath, I caught a whiff of liquor.

"Prove it," I said. "Tell me what you know."

"About what? Ask me questions, and I'll answer. I've *been* answering."

I took a deep breath. Either medicinal odors were clinging to his lab coat or he'd been drinking.

"Okay," I said. "What about the insurance policy you carried on Suzanna. It's rather large."

Kemp threw back his head and laughed, a deep-throated roar. "You love pointing the finger at me. I wondered when you'd ask about that."

"Well?" My voice had risen a few decibels, too.

"Maybe three-quarters of a million sounds like a lot to you, but I wouldn't think so. You are a Poole, aren't you? Although you're nothing like your mother." Kemp toyed with the stethoscope hanging from his neck. I felt like choking him with it.

"You're welcome to talk to my accountant, look over my financials," he said. "No jury in the world would believe I'd kill my wife for the money. I simply don't need it." He stroked his chin. "Although I might use it to fund my new association."

The man nauseated me. "What association is that, Dr. Kemp?"

"It's been in the papers," he said. "My father and I may become partners in a medical association." Kemp looked extremely proud of himself and I wondered why. It wasn't abnormal for fathers and sons to go into business together.

"Congratulations," I said, quietly. "I hope you won't have to run it from a jail cell."

Kemp's face turned red, but he kept his voice low. "Do your job and I won't have to. Is there anything else? I have appointments to keep."

When I didn't respond, he opened the examining room door and walked out. I heard an aerosol spray and speculated it might be breath freshener. The man was intolerable. If losing his wife had driven Kemp to drink, he should take a leave of absence.

I headed for the nearest Coke machine and downed the whole can in practically one gulp. At least the caffeine gave me a good excuse for my jitters. Before leaving the hospital, I decided to stop by the receptionist's desk to visit with Sallie McMillan again. Her back to the door, Sallie was busy reapplying her lipstick.

"Remember me?"

Sallie turned, greeting me with a smile. "Yeah, hi."

She closed the tube and dropped it into her purse.

"I just came from Dr. Kemp," I said. "He's in a volatile mood today."

"Today?" Sallie giggled.

"Is he always so obnoxious?"

"Not to his patients. They all love him. But the staff's a different story. I guess you're in that category, too."

"I can't even imagine him being nice," I said.

"I heard that."

"He said he and his father might go into partnership. Maybe you'll get rid of him then."

Sallie looked over her shoulder to see if anyone was within earshot. She lowered her voice. "Probably will. You know Arthur Kemp has a *gorgeous* office on Fannin Street. He'd be crazy to turn down his Dad's offer."

"I guess so." I hesitated, putting a finger on my chin. "Wonder why he didn't go into practice with his father a long time ago. He's not exactly fresh out of med school."

Sallie dropped her voice to a bare whisper. "I think his father was ashamed of him."

"Really?" I pretended that was hard to believe. "Why?"

"Remember what we talked about the other day? It's the women. I've heard he gambles, too. Old Dr. Kemp is a family man all the way. The exact opposite. There was talk about them joining up a couple years back."

The Kemps sounded a lot like Alberto and Vincent Ochoa.

"What happened?" I said.

"That's about when Ed and Suzanna got married. His parents didn't approve of her. They wanted him to marry someone *suitable*. You'd swear he was Prince William or somebody, you know? I liked Suzanna, but I guess they didn't think she was good enough for their son."

Sallie went on for five minutes, telling me all the office gossip about the Kemps—Arthur Kemp's "rich" practice, how he'd excluded his son from it, and talk of his nearing retirement.

When I finally broke away, I couldn't help feeling a teensy bit sorry for Ed Kemp. In different circumstances, maybe he'd have been a nicer person. I knew exactly what it was like to marry someone who wasn't accepted into the family. Nothing I could have done would have closed that invisible gap between David and my mother.

I took the elevator down to the first floor, crossed the green marble, then stopped for a minute at the fountain. The scent of chlorine was strong as I studied the brass statue of a person riding what looked like a porpoise through the rushing water. A light mist fell on my arms giving me goose bumps. My mind slipped back to the day David and I came home to announce our marriage. Dad's ecstatic reaction couldn't make up for Mother's frigid congratulations. The ice had barely melted during our six-year union.

Had Ed Kemp's experience been as bad? He and Suzanna had been married about two years. They were practically newlyweds. Had his family's disapproval turned him into the bitter, sarcastic man I knew?

As I watched the water swirl around coins in the bottom of the fountain, facts swam around in my head. One big question emerged. Had Kemp wanted to get back in his family's good graces badly enough to kill his wife?

Like a needle in a haystack,
One I'll never find.
Lookin' for some payback
Before I lose my mind.

CHAPTER 22

I was preoccupied, thinking about Kemp and his family, and had almost reached the office before spotting the black Mazda lurking five or six car lengths behind me. Him again! I crawled down Kirby, hoping the other traffic would go around so I could get a better look at the driver. The guy wasn't falling for it. He hung back, switching lanes periodically.

Maybe Dad was right and Vincent Ochoa had sent his henchman in hopes I'd lead him to Mitzi. If that was the game plan, I didn't have much to worry about. But what if the guy had a more serious strategy in mind—like running me off the road or carjacking the Ranger with me in it. Kirby Drive isn't an easy place to lose a tail on a weekday afternoon, but I took a chance and cut in front of oncoming traffic to make a left-hand turn.

One driver lay on the horn, expressing his displeasure, but at least I'd left the Mazda behind for a few seconds. I hit the gas, eager to reach the office. How did the man keep catching up with me? No one had followed me to the hospital. I picked up my cell phone and dialed Wade's private office number. He answered on the second ring.

"You have some time?" I said.

He must have sensed my urgency. "What's wrong?"

I hated acting like a wimp, but fear was starting to set in. "Some guy's been tailing me."

"You sure?"

"Positive. I've spotted him off and on for the past couple of hours."

"God, I worry about you. Where are you now?"

"Just around the corner."

"I'll come down and meet you. You know who he is?"

"I have a pretty good idea who sent him. I think Suzanna Kemp's past came back to haunt her. Now they're after me and her friend Mitzi. See you in a minute." I hung up the phone and checked the mirror. The Mazda hadn't caught up with me yet.

If Mitzi figured into this tail, she might be the only living person who knew why Ochoa was so desperate to find her. Maybe she knew some deep dark secret that he didn't want to get out. A secret that Suzanna Kemp may have uncovered. Interesting theory.

And now Larry Rogers was missing, too. I reminded myself that Mitzi and/or Larry might be the bad guys. At this point, I had no way to tell.

My head ached with confusion. Less than an hour ago, I'd been ready to convict Kemp. Now, I didn't know what to think about him. At the moment, Ochoa looked a lot more guilty than Kemp did.

I pulled into the office lot and glided to a stop in my reserved space, exhaling a breath of relief when I saw Wade jogging toward me.

"Are you all right?" He held my elbow, helping me out of the truck as if I were an invalid.

I nodded, feeling teary all of a sudden. "It's not that big a deal. I'm a little spooked is all."

Wade glanced toward the street. "Did you lose him?"

"I think so."

"You get his plates?"

"No, I mean there aren't any. He's driving without

plates."

"Oh, great. Let's get inside."

I grabbed my purse, and we hurried to the elevator. As we rode to the third floor, I told Wade about being followed out of the downtown parking garage, then about the guy in the restaurant. We entered the law firm's lobby and Erin, the receptionist, waved hello. She was busily scribbling a message with the phone propped on her shoulder and covered the receiver with her other hand.

"There's a surprise in your office," she whispered before going back to the call.

I turned to Wade. The skin on my arms prickled.

"I'll go with you," he said.

The scent of flowers hit me when I pushed the door open. An arrangement of long-stemmed yellow roses, baby's breath, and fern fronds stood on the desk corner, the huge bouquet dominating the room.

"Guess she meant a good surprise," Wade said. "Who're they from?"

I didn't read the card aloud. It said—*Hope you're feeling better. Till tomorrow, Clay.*

"A friend," I said. The roses helped chase away the chill of apprehension that hadn't really left me all afternoon.

Wade sat on my sofa, eyeing me and the flowers. Women are generally the more inquisitive sex, but Wade's curiosity honed in on the roses. He looked jealous. "High-ticket item. Is he anyone I know?"

"I don't think so."

"You sure the secret admirer's not the one keeping tabs on you?"

"Positive." I pushed a slight doubt from my mind.

"You can't be too safe these days. Maybe we ought to have the man checked out."

What was he, my big brother?

"Ochoa's the one having me watched," I said, a little too forcefully. "He's tied into this whole thing." I plopped down in my chair and told Wade about my meeting with O'Donnell and about Larry Rogers' disappearance.

He listened intently. "So all this somehow ties in to your theory that someone from Suzanna's past killed her? I'm having some trouble following your logic."

"I don't have a clue yet as to what Vincent Ochoa is really involved in," I said, "but David must have known something."

Wade blew out a breath. "You're crazy."

I'd succeeded in taking his attention off the roses.

"No, I'm not. David knew both of the Ochoas. Reba said Alberto handled the family business himself because he didn't trust his son. When they hired a different law firm, David wanted to talk to Alberto about it. He even planned a trip to Mexico to meet with him. He wouldn't make a trip like that without good reason."

I couldn't tell if Wade was paying attention, or letting me talk it out of my system. He wore the same blank expression Dad gets when Mother rambles on about society events.

"It's a feeling I have, maybe a premonition. Call me crazy if you want." I sighed. "That's right, you already did."

Wade's expression softened. He propped his elbows on his knees. "This feeling—it's pretty strong?"

"Very."

He looked at me, no trace of the usual twinkle in his eyes. "I trust your hunches, Corie. But check every angle. Keep your emotions out of it. After hearing all this, I agree you've got something on Ochoa. The part about David knowing is stretching pretty far, but if you find proof, I'll be the one who looks stupid."

I heard his shoe tapping against the wooden desk.

"What I care about is helping Garrett get Kemp off."

"Which reminds me," I said, "you think Garrett will request a change of venue?"

The tapping stopped abruptly. "It won't get that far."

I knew what he was thinking. "If I do my job right," I added.

Wade nodded. "You got it. Now, what did you learn from Jill White?"

I swore his eyes changed whenever he spoke her name.

"She's hell-bent on prosecuting Kemp. Wouldn't discuss the case, but she had the photos from Suzanna Kemp's camera and she showed me those. She doesn't think they're worth anything."

"What do you think?"

I pulled out the pictures I'd had developed from the negatives in Suzanna's study and described the ones Jill had showed me. We brainstormed about why Suzanna might have taken pictures of furniture, cars, portraits, empty rooms, and an office, but nothing made sense. About an hour later, Wade had to leave to meet a client.

***

That night Kit and I sprawled on my living room floor with the Ochoa file boxes from record archives and a large Italian sausage and mushroom pizza. The scent of garlic permeated the room. The weather had turned unseasonably warm and Kit hadn't changed from her basketball uniform—red shorts and a gold T-shirt emblazoned with a red number 22. Pizza sauce spotted the girl's shirt, matching her shorts.

"What do we have to do with all these boxes?" Kit said between bites. She'd already eaten six slices, feeding the crusts to Midnite when she thought I wasn't looking.

"*We* aren't doing anything," I said. "Don't you have

homework?" Proxy Mom on duty. Jean Thompson was "working late" again.

"I already finished it." Kit thumbed through the *TV Guide* she'd brought from home. "Wanna watch television?"

I looked up from a box of real estate documents. "There's nothing fit for kids on TV these days."

"*Wheel of Fortune* is educational," Kit said. "It's on now."

I smiled. "Okay."

Dragging the closest box to my side, I leaned against the sofa and pulled out a handful of manila folders. I glanced at the television screen. It said "PHRASE" across the bottom, and only half of the letters were turned over. A grandfatherly contestant spun the wheel.

Kit clapped. "Come on, it's 'H!'"

The dial landed on five hundred dollars and the contestant guessed the letter "H" and instantly solved the puzzle. "Needle in a haystack."

"Isn't that the truth," I said, looking at the boxes surrounding me. "This project will take days." And the prospect of finding Vincent Ochoa's secret amid twelve boxes of paper seemed unlikely.

Kit scooted across the floor toward me. "I can help."

I started to argue, then realized I had a perfect chore for her. "See the box over there marked McKenna Timesheets?" Kit nodded.

"Go look in the desk for a yellow highlighter. Then I'll show you what to do."

Highlighter in hand, Kit sat cross-legged at the coffee table with a year's worth of David's billing timesheets. She painstakingly highlighted every reference to Ochoa, Rios Entertainment, or the Ochoa client/matter number assigned by the firm while keeping one eye on a television sitcom I'd never heard of. Her work would save me a lot of time when

I read through the pages later.

Meanwhile, I concentrated on the other boxes. Two of them netted only folders of real estate related transactions. Alberto Ochoa owned a lot of land in Houston, including several office buildings.

I flipped through copies of leases for the numerous Rio-Niño restaurant sites. There was one folder for each site. Nearly every section of Houston had a Rio-Niño. I counted eleven, surprised to see that the restaurant had already extended its business to the rapidly growing Clear Lake and First Colony suburbs, but then I hardly ever traveled to those parts of town.

Nothing remarkable in that box. I shoved it aside and moved on. The next one held personal files. I pulled out a folder labeled "Net Worth Statements" and flipped through enough pages to get the picture. The Ochoa family was extremely wealthy. The balance sheet listed a home in River Oaks and one in Monterrey, four automobiles including one Rolls Royce, jewelry, antiques, and huge stock holdings and bank accounts.

Wow. I didn't keep up with my parents' financial affairs, but I doubted they could match the Ochoas' net worth. I laid the file in my lap and stared ahead, thinking. A Century 21 advertisement was on television. Looking at their for-sale sign reminded me of the vacant house Dad and I had gone to the other night. When I was ready to talk to Alberto Ochoa, where would I find him? I remembered the phone books piled on his front porch. Phone books were delivered in the spring if I wasn't mistaken. He must have moved out months ago. I might have to travel to Alberto's home in Monterrey. Just like David had planned to do. If Alberto still lived there. I hummed a familiar tune, making up my own words.

Lookin' for you in all the wrong places,
Lookin' for you, who knows where it'll take us. . .

No, a phone call would suffice. Surely with today's Internet resources the old man could be tracked down. Even if he was as far away as Monterrey, I could schedule a conference call with him. Since I didn't feel like getting on the computer right now, I rummaged through the boxes, pulling out the correspondence files. The last letter to Alberto had been sent to the River Oaks address two years ago. Since he'd hired a new lawyer, Alexander & Glover wouldn't necessarily know when his address changed.

I continued flipping through correspondence, skimming the letters. When I saw one that mentioned the enclosed last will and testament, I went back to the boxes looking for the document.

Reba had mentioned Alberto Ochoa didn't trust his son, and his will confirmed that sentiment. The first bequest left a million dollars to cancer research. No small donation, but the family had plenty of money. I flipped a page. I didn't have much experience reading wills, but it appeared Vincent wouldn't be getting his hands on any cash, except for a moderate salary from Rios Entertainment, until he reached his thirty-fifth birthday. Then he'd be a multimillionaire. His inheritance was to be left in trust until then. I wondered how old he was now.

I read on. The real estate holdings and restaurant business would continue to be managed by Rios Entertainment, under the person named as chief executive officer. Who held that position? If I could find the company minute book, it would include all details about the corporation's set-up.

The phone rang, interrupting my thought. It was Dad.

"The furniture auction's this Saturday at ten," he said. "I talked to Leo Atkins himself. Told him I'm interested in buying the whole lot. He's meeting me tomorrow morning at the warehouse."

"Good work," I said. "I'll go with you."

"I think I should go alone. He might not recognize me."

"You're right," I said with a sigh. Kit stood, stretched, and padded down the hallway toward the bathroom. Midnite followed her.

"You okay? What're you doing?" Dad asked.

"Oh, Kit's here. We're looking through the firm's old files for Alberto Ochoa." I filled him in on how certain I was about who'd been following me, and what I'd found in the file so far. "I plan to find out everything I can about the man," I said.

"What about the Ochoa house?" Dad said. "We could pose as buyers. The real estate agent might have some useful info on Alberto. Better yet, you and that new boyfriend could check the place out."

I smiled to myself. "I don't think I'm ready to involve him in my work. But he did accept my invitation to the gala tomorrow night. In fact, he seemed pleased."

"Watch out," Dad said. "He sounds like your mother's type."

"Uh-oh. I didn't think of that."

Kit came back to the living room. She picked up the pizza box, our dirty paper plates and cups, and headed for the kitchen, Midnite panting at her heels. A kid who picks up after herself. Amazing.

All of a sudden, Midnite started barking.

"I better run, Dad, and see what's bothering the dog." I dropped the receiver into the cradle and hurried to the kitchen.

Kit was at the back door, looking out into the dark moonless night. Midnite stood on her hind legs, front paws scratching the door window, barking like crazy. I switched the kitchen light off and the patio light on in the same motion and joined them.

"Is somebody out there?" I said, patting Midnite's side and staring into the darkness.

"My mom just came home," Kit said. "I saw the living room light turn on. Midnite doesn't like her very much."

"Maybe that's it," I said, but I'd never heard Midnite bark at Jean before. My heartbeat wouldn't slow down. Maybe someone was lurking around again. I moved to the front windows and checked the street. It was garbage collection night. Metal and plastic cans stood out on the sidewalk. Probably some hungry animals got into the containers and started the ruckus. At least that's what I wanted to believe.

I joined Kit in the living room, noticing the evening news had begun. "It's ten o'clock. Better get you home to bed." Midnite had stopped barking, but I could hear her nails clicking on the tile kitchen floor as she paced.

"Okay," Kit said, disappointed. "But I wanted to finish this for you." It looked like she'd already gone through a three-inch stack of timesheets but there were plenty more.

"Don't worry about it," I said. "You can come back and finish tomorrow night. I won't have a chance to look at them before then anyway."

The evening had passed quickly, but I'd spend a few more hours poring over the files. I straightened the folders I'd already read while Kit gathered her school books, stuffing them into her backpack. Highlights of the stories coming up droned in the background.

"Carjacking. . .robbery. . .a stabbing in the Fifth Ward." Houston news never had much good to say. I tried tuning out the TV.

"The big story. . .our very own Maggie Robbins. . .in Methodist Hospital tonight. . . victim of a drive-by shooting." I dropped the folders, staring at the television.

The picture on the screen zeroed in on a balcony at a

condominium complex on West Alabama. I'd never been to Maggie's place, but I knew the area.

"Ms. Robbins was on her way to a Rockets' basketball game this evening," said an on-scene reporter, "when the incident occurred. A witness saw her fall down these stairs and he ran to her aid." The reporter gestured to steps leading to the second-story units. "At last report, she is in stable condition, but it is not yet known whether this was a random act of violence or if those shots were meant specifically for Maggie Robbins."

Within minutes I had delivered Kit to her mother and was on my way to the hospital. Even though Maggie wasn't my favorite person, I wanted to make sure she would be okay. The television account of the shooting gave me an eerie déjà vu feeling, and I was eager to talk to Maggie and the witness about exactly what had happened.

I got a bad feeling
There's more trouble ahead.
Unless we start revealing
Someone else might end up dead.

CHAPTER 23

A woman cradled a screaming toddler with a bloody forehead in Twelve Oaks Hospital's emergency room lobby. Blood soaked the front of the woman's denim shirt. I couldn't believe the nurses weren't rushing to help the child. The place didn't seem crowded, at least not in the waiting room. Five other people occupied the blue cushioned chairs. Two men and one adolescent girl stared at the television screen, watching the evening weather report. One woman flipped through a *Good Housekeeping* magazine, while another stared out the window. Except for the injured child, everybody was quiet.

I turned to the check-in counter. No one sat behind the desk, but a heavyset nurse scurried past the window. A tall man in green scrubs whizzed by. It sounded like ten phone lines were ringing at once. I wondered if Maggie was back there being attended to. Or maybe she was resting comfortably in a private room. God, I hoped she'd be okay.

Standing at the counter, my breath came in shallow gasps. The wailing child didn't help my nerves. Until last Friday, I'd never known anyone who'd been shot. Thinking about the murder and now this, my body broke into a cold sweat. The odds of two people I knew being shot within days of each other were minuscule, so were the shootings somehow connected?

I jumped when the swinging door to my left opened.

A nurse beckoned to the woman with the injured child, and they quickly disappeared through the door. The youngster's screams echoed down the hallway. I massaged my throbbing temples. When I looked up, the chubby nurse was seated on the other side of the partition.

"What can we do for you?" She punched out some words on her computer keyboard.

"Maggie Robbins." I managed to stammer her name. "What's her condition? Is she going to be all right?"

"You and every Tom, Dick, and Harry reporter in the city's asking about her. We can't give out private information. Sorry."

"But, but," I said, my mind racing. "I'm her sister. Is she okay?" Sorority sisters counted, didn't they?

The woman's expression softened a tad, but I don't think she believed me. She lowered her voice. "She's in surgery, dear. That's all I know." She pointed to the waiting area. "But she did speak to your *other* sister before they took her back. Did you see her in the waiting room?"

"Yes, thanks." I nodded, wondering which of the women she was referring to. I guessed Ms. Good Housekeeping's age at about forty-five. Probably too old to be Maggie's sister, but she was perfectly groomed and had hair bleached about the same shade as Maggie's. I studied the younger woman sitting at the window but couldn't imagine Maggie being related to her. Light brown hair hung limply around the girl's blotchy red face. She wore jeans, scuffed Reeboks and a navy hooded sweatshirt with a pacifier tied to a ribbon pinned to the pocket. Diapers protruded from her bulging denim purse. There were five empty chairs between them so I picked one in the middle. I looked from one woman to the other, but neither paid any attention to me.

I glanced around the room. A man was helping himself at a coffee bar in the back corner. I joined him and poured myself a cup, then returned to my chair.

The warm Styrofoam felt good on my cold hands. I inhaled the steam rising from the cup. The coffee smelled old, but I didn't care. After taking a few tentative sips, I put the cup down and leaned forward, putting my elbows on my knees and clasping my hands.

"Maggie has to pull through this." I whispered, just loud enough for both women to hear me. When red-rimmed eyes turned away from the window, the resemblance shocked me. Bleach the hair, give her a body wave and a professional makeup job, and the young woman would be Maggie's twin.

She must have seen the recognition in my eyes and flicked her head back to the window. I drank more of my coffee before moving to the chair beside her.

"The nurse told me you talked to Maggie," I said. "How is she? What did she say?"

The woman didn't look at me. "I don't think she'd want me talkin' to anybody. Excuse me."

"I heard about the shooting on the news," I continued, "and rushed right over. I'm frightened for her."

She leaned against the chair back and looked at me thoughtfully. "Are you a reporter?"

"No, thank God." I smiled. "I'm Corie McKenna. Maggie and I went to college together. She stopped by my office yesterday afternoon for a visit. What's your name?"

"Penny." She reached into her purse, pulled out a wad of tissues and began to cry. She turned away from me, wiping her eyes.

I touched her arm. The fabric of her jacket sleeve felt sticky. "Hey, she'll be fine. She'll pull through this. Are you here alone?"

"Uh-huh." Penny's body heaved, and I put my arm around her shoulders.

"Don't worry. I'll wait with you."

The tears kept coming, like she'd turned on a faucet.

"Calm down," I said. "It won't do Maggie any good to have you all upset."

Penny sniffled, then blew her nose loudly. She looked around the room before speaking. "Maggie is the most wonderful sister anyone could have." I had to lean closer to hear her. "Mama and I are so proud. Even Dwayne. That's my husband." She hiccuped. "And the kids, they think their Aunt Maggie is the most famous person in the whole world. Right up there with Walt Disney."

"Course they don't go braggin' on her to their friends," Penny went on. "They know she needs her privacy."

"How many children do you have?" I had a hard time fitting Penny and her kids into my preconceived image of Maggie Robbins' personal life.

"Four." Penny beamed. "And another one on the way." She touched her abdomen.

"That's wonderful," I said. "Your family must be very happy."

Penny played with the sweatshirt zipper, pulling it up and down, up and down. "We usually are. Maggie helps out when she can."

"I'm sure she does."

"She loves her career," said Penny, letting go of the zipper to wipe her eyes again. "But I wish she would quit. It's so dangerous."

"Can you tell me what happened?" Now that I got Penny talking, I wanted to know everything Maggie had said to her.

"The shot hit her shoulder." Penny clenched her left shoulder with her right hand. "It looked awful." She winced. "She was in so much pain." Her hiccups were coming closer together.

"I'm sorry," I said. "How did you find out what had

happened? I saw the news, and they said it was a drive-by shooting."

"Maggie told them to call me. I ran out of the house, left poor Dwayne with puttin' the kids to bed." She straightened in the chair and took a deep breath. "There's too many crazy people—that's the bad part about gettin' famous. I told the police to find that weirdo who stalked her. He shoulda been locked up long ago."

"Maggie had trouble with a stalker?"

"Yeah. She met him last year at a party. Never went out with him, but he won't quit botherin' her."

"Do you think he shot her?"

Penny shook her head. "I don't know. The security guard at her complex had a couple run-ins with the guy and knows to watch out for him. He hasn't been there since last summer, far as I know. But there's a lot more weirdos where he came from."

"I guess being on television's not all that great," I said. "Sets her up for a lot of hassles."

"You're right about that. She gets hate mail, too. You'd be surprised. Women jealous 'cause their husband's been glued to the TV at night, watchin' Maggie a little too close. As if it's her fault." Penny was getting over being upset. Now she looked angry.

"They better find the person who hurt her," she continued. "And I'd love to get a hold of him." She stood abruptly. "I need some coffee."

Penny stomped across the room before I could offer to get her a cup. She never returned to her chair. A male nurse walked down the hallway, stopping at the waiting room entrance and called for Penny Ernst. Maggie's sister left her coffee cup and followed him. Maggie must be out of surgery. She'd be fine, I told myself. A shoulder wound wouldn't be fatal.

***

Despite having drunk three cups of coffee, I dozed in my chair. Just before two in the morning Penny's tapping on my shoulder woke me up.

"Maggie's in a room now," she said. "She's going to be okay." She pulled her lifeless brown hair away from her face, securing it with an elastic band.

"That's wonderful news." I stood and stretched. "May I see her?"

"Yeah. When I told her we'd met, she asked me to come down and see if you were still here. She wants to talk to you."

Penny gave me directions to Maggie's room before she left. Her husband worked a night shift and was already late. She needed to go home to be with the kids. I took an elevator to the third floor and shuffled through the labyrinth of hallways to the north corner. In the still of the night, the place seemed deserted. The only noises I heard were hums and beeps, signals from the paraphernalia they always hook up to people who already feel sick and feel worse with all the needles and gadgets attached to their bodies.

At a nurse's station, two women huddled behind the counter, transferring data from charts. They didn't seem to notice me. I glanced into one room and saw a woman in a pink robe sitting at the foot of a bed with her head bowed. The patient, an elderly man, had an oxygen mask strapped to his face, and his breathing was so ragged the bed railings rattled. I walked faster.

Reaching room 320, I hesitated. Comforting the sick wasn't one of my strong points, and I wasn't sure if I had the stomach for it. I summoned my courage and opened the door.

Maggie looked incredibly tiny lying on the hospital bed in a green print gown. Her left arm was in a cast and thick dressing padded her shoulder. Her blonde hair was dirty and matted, and her ghostly white complexion contrasted with one black and blue eye and the purple knot on her forehead.

"Thank you for coming," she whispered as I approached the bed.

"When I heard the news, I had to come over."

Maggie managed a weak smile. "You don't even like me. I'm trying to figure out why you're here."

"I was concerned." I walked around the bed and sat on a straight-backed chair next to the nightstand.

"That's bull. Tell me the truth. Why'd you come?"

"Have we reversed roles? You're always quizzing me, but I don't think I should bother you with questions right now."

"I don't mind." Maggie closed her eyes. "I can't believe this happened. First, I heard a loud 'thunk' kind of noise. I couldn't place the sound, so I turned around and looked at my front door. Then there was a 'ping.' I think the second bullet hit the wrought iron railing on my patio. I felt a godawful pain in my shoulder. Then I fell, twisted my ankle, rolled down the steps." She looked at me. "It was all a horrible nightmare."

I rubbed goose bumps on my arms. "You think someone you did a story on decided to take revenge?" I asked. The idea sounded plausible enough.

"I don't know what to think. I didn't see anyone."

I put a hand gently on her arm. "You should rest. Can I get you anything? Water?"

"I'm okay, considering, least 'til the drugs wear off. Doc says I'm not as bad as I look." Maggie cringed, trying to shift positions.

I adjusted her pillows.

"So, tell me what you think," she said. Even in a life-threatening situation, Maggie was eager for a story. For once, I wanted to help her construct one.

"I'm wondering about a connection to the Kemp shooting," I said. "But it doesn't work unless you know some of the characters I've been investigating this week. How well did you know Suzanna?"

"I'd never even met her. Who else?"

I ran down a list of names and occupations—she didn't know anyone connected with Whispers Nightclub. She'd never done a story about topless clubs or any of the Ochoa family's restaurants. She'd never heard of Larry Rogers. I pleated the edge of the bedsheet, frustrated because we couldn't find any link. Unable to ignore the range of blue, purple and black shades decorating Maggie's face, I wanted to know more about the stalker Penny had mentioned.

"Your sister thinks your career is dangerous."

Maggie moved to sit up. "She worries too much."

"Is someone stalking you?"

"No." The word seemed to take whatever energy Maggie had left. Her body sagged into the pillows. "That's old news, and I'd rather not discuss it."

A hefty black nurse came in then, as though Maggie had pushed some invisible button to keep me from asking any more personal questions. The legs of the woman's uniform pants swished together as she crossed the room. The way she eyed me, I wondered if my skin looked worse than Maggie's did.

"You best leave her to rest now," the nurse said. She checked Maggie's chart, then inspected the IV in her arm. Too worn out to fight the stern nurse, I decided to call it a night.

On the way home, I chastised myself for upsetting Maggie, at the same time wondering if she'd recognize any names if I mentioned them again after the painkillers wore off. I couldn't shake the feeling that her shooting had to be related to Suzanna's murder.

Maggie had never discussed her personal life with me

in the past, so I wasn't surprised she didn't want to talk about the stalker. Rumors about hate letters and stalkers wouldn't enhance her reputation. But I certainly hoped she'd confide in the police to increase their odds of bringing her shooter to justice. After she felt better, I'd be sure to bring up the subject again.

By the time I pulled into my driveway, my brain cells scurried around hypothetic scenarios like the bugs fluttering around my back porch light. I punched the garage door opener.

Midnite scooted out from under the garage door and ran toward the truck. I shifted into park, turned off the ignition and opened my door. Had I been in such a hurry to leave that I hadn't noticed her following me into the garage?

"What is it, girl?"

The dog barked once, then ran to the gate. I followed. She rushed to the back door, whining until I opened it, then leaped over the door sill and charged down the hallway. I sprinted behind her. In the living room, the dog ran in circles, sniffing the carpet.

My brain cells were getting more confused by the second. Midnite looked like she'd been watching too many silly dog food commercials. It took me a minute to realize what was wrong.

I had left a dozen file boxes on my living room floor. They were gone.

Nothing's getting clearer.
I'm not any nearer
Than I was the day before.
I can't take it anymore.

CHAPTER 24

"Girl, you look a mess," Reba said at our status meeting the next morning. "What you need is a nice long vacation. I hear Nashville's gorgeous this time of year."

She licked sugar off her fingers, then grabbed another glazed doughnut and passed me the Shipley's box. I selected a chocolate iced doughnut hoping the treat would improve my mood. Wade declined when I offered him the box. Though he often brought doughnuts to the office, he'd started an uncharacteristic health-food kick about six months ago and hadn't eaten one since. At least not that I'd seen. If I kept on eating them, I would have to join Weight Watchers before the year was out.

Thinking about that possibility, I dropped my half-eaten doughnut on a napkin. "Cut the Nashville talk, Reba. I'm not going anywhere until I figure out why someone would steal boxes full of boring documents."

"That's a damn good question," Wade said. He drained his coffee cup and got up to refill it. "Are you sure they didn't take anything else?"

"Not a thing. The West U police think I'm a nut case. Asked me a few questions about what was in the boxes, but didn't show much interest when I started talking about attorney timesheets and lease agreements."

Reba finished off her doughnut with one big gulp. "I sure can tell you what I'd find interesting about those files—nothin'—with a capital N." She licked her fingers again. "Archives kept an inventory of the folders in each box. They're faxin' me a list. Not that it'll be much help." She brushed crumbs off the fringe decorating the yoke of her fitted black shirt. Silver and turquoise button covers accented the plain fabric, and howling coyote earrings peeked out between her curls.

I twisted my paper napkin. "There had to be something very important in those boxes. Secrets—details—insinuations—threats. What could it be?" Frustrated, I tore the napkin in half.

"We did some litigation for the restaurants, but not much," Wade said. "A couple slip-and-falls. There'd be some medical records, settlement agreements. Aside from that, the normal documents associated with contract negotiations and setting up new restaurant sites." He shrugged, stirred another packet of Equal into his coffee and leaned against the counter, his frown lines deepening. "We can't expect to make any big discoveries without the file and based on what little we know."

David had made a big discovery, a voice seemed to whisper in my ear, as though Jiminy Cricket were sitting on my shoulder. I rubbed my arms against a sudden chill.

"I'll go dig out my old computer diskettes," Reba said. "See if I can find anything interesting." She grabbed a third doughnut and took off to her desk. I followed Wade to his office, eager to shed the eerie feeling that had washed over me and glad this latest development had piqued his interest.

"So, you still think I'm crazy?" I sat on the sofa, watching Wade lift his briefcase to the desk and snap it open. He took his time removing several file folders, a tablet and a couple of pens, shifting them around on his desk before answering.

"No, you're not crazy, but I'm going crazy worrying

about you. Anybody following you today?"

I shook my head. "Don't think so."

"Tried to call you last night. Late." He didn't look up, busying himself with closing the briefcase and settling it under his desk. "Guess you were out with that secret admirer, huh?" He made the phrase "secret admirer" sound synonymous with "convicted felon."

"No, I went to see Maggie Robbins at the hospital." I didn't suppose he'd want to hear me hypothesizing about why Kemp may have murdered his wife and tried to kill Maggie.

"Corie, under the circumstances, you can't run around at night by yourself like this." Wade rounded his desk to come and sit beside me.

"I *can't?* Mother's the only other person who tries to tell me what I can or can't do. And you know I never listen to her."

Wade punched the sofa cushion. "You know what I mean. It's not safe, with people like Vincent Ochoa out there taking an interest in what you're doing."

"So, you agree Ochoa may have hired the guy to follow me?"

Wade nodded. "I'd say we have probable cause to suspect him at this point. Or somebody working for him. They probably stole the boxes, too. Who else would want them?" He stood up to hit the intercom button on his telephone. "Reba, how's it coming?"

"Yo, boss," Reba answered. "I must have a zillion diskettes on this client."

"Fill up your paper tray. And print out everything remotely associated with Alberto Ochoa's companies." Wade turned to wink at me. The "Alexander wink" wasn't a flirting maneuver—and it didn't mean his worries had melted away — it meant Wade had a plan. His helping made me feel better since my brain couldn't focus on anything except the knot in my stomach. I might have blamed it on doughnuts wreaking havoc with my intestinal tract, but I knew it was apprehension. Maybe fear. Wade and I were on the trail of something David had known before he died. Something that had snagged his curiosity the same way it had snagged ours.

***

We spent several hours paging through and scanning documents as Reba printed them. In the end, she'd used five reams of paper, nowhere near the quantity of documents occupying the dozen stolen boxes. After going to all that trouble, we found absolutely nothing worthwhile, but Wade planned to use what she'd printed as a prop.

Reba had called Niño Fine Foods and been told that Mr. Ochoa was semi-retired and didn't come into the office anymore. Wade wanted to arouse the curiosity of whomever Alberto had left in charge of his business by taking a box full of paperwork with us on an unannounced visit. We'd pretend the entire file *had* been preserved on microfilm, then wait to see what happened next.

On the outskirts of downtown Houston, the Niño Fine Foods office was wedged in a strip between a Chinese restaurant and a drycleaning establishment. Graffiti decorated the building across the street. The cracked sidewalks looked like bait for lawsuits against the city. A white van advertising "Ray's Remodeling" was parked out front, and a man wearing a carpenter's belt hoisted a ladder over his shoulder and disappeared through a door with Niño's logo on its window. Wade made a U-turn and parked behind the van.

"Looks like they're doing some maintenance," he said. "It's long overdue." We got out and Wade walked around to open the trunk, lifting out the file box. As he approached the front door, I dawdled, taking in the building's dilapidated brick facade. So much mortar had fallen out I wondered how the bricks stayed in place. The carpenter hadn't shut the door completely, and Wade pushed it open with his foot.

Inside, we ran into a wall of boxes, much like the one Wade carried. He set his box on top of the others, and we stared at the bare, dingy walls. I hoped Ray's job would include repainting the interior. The last coat had to be decades old. Despite the fluorescent lights in the ceiling, the room's only bright spots were lighter paint squares on the wall where things had been hanging.

"Well, that's exactly what I don't need today." A loud feminine voice shot out over the cardboard wall, from our right. "Another box!" A permed head of light brown hair bobbed up and down on the other side of the row eight-boxes-long and five-boxes-high. It sounded like she was throwing files around. "The year-end records, I bet. Only two months late."

Wade and I exchanged confused glances. He shrugged and started to say something, but the woman hadn't finished. "I'm not doing any more reports. My clock's ticking. As soon as the packing's done, I'm out of here. You should have taken 'em straight to the new place. Let them handle it." A metal file cabinet vibrated when she banged the drawer shut. I could hear the remodeler's aluminum ladder rattling in the next room.

With a huff, the woman heaved a box on top of the last row in the pileup. Judging from the slap of that carton hitting the one beneath, I figured it must weigh at least forty pounds. If the lone woman had filled all these boxes by herself, no wonder she sounded so testy. Turning and shifting to a full standing position, she got her first glimpse of Wade. He looked good in a light blue oxford shirt, the collar open enough to show some dark chest hair.

The woman's lips at first seemed permanently set in a frown, then turned up. She tried to smooth her unruly hair and walked around the boxes toward us, wiping her hands on her denim skirt. She smiled in approval after a head-to-toe appraisal of Wade, but didn't even acknowledge my presence.

"I thought you were someone else," she told him, batting abnormally long eyelashes that looked more like spider legs to me. "Things aren't exactly normal around here today. What can I do for you?"

I rolled my eyes. Wade made introductions, using a provocative tone. I knew he was playing a part, but he didn't have to take it so far. His appearance alone had obviously elicited the woman's complete cooperation. By the goo-goo eyes she was making, I'd bet she'd have jumped off a bridge for him if he asked her to. Why the woman thought somebody tall, dark, and handsome like Wade would be attracted to short, mousy, and plain her, I couldn't imagine. Even if her huge bosom *was* practically nudging his arm as she listened to him explain why he had to speak with Alberto Ochoa immediately.

Trying to ignore her blatant flirting, I circled the office, dodging boxes. The room we were in was long and narrow, with a grimy window facing the street. A metal secretarial desk stood in front of the window. File cabinets marched down the walls. An oval rug in the room's center had probably been surrounded by waiting room furniture before the remodeling started. The rug looked like something handmade by Indians, with a tan, green, and rust zigzag border.

I stopped walking and studied the wall opposite the entrance. On each side of the center, an archway opened into another room. Suddenly, the place seemed familiar, though I was certain I'd never been here before. Confused, I turned back to Wade.

"You understand, Debbie," he was saying, "why it's imperative I speak with Mr. Ochoa. I'm afraid his client confidentiality has been breached. When do you expect him?"

Debbie's smile faded a bit. "You're kidding, right? I've been working contract here for almost six months and never laid eyes on the man. He's semi-retired, living in Mexico. Takes care of business by fax and Fed Ex." She took a step toward Wade. "I prefer more personal contact myself—"

The phone rang, interrupting her. Debbie strutted over to the desk, piled high with file folders, framed pictures, and miscellaneous office supplies. Her short skirt rode up as she stretched to reach the phone. I looked at Wade, but he had turned the other way. I was about to mention my sense of déjà vu when Debbie's conversation captured my attention.

"No, I'm sorry, Mr. Atkins isn't in right now." She turned to glance at the wall clock. "He went out to an appointment, but I expect him any minute. Yes, I'll tell him to call you." She hung up and smiled at Wade.

"By the way," she continued, not missing a beat, "my contract here ends today. They didn't give me any notice, so my budget's in a pinch. Need any help at your firm?" The spider-leg lashes worked double-time.

"I, well—" The question had taken him by surprise.

Suspicious of exactly what type of work she had in mind, I jumped in. "That depends on your responsibilities here at Niño. Who do you report to?"

Debbie turned a cool glance my way. "Leo Atkins. He's the CEO."

I tried to keep a neutral expression. Leo Atkins, first known to me as Whispers' bouncer, who supposedly owned a warehouse full of expensive furniture, also ran Alberto Ochoa's company? Wade didn't react to the name, probably didn't remember it from the case report I'd typed up for him. I sure didn't want to run into the bouncer now. He would report to Vincent Ochoa that we had been there nosing around.

Debbie made a face at me, then picked up a perforated piece of cardboard and started forming it into a box lid. She was not nearly as charmed with me as she was with Wade. While she was looking away, I mouthed "let's get out of here" to him. He gave me a puzzled glance, palms up, then dropped his hands as Debbie turned around.

"We really need to be going," I said, edging toward the door.

Wade ignored me, trying to smooth things over with the woman. He wasn't finished asking questions. "Debbie, I realize your knowledge about the company is privileged, and I won't risk any appearance of impropriety. If you can get Mr. Ochoa on the phone for me, I'll speak directly with him about the problem I'm having with his file."

Debbie shook her head. "Wish I could, but he's *always* traveling. We communicate strictly through Sanchez & Sanchez, his lawyers in Brownsville. I can try Leo's car phone if that'll help. He makes all the decisions here, anyway. Every once in a while he has to call Vince to get an okay. But Leo's the one who told me this morning about them selling this building and that I had to pack up all this stuff today 'cause it's being moved tonight." She sighed.

I checked my watch, worried that Atkins would appear any second, but Debbie was giving us good information. We had to find out all we could. "I can't believe they didn't get you any help," I said, trying to ingratiate myself to the woman. "Where are they moving to?"

"Someplace on the Loop," she said. "In with Vince's company. Said his staff will be taking over all my duties."

"What a shame for you." Must be moving in with the Othello Corporation, I thought. Combining the food business with the topless club business might make sense to the men involved, but it sounded like a dumb idea to me.

Wade walked across the room to stand closer to

Debbie. "I really must deal with Alberto personally," he said, making it sound like an apology. "Under these circumstances, I think the proper thing is for me to contact Sanchez & Sanchez. If you have the address and phone number handy, that would be a big help."

When he smiled, Debbie dropped the box lid and practically ran into the next room. "One computer's still hooked up," she called out. "No problem." Wade followed her, and I rushed to the window to check the street. No sign of Atkins yet, and this was my chance to snoop around the office. I hurried across the room to look at the junk piled on the secretarial desk.

First, I quickly flipped through the framed things that had no doubt hung on the office walls. There were certificates and awards from food-related organizations and many favorable newspaper and magazine reviews of Rio-Niño and the Grandioso dinner theatre. I read a few of them before seeing one newspaper article with a group picture of several Houston businessmen, the ex-Governor of Texas and, according to the caption, Alberto Ochoa himself. The clipping was dated over ten years earlier.

I heard the printer clattering in the other room. Debbie must be printing something for Wade. It was hard to believe Niño hadn't converted to lasers. Alberto Ochoa might be old-fashioned considering his age, but if Atkins was in charge, why hadn't the office been modernized? Maybe he and Vincent Ochoa ought to consider dropping their topless dancers' salaries so they could afford to update their office equipment. By now, my brain was assuming the two of them were partners in every endeavor.

I bypassed the rest of the framed clippings to look at a large picture that was setting on its side. Holding the edge of the picture frame, I cocked my head to get a better look at the portrait of a man who had to be Alberto Ochoa. He looked much younger than when the newspaper photo was taken, but the resemblance was unmistakable.

Then it hit me. I had seen this portrait before. I had seen this office before, too, in a manner of speaking. Suzanna Kemp had been here. She'd photographed it.

Wade cleared his throat behind me, and I dropped the portrait as if the frame were on fire. I checked my watch, then caught Wade's gaze, wishing he could read my mind. Debbie, intent on Wade, hadn't noticed my snooping.

"If we don't leave now, Mr. Alexander, we'll miss our appointment," I said. "Don't forget your box."

Wade, finally taking the hint, said "Thanks for your help, Debbie. If you do happen to communicate with Alberto, please tell him I'm locking these documents in my vault for safekeeping. And I'll be in touch with his lawyers."

I was already out on the sidewalk as Wade told Debbie she could stop by the firm and fill out an employment application.

"What's going on?" he insisted, after the door clicked shut behind us.

"Let's get out of here quick," I whispered. "I'll explain in the car."

We hadn't pulled out of our parking space yet when a red Bronco came down the street toward us. I didn't focus on it until the driver U-turned and parallel parked in front of the carpenter's van. Then I held my breath, watching the man who climbed out. He seemed a lot bigger than he had the first time I met him. Even through the closed car windows, I could hear the heavy clump of Leo Atkins' cowboy boots as he crossed the sidewalk toward the office building.

So, Leo Atkins drove a red Bronco. No doubt it was the same red Bronco Kit had seen outside my house the night the prowler had frightened her—the red Bronco from the scene of the apartment explosion.

You're makin' it real clear,
You say my work is finished here.
Why can't you understand,
That's not what I have planned.

CHAPTER 25

"What is your problem?" Wade asked, following my stare, directed toward the husky man entering Niño's office. "Who's that?"

"Leo Atkins," I said, keeping my eye on the door.

Wade shifted the car into park and moved to turn off the ignition. "So, let's finish what we came to do. What's the big deal?"

"No!" I grabbed his arm. "We can't go in there now. Let's get away before Debbie tells him we were here. He's the one who set Mitzi's apartment on fire. Snooped around my house, too." I chewed my lower lip. "Maybe even killed Suzanna Kemp."

Wade looked surprised, but he took my advice, yanking the gearshift into drive. The Lexus jerked out of the parking space.

"Explain your logic," he said, as we sped down the street.

My brain felt like I was trying to run a computer program without enough memory. "In those pictures on Debbie's desk, there's a portrait of Alberto Ochoa."

"So what?" Wade said. "Isn't he the company's founder?" He stopped at a red light and faced me.

"Some of Suzanna's pictures were taken inside that office," I explained. "They're in the batch Jill White showed me."

Wade smiled broadly. "That's great! I love it. Garrett can put Suzanna in that office, skulking around a warehouse, breaking and entering, bring in her history as a topless dancer, add a few unsavory acquaintances. The D.A.'s case against Ed won't get off the ground."

I was in no mood to listen to his defensive strategy. "But who killed her? We still don't have the most important answer."

Wade's light mood vanished. "On that front, it's time to get the police involved. Tell them everything and turn it over."

"I can't do that." I grabbed my purse, fishing around for some gum, a LifeSaver, anything to get the dry taste of fear out of my mouth. "What do you want me to tell them? That some clown is having me followed, watching my house, that I have no idea why? They already thought I was a nut when I reported the stolen boxes. What do you expect them to do, assign me a bodyguard?" I popped a stick of bubble gum into my mouth. "No, I'm not ready for them yet," I muttered. "Maybe when I'm closer." My teeth gnashed on the gum.

"You're *too close* to something. That's the problem." Wade shot me a look. "And I don't want that man getting any closer to you than he's already been. Your job is over."

That's what he thought.

Somehow I had to find Alberto Ochoa. His office was moving, and his house was up for sale. Odds were that the furniture in the warehouse belonged to him, too. He was selling out. Why?

My mind raced ahead. Suzanna Kemp had been taking pictures of things related to the man. His office. Maybe his furniture. She'd been doing it at night, when she wouldn't run into anyone. What purpose could the photographs serve? Blackmail photos usually featured human subjects. Had Suzanna snapped these pictures for her own use or at someone's request? Mitzi's? I stretched the gum over my teeth and blew a bubble.

"Are you listening to me?" Wade touched my shoulder.

"Huh? Sure. You said my work's finished." I gave him a half-smile. "I never liked working for Kemp anyway. So, what are you planning to do now?" We were about a mile from the office, and I was eager to part company.

Wade's lips molded into a frown. No doubt he'd sensed my phony reaction.

"I'll put in a call to Ochoa's lawyers in Brownsville. I don't think that's out of line. Then I'll touch base with Garrett. I'm sure he'll agree it's time to turn over everything we know to the police." He glanced at the dashboard clock. "And I have a client coming in at four. How about you?"

"Guess I'll start typing up a statement for the cops," I said, making another move toward false cooperation. "And I'll be leaving early today. Mother asked me to help her out with the Thomansen Gala, one of her famous fundraisers. It's tonight." I wasn't actually helping, but it sounded like a good excuse to get away.

"Lucky you." The Lexus hugged the curb turning into the office parking lot and brushed the shrubbery lining the curb. The tension between us was evident in Wade's erratic driving. "Hope she's not setting you up with some boring executive again."

"Don't worry. I'm taking the man of my choice tonight."

Wade pulled into his parking spot and stomped the brake. If I hadn't been wearing my seat belt, my head might have cracked the windshield.

"Good for you," he said.

We parted in the hallway without further words. I was surprised Wade hadn't lectured me about staying off the case. Did he realize that at this point I wasn't concerned about Kemp's murder charge? My one-track brain was stuck on finding out what David had been investigating before he died.

I unlocked my office door and was greeted by my blinking voice-mail light. I punched in my code, and the recording said there were two new messages. The first was from Dad.

"I'm in from meeting with Atkins at the warehouse. Thank my lucky stars the hulk didn't recognize me. Hoo boy, I'd hate to get into a fist fight with him. He's over-anxious to sell, for sure. Has a fabulous Bardwell original your mother would die for. Asking thousands less than it's worth, but I told him the price was still too rich for my blood. He wants to negotiate. No hint why he's selling. Nothing else to report for now."

Even when Debbie had mentioned Atkins being out at an appointment, I hadn't remembered Dad's plans to meet with him. Well, his visit hadn't amounted to much, anyway. I punched the buttons to discard that message and the second one began.

"Hi, it's Clay. Looking forward to the party tonight. And to seeing you again. Black tie, right? Give me a call. I'm at the gym."

I hit the button to review that message merely for the relaxation value of Clay's deep, sexy voice tickling my ear. This gala might be the first of Mother's functions I'd ever looked forward to. Apparently, Clay owned a tuxedo. The fact didn't fit with my impression of him during our brief acquaintance, but that was okay. What would I wear? I chuckled, unable to remember any occasion when I'd actually worried about what to wear.

After straightening my desk, returning Clay's call, and deciding on a black beaded dress Mother had bought for my last birthday, I turned my full attention to the Ochoa problem. I picked up the phone and called information for Monterrey. Alberto wasn't listed. That would have been too easy. There had to be a way I could reach the man personally. Sitting in my office, no brilliant ideas came to me, but I thought a closer look around his house might jog my brain cells.

I arrived at Ochoa's River Oaks neighborhood in less than fifteen minutes. Mindful of the threat Leo Atkins, Vincent Ochoa, or their cronies might pose if we crossed paths, I parked the Ranger about half a mile down the street from his mansion. Then, hoping I'd pass for a fitness enthusiast out running despite the cold drizzle that had begun to fall, I headed for the house on foot. Raindrops hit my face, chilling me to my toes. My fleece jacket wouldn't fend off the moisture forever. I picked up my pace.

When I reached the property line, I ducked through the hedge instead of walking down the driveway. Though the huge homes were set far back from the street, I didn't want to attract the attention of some nosy neighbor who might call the police. As I'd already pointed out to Wade, I wasn't ready to talk to them yet.

Traipsing through the woods, the thick cover of trees shielded me from the rain. I reached into my pocket for a tissue and tried to dry off my face. The day had started out sunny, but now gloom hung in the air with the dark clouds, making it seem a lot later than it was. I hurried through the trees, hoping the clouds wouldn't open up until I had finished snooping around.

I approached from the north side of the house and looked through the long double-paned windows. Nothing but empty bedrooms. In one of them a real estate "For Sale" sign advertising Sharon Silverthorn Realty leaned against the wall. It had a "Sold" sticker pasted across the corner. I headed toward the front door. The phone books and cardboard box Dad and I had seen the other night were still on the stoop. I picked up the box. It was addressed to Alberto in a feminine hand and had been mailed from Mexico City. I balanced the box on my hands. Wrapped in plain brown paper, it was a little smaller than a shirt box, and I guessed the weight at no more than two pounds. I felt like a little girl in mid-December holding a gift that said "Do not open until Christmas."

In this case, opening the box would be a federal crime. *If* anyone caught me. I debated with myself, then moved on, still holding the package. Peeking in the windows to the left of the front door, I recognized the huge kitchen. Suzanna had photographed it. Surprise, surprise. Then I heard a vehicle coming up the drive.

After a frantic glance at the small black car, I darted around the corner, returning the way I'd come, praying my dark jacket and jeans blended into the landscape and I'd escaped notice. I flattened my body against the rough stucco, gasping when I realized the car was a Mazda. My grip on the cardboard box crushed one corner.

The rain was falling harder, drops pelting the fallen leaves. The car's engine stopped and two doors slammed.

I waited at least five minutes before my patience gave out. If I hightailed back through the woods to my truck, I might live to regret it. If I took too many risks, I might not live at all. Bravery, or maybe it was curiosity, overcame my better judgment. I crept around the perimeter of the house in the opposite direction I'd gone before. Voices drifted through the murky air. They were speaking Spanish. Damn, why hadn't I paid better attention in high school?

I held my breath and peered around the corner of the house to the detached garage. Two of the four garage doors were open. Light flooded the inside, bouncing off the black Rolls Royce and an old model red Corvette. Surprise again. Suzanna had been in that garage, too. How had she accessed all these places?

Two dark-haired men were staying dry under the garage eaves. I recognized the taller one as my tail from Manuel's Cantina. I'd never seen the other guy. He wore a dress-length leather coat, and pricy shoes that gleamed through the mist. A third man was out of my view, though I could hear him.

My sketchy remembrance of Spanish said they were talking about some sort of deal. The hidden man took a step forward. Vincent Ochoa. The classy stranger removed a manila envelope from his inner jacket pocket and exchanged the envelope for the car keys Vincent held. Then the stranger climbed into the Corvette and left. A car sale?

Vincent turned to the other man, reached into the envelope and pulled out a sheaf of bills. He counted ten of them into the palm of the guy who'd tailed me. I wondered what denomination they were.

After pocketing the money, the second man said *adiós* and drove away in his Mazda. Vincent stood, watching the tail lights recede in the mist for a minute, then disappeared into the garage. I hoped the other guy didn't recognize my Ranger parked on the street.

The rain had intensified, and I knew I'd be soaked seconds after leaving the protection of the overhanging roof. But I had to go, the sooner the better. I wasn't ready for a face-to-face with Alberto's son.

I stepped away from the building's cover and shoved the cardboard box inside my jacket, intent on taking it with me. Halfway across the lawn, I caught sight of Vincent running toward the house. His head was down and he wasn't heading in my direction, so I kept moving. Rain streamed down my face as I kept my eyes on him, praying I wouldn't trip over anything. When I reached the edge of the woods I slid, like a baseball player approaching home plate, and scrambled behind the trunk of a large live oak.

My heartbeat seemed to echo, pounding off the box under my jacket. I turned to look at the house, blinking away raindrops. Lights flicked on downstairs. For the first time I noticed smoke coming out of the chimney. The house was vacant—why would he start a fire? Suspicion nagged at me, and I knew I had to go back despite the chattering of my teeth in the chilling rain.

I followed my soggy footprints to the house. Dusk was falling rapidly. I moved around the familiar territory more quickly than before, stopping to look in every window I hadn't checked out the first time. About halfway around, I saw the fireplace and jumped back, then inched up until I saw Vincent inside. He was tossing papers into the fire, as if he'd run out of kindling and was desperate to stay warm. File folders. More papers. He tossed them in by the armfuls.

Risking discovery, I edged forward for a full view of the room and saw the boxes that had been stolen from my house. They were clearly marked with the client's name, except they were almost empty now. Papers that held some unknown significance had been reduced to a pile of ashes.

The sight made me so angry I wanted to jump through the window and attack the man. Before I could make any such foolish moves, he turned and his sport coat flared away from his body. I saw the shoulder holster, but couldn't make out the type of gun he carried. I had no weapon, not even my purse to slug him with. All I had was the stupid box bulging under my jacket. I meant to open it, too. I didn't care about violating anybody's privacy now.

With rasping breath, I ran through the woods, back to the Ranger. The cell phone kept slipping in my wet grasp, but

I managed to call the West University police. I didn't know whether they'd be able to do anything about the lost file boxes now. This address wasn't in their jurisdiction, but I urged them to contact the Houston police. Maybe they'd interrupt Vincent and some of the file would be spared.

Then I yanked the box out from under my jacket and ripped at the damp paper, careful not to destroy the return address. Inside, a smaller box was wrapped in birthday wrapping paper with a card taped to the front. I pulled the paper off to uncover a book of Spanish poetry. Big deal! Then I opened the card. There was a long handwritten note. In Spanish. Disgusted, I threw the card and the book on the passenger seat.

I drummed my fingernails on the door handle. Remembering the real estate sign, I called information for Sharon Silverthorn's office number. Real estate agents kept in touch with homeowners so she might be able to help me out with a number for Alberto. I wouldn't rest until something broke on this case. After telling the receptionist my name was Corinne Poole and that I was interested in buying in the River Oaks area, I didn't have to hold very long. Ms. Silverthorn snatched up the line with a cheerful hello.

"I'm calling about the property on Winding Trail," I said. "But I heard a rumor you've sold it."

"Yes, dear, that's right," Sharon groaned, but with a quick recovery. "I have several other lovely properties—"

"That house belonged to Alberto Ochoa, didn't it? I interrupted. "He was an old friend, but we've been out of touch. How is he?"

Sharon held back her sales pitch for a second. "Why, he's fine. I'd love to meet with you and show you a couple of places that would be perfect for your lifestyle."

What did she know about my lifestyle? Imagine me and Midnite roaming around a twenty-room mansion.

"He had a lovely home, didn't he?" I said. "I would love to see Alberto again, but I don't even know where he's living now."

"He's been in Monterrey, dear, for quite some time," Sharon said. "But you're in luck. He's coming to Houston day after tomorrow for the real estate closing. If you'd stop by my office around three, you might chat with him. Then I can spend the rest of the evening showing you—"

I tuned out the rest of her conversation. Finally! The break I needed. Alberto Ochoa would certainly be able to answer a lot of my questions. I picked up the book of poetry, wondering if I could salvage the wrapping paper, feeling silly for spoiling the poor old man's birthday gift.

What if I should discover
We're not perfect for each other?
Want to make my choice alone,
Without the help of Mother.

CHAPTER 26

Chandelier light glittered off the diamond jewelry, sequined dresses, and capped teeth of an elite Houston crowd in the Doubletree Post Oak's ballroom. I felt confined in my slim black evening dress, but surprisingly at ease with Clay's arm hooked through mine. The hubbub didn't die down when we entered the room, though I noticed several women turning to get a better view of my date. Who could blame them? The man looked almost as good in a tux as he did in workout shorts and a T-shirt. The snobs in the room would never guess Clay was a small-time business owner.

"Ready to party?" Clay said, looking completely at ease in the high-brow setting. "Shall we find the champagne, or would you rather I locate a Coke machine?" He already knew my vices and seemed to like me anyway.

"I better opt for the ahh. . .ahh. . . ." I pressed a forefinger under my nose and squeezed my eyes shut, holding back a sneeze. My escapade in the rain would probably result in a full-fledged cold. When the tickle had passed, I opened my eyes. "Champagne," I answered. "Don't you think a crystal glass will complement my dress much better than an aluminum can?"

"You could pour the Coke into a glass." Clay chuckled as we walked deeper into the room, passing layers of silk and velvet, elegant tuxedos, expensive colognes and trivial conversation.

On the way to the gala, I'd admitted drinking two glasses of wine before he picked me up, to de-stress after work. Clay didn't press me for any details. The alcohol had somewhat eased my apprehensions about Vincent Ochoa. When the police investigated the box-burning I'd reported, they'd found no sign of him or any boxes, empty or otherwise. My game plan for tonight was to relax and have a good time. When Alberto came to town, I'd get some answers—answers I hoped would put to rest my nagging questions about David's visits to Whispers.

My immediate concern was how Clay would react to meeting my mother. Since she was chairing the Thomansen Gala this year, I hoped she'd be busy enough for us to mill around and have a few drinks before introduction time. I should have known better.

"Darling, I didn't see you come in." The cooing sounded from behind me. Turning, I was immediately enveloped in deep purple satin sleeves. Mother stepped back, smiling, holding my hands in hers. Her sparkling violet eyes looked from me to Clay, then swept over my outfit. Her once-overs always made me feel like a head of cattle about to be auctioned off. Her eyes stopped for a second on my plain black five-year-old pumps, but she mercifully held her tongue.

"Mrs. Poole, you look every bit as lovely as your daughter this evening." Clay interrupted her inspection, no doubt sensing my discomfort. "And what a turnout." He glanced across the crowd.

Compliments entice Mother like rawhide bones attract my dog. Without giving me a chance to introduce Clay, she launched into a vivid description of the gala activities, beginning with the first committee meeting. I didn't know why she thought Clay would care about the kick-off dinner at Maximillian's. She had turned the charm on high, and I hoped

Clay's patience held out. Noticing his rapt expression, I wondered if he had some acting experience.

When she turned to point out the gala's emcee, one of Houston's most respected heart surgeons, I caught sight of Dad rushing toward us. "Sorry, sweetie," he whispered, kissing me on the cheek. "Tried to keep a rein on her, but it's a losing battle."

He straightened, turning to shake Clay's hand. "Good to see you." Before he could say more, Mother had taken Clay's arm, leading him toward a group congregating nearby. Short of starting a tug of war using Clay as the rope, I didn't know what to do.

"Oh, well," I said, shrugging. "She'll turn him loose as soon as somebody more important shows up."

Dad laughed. "How well I know." He snagged two glasses of champagne from a passing waiter's tray and handed me one. "What's new with the case? You get my message?"

I nodded and filled him in on my recent discoveries about Atkins and Ochoa.

"Betcha old Alberto will shed some light on the situation," Dad said. "Never met the man, but always heard he was a wizard in business." He drained his champagne glass. "I think you'll get the truth from him. In that family, the apple fell a *long* way from the tree. Speaking of his sleazy son, any word on the missing dancer?"

"No. I'd like to question Mitzi's co-workers again, but not when Vincent is there." As I sipped my champagne, a vivid memory formed. Glowing flames reflected off Vincent's face as he threw papers into the fire. Like a slide show in my head, the next frame clicked into place. Fire licking Mitzi's apartment. In this age of computers and copy machines, I wondered if Vincent had succeeded in destroying whatever it was he was trying to hide.

"Don't look now, sweetie," Dad said, his elbow

tapping mine, "but I think you should pay some attention to Mr. Mitchell before someone else steps in. Can't turn your back on these women. I'm off to save some other poor soul from your mother."

Trying to appear casual, I turned to spot Clay deep in conversation with Ed Kemp's friend, Vivian Coulter. Walking across the floor toward them, I wondered how Dad knew Clay's last name even though I hadn't had a chance to make introductions. I stopped a waiter and exchanged my empty glass for a full one.

Vivian wore a slinky mustard-colored crepe gown. A barrette that looked like real gold with inset diamonds pinned her brown hair back over one ear. Clay was speaking when I walked up, but Vivian wasn't paying attention to him. Her gaze darted around the room. Her hands fidgeted with the ornate gold clasp on her yellow fabric-covered belt. She was making me feel jittery. I emptied my glass in two gulps.

When Vivian's stare fixed on me, her brows drew together for a moment. Then her expression changed suddenly and she smiled, looking from me to Clay. "Are you two together?"

I nodded, but she didn't give me a chance to say anything.

"How nice. I've known Clay for ages. He was such a malicious little tyke back when I was a teenager." Her twitter had a Julia Child-like accent. I wondered if she'd picked it up by watching the famous cook on television.

"Vivian's younger brother, Winston, was a friend of mine," Clay explained. "We enjoyed harassing Viv. We'd collect frogs, snakes, spiders, you name it, and leave them everywhere—in her shoes, her closet, the bathtub."

"Ugh," I said. "I suppose I'm lucky, being an only child."

Clay laughed. "Remember those hunting trips your

dad took us on, Viv? You loved everything about hunting except being out in the woods."

Vivian didn't respond. Her gaze darted again. Clay looked at my empty glass. "We're going to refresh our drinks, Viv. Say, I haven't seen you around the gym for a couple of weeks. You were getting to be one of our regulars. Don't be a stranger."

Her head jerked toward him, and her lips turned up slightly as she shook her head. "No, I won't." She wiggled her fingers in a goodbye gesture. I expected her to say "toodles," but she didn't.

Halfway across the floor, I turned to look back at Vivian. "Did she seem jumpy to you?"

"No. Viv's always been like that." Clay steered me toward the hors d'oeuvre table. "Has some emotional problems. The family sent her to a private hospital in London when Win and I were in college. He was always worried about her. Tell you the truth, I thought she was still there."

Funny, Vivian hadn't seemed the least bit nervous on the previous occasions I'd run into her. Maybe she took antidepressants and had forgotten them tonight. I shrugged off Vivian's behavior as none of my business, but Clay's reminiscing had confused me. He was holding one of my hands as we weaved through the crowd. I stopped walking.

"You went to school with Winston Coulter? One of the oil company Coulters?"

"Sure. Winston, Jr. His dad owns the company."

My ordinary-boy-next-door-turned-small-businessman image of Clay faded fast. "You knew him pretty well?"

"We lived right across the street." Clay's eyebrows scrunched together.

Realization hit hard. "Oh, my God," I said, loud enough to stop conversation in the circle nearest us. I shuffled past a hippy lady in an unflattering white dress, dragging Clay with me, headed for the door. All of a sudden, I was uncomfortably hot. Maybe it was the alcohol. Maybe *I* should be taking antidepressants. When we reached the relative privacy of the foyer outside the ballroom, I whirled to face Clay and had to grab a column to steady myself. "Don't tell me you're Dorothy Wells' son."

"As a matter of fact, I am." He dropped my other hand. "What is wrong with you?"

"My mother has been trying to set me up with Dorothy's son for the past year." Dorothy had remarried but her children retained the Mitchell surname. I'd had no reason to make the connection earlier. My eyes were watering, either from the champagne bubbles or the brewing head cold. I knew I sounded childish, but couldn't help feeling like I'd fallen into a trap.

A matronly white-haired woman in a bright red dress seemed to be edging closer to us, eavesdropping. Clay grabbed my hand and led me to a side hallway, pulling me down beside him on a bench.

"I should have bought you a Coke," he said with a grim look. "Alcohol seems to have an adverse effect on you."

I looked up, embarrassed. "I'm sorry, but—"

"You're sorry that I'm Dorothy Wells' son? Why? You don't like my mother?"

"Your mother is a fine person," I said.

"Or I was okay before, being a nobody, but now you know my family, forget it. Is that it?" His smooth tanned face had reddened.

He'd hit the truth. He must have been a psychology major. "I'm acting ridiculous, I know."

"A definite understatement." Clay stood and paced in front of the bench. "I've had women chase me for money before. But you're the first who's treated me like a leper after finding out I'm rich." He stopped in front of me and sighed heavily before meeting my eyes. "If it bothers you that much, I can ask Mom to disinherit me." His eyes hinted at a smile.

"I'm such a dunce," I said, trying to dry the corners of my eyes without smearing my mascara. "You've met my parents before, huh?"

Clay nodded. "But I didn't know you were their daughter until you invited me here tonight. And I never heard about anyone trying to set us up." He touched the corners of my mouth with two fingers, trying to force me to smile. "You came to my place, remember? It was your sharp investigator's wit and those basketball shorts that attracted me."

Remembering the ancient clothes I'd worn to the gym the day we met, I had to laugh. "Maybe I should eat something to soak up this alcohol. I'm much less obnoxious with a full stomach, I promise."

Sitting at the dinner table an hour later, I was glad Mother's friend Muriel occupied the seat between me and Clay. I had a feeling the tension between us hadn't completely passed yet, maybe never would. Every time Mother looked at us I imagined her planning Houston's wedding of the century. The thought made me shiver. When Muriel started talking about Ed Kemp, I was glad for the diversion.

"It's too bad he couldn't come tonight," she said, leaning toward me, "and see his father accept the donation for cancer research." She speared a cherry from the cheesecake topping and nibbled it daintily. "Especially since they're going into business together soon."

"I heard about that," I said, sipping coffee.

"Of course I don't blame him for staying out of sight, what with the preposterous murder charge dangling over him. And would you look at that woman," Muriel whispered, leaning even closer. "I'm sure she counted on Edward being here." I followed her gaze to a table where Vivian Coulter sat, staring at her plate.

"She does seem to enjoy spending time with him," I said, sliding my fork into my cheesecake.

Muriel laughed. "You noticed. What really surprises me is that she would take her hands off his baby long enough to come to this gala."

Before I could question Muriel about the comment, Mother rose to a round of applause and approached the stage. After a solid five minutes of gushing her thanks to everyone involved with making the gala a success, she introduced Arthur Kemp, who accepted a check for the funds raised by her efforts. As he spoke, I found myself feeling sorry for Maggie Robbins and wondering if she would ever get the interview with him she had so desperately wanted. If it wasn't too late, maybe Mother would agree to ask him to meet with Maggie.

The elder Kemp kept his speech short and to the point. He thanked all of the "fine Houstonians" for their generous donations and mentioned several late public figures who donated the bulk of their estates to medical research. Muriel's husband muttered "Sounds honorable, but my kids would contest the will." Dad laughed along with him.

My thoughts drifted. I remembered scanning Alberto Ochoa's will. He'd left a million dollars to cancer research. I doubted Vincent would appreciate his philanthropy. Personally, I didn't care what Mother and Dad decided to do with their money. I'd been called a trust fund baby, rich bitch, spoiled brat, and lots of other names denouncing my birthright, and I'd hated it every time. I probably needed a therapist. Clay would no doubt agree.

By the time we'd escaped Mother and her friends and their comments about how wonderful it was to see us together, I felt like screaming. My eyes wouldn't stop watering, and I was fighting sneezing fits. Every man I'd come in contact with had offered me his handkerchief.

"I can see how your Mom's matchmaking might get on your nerves," Clay said, pulling into my driveway. "One night, and I've had my fill."

Sounded like I wouldn't have to fend off future dates with the man. A full moon dimly lit the inside of the car, outlining Clay's stern profile. Despite everything, I didn't want him to leave angry and wasn't sure I wanted him to leave at all. He didn't move to turn off the ignition. I'd have given anything to see him smile.

I touched his arm. "I really am sorry. For everything."

"Don't worry about it," he said, turning to me. He laid his hand on my shoulder, massaging it. "How's the sore neck? Have you been icing it? Taking ibuprofen?"

I nodded, though I couldn't remember doing either. It had been a hellish week. Clay got out to walk me to the door.

"You're letting this case you're working on get to you. If you ever put it behind you, give me a call." He took my key and opened the front door, then put his hands on my shoulders and might have kissed me goodnight if I hadn't sneezed. Just as well, because I didn't want to pass on my germs.

After he drove away, I shuffled through my bathroom vanity drawers and found a bottle of cold pills, hoping they'd put me to sleep fast. After about two hours of lying in bed wide awake, sniffling and sneezing, I decided the pills must have been one of those non-drowsy formulas. Frustrated, I threw back the covers and got up. I didn't think reading or drinking warm milk or hot tea would help put me to sleep or stop the questions racing through my mind.

I paced the bedroom floor, shuffling back and forth on the carpet until static electricity made the hair on my arms stand up. Was the medication making me edgy? I didn't think so. Clay was right about my needing to put the case behind me. I wished Suzanna's murder hadn't affected my life so much, but I had to figure out who killed her and what David had been investigating before I could put it to rest. Then maybe I could face the future.

I pulled on a black sweatsuit, threw David's flannel shirt over it, and slid into my Reeboks. There was one place Suzanna might have visited that I hadn't checked out: Othello's offices. I grabbed my copies of her keys and headed out the door, pausing for a minute to pat a drowsy Midnite on the head.

At the ten-story office building on the West Loop, I didn't have to break and enter. Cleaning people pushed vacuum cleaners past the lighted windows, and I spotted a mid-size moving van out back. Double doors into the building were propped open to aid two men in tan uniforms who were moving the furniture and boxes I'd seen earlier that day at Niño's office downtown. After parking in the lot next door, I was able to slip around the corner and through the doors without the movers noticing me.

A sign in the lobby indicated Othello was located on the fifth floor, so I huffed my way up the stairs, breathing through my mouth because my nose was thoroughly congested. Stifling a cough, I felt insane for being here when I ought to be home asleep. I might have run into less building traffic during the work day. When I reached Othello's floor, I cracked the heavy stairwell door and peered into the hallway. A third tan-uniformed man appeared. His blond hair curled around the bottom edge of a tan cap. He looked familiar, but I didn't want him to spot me, so I shut the door.

The three moving men had paced their trips upstairs in such a way that I couldn't chance leaving my hiding place. Every few minutes, I checked again. Othello's door was apparently on my side of the hall, about three-quarters of the way down. I was trying to come up with a believable scam to get me inside the office, when a man's shout echoed down the hallway.

"It's the middle of the night, and I don't give a crap. Shove the stuff inside the door and be done with it. I'm locking up now. Send me the bill." A door slammed. I pushed the stairwell door open slightly and saw Vincent Ochoa staggering in my direction. The blond mover rolled an empty dolly behind him. Holding perfectly still, I watched Ochoa until he reached the elevator. When he turned to get inside, I saw the black plastic garbage bag slung over his shoulder.

Before the elevator doors slid shut, I hit the stairs running. Business owners didn't take out their own garbage, and I wanted that bag. Clutching the stair railing, I swung around corners, down to the fourth floor, third, second. Before reaching the ground floor, I heard the elevator ding. The moving van was parked on that level, but I hadn't seen any cars out back. Executive parking would be covered. Probably underground. I made it to the lower level before the elevator, took note of three parked cars, and hid behind the elevator bank.

Watching Ochoa stumble toward a black Jaguar, I wondered how much he'd had to drink. My own combination of alcohol and medication had me on high alert, but Ochoa looked lethargic. His straight black hair was greasy, and his charcoal suit looked like he'd grabbed it from a pile heading to the cleaners. Struggling with the shifting weight of the bag, he managed to punch a button on his key ring to disarm the car's alarm system. Then he yanked the back door open, almost falling backwards in the process, and dropped his keys.

I saw my chance. Emerging from my hiding spot, I ran silently across the concrete floor, wondering again about my sanity. Ochoa had stolen things from me, and I was ready to steal something from him. As he bent to retrieve the keys, I aimed a flat-footed kick toward his buttocks, hoping to send him crashing into the car's rear quarter panel. My foot slipped, hitting further south than I'd intended. Ochoa collapsed in a moaning fit, clutching his crotch. Whatever works.

I snatched the garbage bag and took off. My running shoes had rarely been put to such good use. I ran full speed, following the exit arrows. The bag, not weighing much more than twenty pounds, swung wide off my shoulder as I leaped around the driveway barricade gate, aiming for the lawn outside the garage. Remembering Ochoa's shoulder holster and expecting to hear gunshots at any moment, I tried to decide whether to hide in the bushes or make a run for my truck.

A hand grabbed my arm, pulling me down on the wet grass.

In my tumble, I saw a flash of a tan arm and realized one of the movers had attacked me. Then I heard a click that sounded frighteningly like a safety being released on a gun. My right hand clenched the neck of the plastic bag as someone tried to pull it away from me.

"Give it to him." The feminine, Spanish-sounding voice startled me.

I turned my head slowly. By the light of the full moon I recognized Mitzi Martin immediately.

Girl, we have a lot in common,
We both want to know the truth.
Tell me what you know,
Then we'll try to shake him loose.

CHAPTER 27

"It's you," I said. "I've been dying to talk to you."

An unfortunate choice of words, considering Mitzi's gun was aimed at my chest. Her petite hand had a steady grip on the weapon. Her dark eyes blazed as if she could pull the trigger without feeling any remorse.

"What do you know about me?" Mitzi snorted. "I have never seen you before."

"She's the investigator I told you about." The male voice came from behind me. "She's on our side."

Mitzi glared at her accomplice. "I can trust no one."

I thought I recognized the man's voice, but was afraid Mitzi might shoot me if I turned my head. I wondered whether a wound made by her revolver would resemble the ones that killed Suzanna. Probably not. Suzanna had been shot from a considerable distance, likely with some kind of rifle. And by someone else, not her friend Mitzi.

She muttered in Spanish, darting a quick look over her shoulder. Too quick for me to try anything even if I'd had a sudden burst of bravery. I looked across the parking garage but couldn't see Ochoa's car from where I sat on the wet grass. Why hadn't he yelled or come after me by now? Maybe I'd hurt him worse than I realized. If he headed in the direction I had run now, he would surely notice Mitzi where she stood on the crest of the sloping garage exit ramp.

"Here, you can have the sack," I said, releasing my grip on the garbage bag, "but we can't stay here. He'll see us."

Mitzi looked uncertain, but she didn't respond.

"Vincent is hiding something," I said. "You want to know what it is, and so do I. You're afraid he killed Suzanna. If he did, he must be punished."

Some of the fire left Mitzi's eyes.

"We have to get out of here," I urged. "He'll be chasing after me any second."

"She's right. Let's move." The man reached for the cap he'd lost when he tackled me. I stole a glance that confirmed his identity, surprised that Suzanna's ex-fiancé had been clever enough to get himself hooked up with the company moving Ochoa's boxes. Apparently, he and Mitzi and I were on the same trail.

"Why don't we help each other out here, Larry?" I said. "We were all Suzanna's friends." Well, they'd been her friends, but I felt like I'd known her.

Mitzi wasn't buying it. The arm holding the revolver didn't waver.

"Leo Atkins destroyed your apartment," I continued, "on orders from Vincent, I'm sure. If we compare notes, we'll figure this thing out. We can do it."

"We know nothing about each other," Mitzi said, shaking her head. "Why do you trust me?"

As I searched for a compelling answer, footsteps echoed throughout the garage.

"It's Vincent," Larry said.

Before Mitzi could turn to look, a shot rang out. It wasn't from her gun. She dropped to a crouch and scooted down the exit ramp. I jumped up, taking refuge behind a concrete pillar.

"Mitzi. Mit. . .zi, sweet. . .heart." Vincent Ochoa's call resounded in the garage. "Don't leave me again."

Larry shimmied across the concrete. He grabbed Mitzi's gun with one hand and her arm with the other, startling her.

"What are you doing?" she said, looking in Vincent's direction.

"Jesus, he's trying to kill you. Don't you dare answer him. We're getting you out of here." He looked around frantically. "Shit, the car's one level up."

"My truck's in the garage next door," I said. "You can come with me. Hurry."

"Go with her, Mitz," Larry said. "If he follows you, I'll stop him."

Mitzi's gaze flitted from Larry to me, then toward Vincent again. "But—"

"Please," I said, "you can trust me." Tugging on the sleeve of Mitzi's suede jacket with one hand, I grabbed the garbage sack with the other. Her feet seemed rooted to the concrete floor. What would it take to make the woman budge?

"Clay Mitchell told me what a nice person you are," I said, "but he never mentioned your damn stubborn streak."

"Mitzi!" Vincent shouted once more, before his shoes started clattering across the garage floor, coming closer. Larry, staying out of sight, fired a shot from Mitzi's revolver into the air. Vincent stopped running. For the moment.

Mitzi's eyes met mine. "How do you know Clay?" I figured her parents must have really stressed the danger of accepting rides from strangers.

"I met him at the gym when I went looking for you," I answered, talking faster than a used-car salesman on the last day of a bad month. "He's a great guy. Damn, if we had more time, you could call him to check my references." I pulled on her arm again and she gave in this time. I swung the sack over my shoulder, feeling like Santa Claus, but I didn't have to tug on Mitzi anymore. She was ready to go.

"Be careful, Larry," Mitzi said. "We'll meet at the hotel?"

"Yep. Don't worry."

Larry fired one more shot as we stole away. When I looked over my shoulder, he was rounding the far side of the garage.

***

An hour later, Mitzi and I sprawled on the double beds in a room at the Sheraton Astrodome with the contents of Vincent's garbage bag spread around us. The medication I'd taken had worn off, and I'd confiscated the tissues from the hotel bathroom. The box sat right beside me on the bed because my sneezing attacks were coming minutes apart. The rough, off-brand tissue had rubbed the skin under my nose raw.

Though we had talked non-stop during the ride, Mitzi didn't seem entirely comfortable, maybe because of my cold germs. But she'd explained openly how she and Larry had been hiding out at the hotel since her apartment fire, trying to solve Suzanna's murder themselves. She'd also admitted she was still in love with Vincent, and I knew she desperately wanted to absolve him of any wrongdoing. Considering he had taken a shot at her, the chances for reconciliation didn't look too good to me.

I leaned against the headboard, flipping through Ochoa's company checkbook register, sandpapery tissue in hand.

"So, you think your apartment fire was meant to destroy the computer disks Suzanna gave you—the things she copied from Vincent's computer?"

Mitzi lay on her stomach, elbows propped on the mattress, her chin resting on her hands. She stared at the wall. "I'm not sure. Suzanna said she would bring a laptop computer over one day and start going through them. She had not done that yet. I hid them in a box of tampons. She was not sure if someone would be able to tell the files were copied. He had special software, she said, and she broke his code to make the copies. Leo Atkins is not a patient man—if he came looking and couldn't find them, he'd get violent. Or, maybe Vincent only wanted me to know he is boss."

"You mean he would destroy your apartment to make a point?" What a guy.

"It is a possibility." Mitzi stretched her long dancer's legs, slim in black skin-tight leggings under a pink tunic.

"You told me Vincent had changed," I said. "When did you first notice a difference?"

"There are so many things. When his mama died, he was a crazy man. Such a sad time. She had cancer, you know. He was not thinking straight."

"When was that?"

"Over two years ago, when I worked at one of the restaurants. It was before Whispers." Mitzi sighed. "Vincent was Mama's boy. They were very close. She always took his side."

I remembered Reba saying that Alberto Ochoa didn't trust his son with any important tasks. Was it because Vincent didn't have the mental ability? Or maybe he had a proclivity for doing things wrong. I was scanning the check register, not wanting to spend too much time on it right now. There were a lot of large deposits, but also eight or more five-figure checks written out to Vincent himself each month.

"He spent a lot of money," I said. "A hundred thousand or so taken out of this account every month. Did he hand out cash on paydays?" I snatched a new tissue and sneezed into it.

Mitzi rolled onto her side. "No, he paid us by check. But he had big money problems. For the past year, I have worried. Vincent used to talk about marriage, but he thinks

I'm stupid. That I would never notice problems. He spends and spends, like money grows on trees, and maybe it did for him once. I do not know. But he will not listen when I try to discuss it. So I decided to call his father. Somebody must do something, or they will be bankrupt. When he found me looking in his desk for the phone number, he hit me." She placed the palm of her hand on her cheek, remembering. Her dark complexion was flushed.

"He threatened me," she said. "Told me if I did not mind my own business, he would leave me. Forever." Mitzi pushed herself into a sitting position. "Suzanna and I talked often about our men. She was angry with her husband, bored because he never came home to be with her. She followed Edward herself and proved his affairs. Suzanna was good at finding things, and she offered to check out Vincent's trouble for me. I could not do it myself because he was with me every night, watching me dance. So I sneaked his keys away one night when he was sleeping and made her a copy. If only I had not." Mitzi covered her face with her hands for a few seconds, then stood. "Excuse me." She went into the bathroom and shut the door.

I put down the checkbook, blew my nose again, then picked up a pile of papers. Leafing through them, nothing seemed particularly important. There were leases, minutes from Niño's board of directors meetings, unanimous consents. The documents only had one thing in common—Alberto Ochoa's signature. Near the bottom of the stack I found an invoice from Sanchez & Sanchez, the new attorneys.

Running a forefinger down the page, I skimmed the entries. Review and revise lease agreement, draft correspondence to lessee, all boring stuff. On the third page I spotted a reference to a will. "Prepare Last Will & Testament, meet with Mr. Ochoa to execute final Will, 2 hrs." The entry was dated six months ago. Another entry mentioned preparing powers of attorney for Mr. Ochoa. I found them further down in the stack. Four identical originals wherein Alberto gave his son Vincent the power to do just about anything a person might need to have done. Curious behavior for a father known not to delegate things to his son. There was no will in the stack of papers.

When Mitzi came out of the bathroom, her large dark eyes were bloodshot and she dabbed at them with a section of toilet tissue. She sat on the corner of the bed and picked up a double-framed picture Ochoa had included in his stash. She stared at the photos for a moment. "His mother and father. Is he hiding these pictures? Why would he?"

I moved the stack of papers I'd been holding in my lap and tried to uncross my stiff legs. "I wish I knew."

"I'm surprised there are no disks, no computer things, except for this." Mitzi picked up a gadget that looked like a hand-held calculator, but was some sort of electronic organizer. She punched its buttons. We couldn't figure out how to call up any of its data, so Mitzi gave up, throwing it down on the bed. "If we could make this work, I could find Vincent's father and talk to him."

I started to mention Alberto's planned visit to Houston but decided against it. With Vincent's power of attorney, Alberto didn't have to make the trip for his real estate closing, and I wondered if he had other reasons for coming and what they might be.

"When's the last time you saw Vincent's father?" I said.

Mitzi shrugged. "He went to Monterrey soon after his wife's death, and I haven't seen him since. Vincent says his father is still mourning."

Funny. I heard he'd been doing a lot of traveling. The phone rang, interrupting my thought. As Mitzi answered, I went to the window and parted the drapes, looking out to the day's first streaks of light. It was nearly dawn. Exhaustion had drained my ability to reason.

"That was Larry," Mitzi said, hanging up the receiver. "Vincent didn't follow us, but Larry followed him. To the airport. He left on a flight to Mexico."

***

After finding and swallowing a cold tablet that promised deep rest, I slept straight through until noon on Friday. Midnite's nails, clicking as she paced the hardwood floor in the upstairs hallway, woke me. Groggy, I squinted at the clock. The poor dog was anxious for breakfast and I couldn't blame her. My own stomach let out a deep growl. I dragged myself out of bed and down the stairs, noticed the blinking answering machine light, but ignored it on my way to let Midnite out. As she wandered about the yard, I staggered around the kitchen and managed to start a pot of coffee, then filled her bowl.

When I pushed open the storm door to let the dog back in, I noticed a manila envelope that must have been wedged in between the doors. A note was scrawled on the outside—"I finished the papers. Here they are. See you later. Kit." What papers? Something for school? I opened the envelope and reached inside. The contents woke me suddenly, more effectively than if I'd drunk the whole pot of coffee. David's timesheets.

Ochoa thought he'd destroyed the entire file, but he hadn't. Kit had taken these timesheets with her. Bless her little efficient, wonderful heart.

I let Midnite back inside, plopped her dish on the floor, and headed for my desk to study the entries Kit had highlighted. Afraid of missing important news, I stopped at the answering machine and pressed the message button.

Reba had called, of course, to see why I hadn't showed up for work yet. Really, she wanted to nose into my investigation and find out the latest. That, or work on persuading me to go to Nashville with her. Clay had left a short message about enjoying the gala. Mother had left three pleas for a return call. I reset the machine and almost ran to my desk to read the timesheets. I had spread the pages out on my desk and begun studying the paperwork when the phone rang. I jumped in my chair, banging my thighs on the middle desk drawer.

Damn. I grabbed the receiver, rubbing my legs with the other hand.

"Hi, it's Dad. Interesting news just came in."

"What is it?"

"Alberto Ochoa died a couple hours ago." He paused to let that sink in. "In an explosion."

My head fell back against the high desk chair. "Where? How? What kind of explosion?"

"In an office he rented in Mexico City. I called as soon as I heard. Thought it might have some bearing on your case."

"I'm sure you're right, Dad. How'd you get the news so fast?"

"One of my men was on the horn with a contact in Mexico City on another matter. In the course of the conversation, the other guy mentioned an American businessman from Texas dying in an explosion. My guy got the details, thinking it'd make a cover story in Houston."

"Well, was the building bombed or something? Were other people killed, too?"

"Only him." Dad hesitated. "Preliminary reports say there was a gas leak. I hate to bring this up, sweetie, but the whole thing reminds me of what happened to David."

I am onto something here,
Let me try to make it clear.
This man is the guilty one,
Let me tell you what he's done.

CHAPTER 28

The evidence I'd brought Wade to help prove Ed Kemp hadn't killed his wife littered the desktop. Though excited about clearing Kemp, Wade scowled as I paced his office. Reba sat on the edge of the desk, absorbed with trying to extract information from Vincent Ochoa's electronic organizer. I had the feeling neither of them was taking me seriously. Trying to hold back the panic rising in my chest, I pushed sweaty bangs off my forehead.

"You're not making sense. How can you believe this stuff is somehow connected to David?" He scanned the things I'd stolen from Ochoa's car, then watched me pace. "Are you on something?"

I had switched back to the cold tablet that kept me awake and hyper, but I ignored his question. "Don't you see what I'm worried about? Alberto Ochoa is dead! I wanted to talk to him. Mitzi wanted to talk to him. Two years ago David was searching for him. His son has been hiding things, moving things, he's in financial trouble. He *burned* our files. The man's a lunatic. What if he went to Mexico to get rid of his father?" Unspoken words echoed in my head—what if he murdered David to keep him quiet?

Wade leaned forward, eyes riveted on me. "That's far-fetched. I'll look through these papers, but you'll have to make a better argument for me to buy such an outrageous story."

"I agree," said Reba. "I've seen father and son together

more than a few times. First of all, Vincent Ochoa doesn't have any guts. He's all talk. Second, even though the old man didn't trust him with anything important, I think Vincent respected his father. The part I can't buy is Alberto signing those powers of attorney and allowing Vincent to run the company." Punching the organizer buttons faster, Reba said, "I think I'm onto something here." She grabbed a tablet and pen and began copying information from the organizer.

"Well, Alberto's been out of town," I said, looking over Reba's shoulder. "Somebody had to run it." I shoved my hands in my jeans pockets and kept pacing. Reba and Wade didn't realize I was weighing the possibility of a murder case much older than Alberto's or Suzanna Kemp's. Ideas flooded my brain. Maybe Alberto had hired Leo Atkins to take over after Hal Smith died in the explosion with David. Vincent may have pushed his way in once his father was out of the country, unless something had happened to inspire Alberto's sudden trust in his son.

Wade drummed his fingers on the sheaf of papers from Vincent's garbage bag. "I talked to Sanchez & Sanchez. Looks like this is the work they did. They said Alberto is a good, paying client, but they haven't seen much of him. He makes contact by fax. He's been at their office a couple of times, always with his son. They don't remember much about Alberto—only that he doesn't talk much, just nods his head a lot, and he's always puffing on a big cigar."

Reba looked up. "I never saw him smoke a cigar." She stood and walked around the desk to take a look at the papers herself.

Wade's chair squeaked as he leaned back, pressing the springs to their limit. Afraid I was losing his attention, I grabbed David's timesheets from the desk.

"Okay, let's look at these. I'll summarize." I flipped the page and pointed to the first highlighted notation, feeling like an attorney in closing arguments of a losing case. Where would I turn if Wade and Reba wouldn't listen to my theory? "Here's the day the letter came from Alberto dismissing the firm. David wrote 'Review correspondence from Alberto Ochoa' in the billing description, then wrote 'He fired us???' in the margin."

I quickly turned the page. "Next day, 'Telephone call to Alberto Ochoa's office, leave message on *recorder.*' He underlined recorder, so that must have been unusual. See his note in the margin—'Where's Luisa?' Ochoa's secretary, I imagine."

Reba snapped her fingers. "You're right. She worked for him a trillion years. I remember when David finally got through to a person. It was a temp. She said Luisa had been fired. We couldn't believe it." Reba edged closer to get a look at the timesheets.

"Here's another entry," I said. "'Correspondence to Alberto Ochoa regarding loss of representation.' I know David must have hated losing a long-term client. Did he ever discuss it with you, Wade?"

Wade shook his head. "Not that I recall. Business was booming then. We were in the Fleming trial, remember?"

Of course I remembered. Because of the trial, I'd barely spent any time with my husband during the weeks before he died. Standing here, reading his handwriting on the page, an eerie feeling swept over me, as though we were communicating right now. I shook my head like a wet dog, trying to free myself of the weird sensation.

Reba pointed a long scarlet fingernail to another entry. "I remember this. 'Telephone conference with Vincent Ochoa regarding the file.' David suggested packing up the boxes and shipping them to Sanchez. Vincent told him not to bother. He said they'd call us if they needed anything. When we didn't hear from them for months, I sent the boxes to archives."

"Can you tell if David *ever* got hold of Alberto?" Wade asked. He bent over the timesheets and I pushed them closer to him, desperate to capture his curiosity.

I shook my head. "Not that he didn't try. Look at all the times he called." I pointed to each notation of a call David had placed. My hands wouldn't stop trembling.

"Odd, he kept writing out every little detail," Wade said, "after they fired us. We obviously couldn't bill anybody for it."

"I remember David was obsessed about talking to Alberto," Reba said. She picked up the framed picture of Alberto and his wife. "He was a nice old man. I don't understand why he didn't call David back."

"Maybe he was sick," Wade said. "He probably wanted to retire in Mexico, go back to his family's roots at the old homestead. Sounds reasonable. It makes sense he'd hire a lawyer closer to home."

"Here's David's last mention of this case," I said, holding the page in front of Wade's face to make sure he paid attention. "'Investigate Vincent Ochoa's new club.' And look in the margin—'Alberto would die if he knew!'"

"We know that didn't happen," Reba said, "unless he just found out about it today."

Wade got up and walked toward the office door. "Let's look at Alberto's will. Reba printed it from her backup diskettes."

"Don't bother," I said. "There's a new one. I read about it on an invoice from Sanchez in that pile of documents. Alberto executed it at their office. But I saw the one we prepared in our file boxes, before they were stolen. It set up a trust for Vincent—he wasn't inheriting until he turned thirty-five. Plus, Alberto left a million dollars to cancer research. What are the odds of those provisions being intact in the new will?"

"I'll bet Vincent's barely thirty now," Reba said. "We talked age once when he tried hitting on me."

Wade looked at the floor, rubbing his chin. He couldn't ignore my facts now that they were starting to add up. "Sanchez can't reveal anything about Alberto's will to us. What about other relatives?" He walked to the desk and picked up the organizer. "You find anything on this, Reba?"

She handed him her notes. "Nothing under Alberto Ochoa's name, but I listed a few numbers in Mexico. Nothing looked particularly interesting, but I'll take this contraption to my computer and type up everything on it."

Wade glanced at her list, then gave it to me. "Ring any bells?"

I scanned it, shaking my head until I noticed the name Maria Umberto. "This looks familiar—I think she's the one who sent the gift to Alberto. A book of poetry. It's out in my truck, with a letter written in Spanish."

"Ooh, a secret love letter?" Reba said. "Maybe I can translate."

Ten minutes later we sat in the firm's kitchenette over a fresh pot of coffee. Reba held the letter while Wade flipped pages of the volume of poetry.

"The salutation says 'dearest brother,'" Reba said. "I'm disappointed already."

Wade put down the book. "Keep reading."

Reba squinted at the letter. "This won't be word-for-word, but I can give you the gist. She misses him. She says families should stick together. Now they only have each other. Sounds like his wife and her husband died." Reba tilted her head, played with a dangling earring, squinted harder. "I think she wonders if she did something to make him mad at her. She understands he's grieving. She's very sad. Sounds like he hasn't visited or written since his wife died."

"Alberto's wife died a long time ago," I said, picking

up the torn brown paper wrapping and checking the postmark. "This package was mailed in July." The warmth of the coffee mug on my hands didn't do anything for the chill running up my spine.

"Maybe they had a family feud and she wanted to make up," Wade said.

"If she's so terribly sad, why didn't she go to see him," Reba said. "Ochoa was rich. I'm sure his sister could afford a little trip. Monterrey and Mexico City aren't on opposite ends of the earth."

"From what I've heard," I said, "he travels a lot. I don't know if *anybody* has seen him lately, except for his attorneys."

"Right." Wade slurped his coffee, looking thoughtful. "But what do they know about the man?"

The hot beverage had unleashed the congestion in my head. I reached for a napkin to wipe my nose. "What are you thinking?"

"Just that anybody might have walked in to Sanchez & Sanchez, claiming to be Alberto Ochoa. The theory is consistent with his company's change in management."

"And it might explain Vincent trying to hide these papers." I clasped my hands around my mug to keep them from shaking. "Maybe Alberto Ochoa isn't the one who signed them."

Reba stood. "This is wild. I think you're both off your rockers. I'm going to scan that picture of Alberto into the computer. We can fax it to Sanchez and ask them to identify him." She left the room, glancing worriedly at us over her shoulder.

"If an imposter signed the will," I said, "I suppose everything's been left to Vincent. I wonder how enormous the estate is?"

Wade sighed. "What I'm wondering is how far

Vincent would go to inherit it. And how we'll be able to prove what he's done."

***

When we finally left the office, the word "murder" had remained unspoken. If we were on the right trail, and if David had been on the same trail, Vincent Ochoa might have planned the meeting David and Hal Smith had gone to on that last morning. Vincent would have known about Hal's chain-smoking. He could have arranged the gas leak at the club. But where had Alberto been at that time and for the two years since the explosion?

Driving home, I reviewed what Maria Umberto had said when we called asking about her brother. She had traveled to Monterrey several times, trying to find him. Much to her surprise, the Monterrey home which had been in the family for generations had been sold. The new owners had never met Alberto in person and had no information about him.

Maria had talked to her nephew about his father's whereabouts. Vincent reported that Alberto was traveling the world. All lies, Maria said. Vincent had always been a liar. The first year after Alberto's wife died, Maria had been busy caring for her sick husband. After his death, she had continued to search for her brother, to no avail. When news of the explosion reached her earlier that day, Maria had been shocked. But she was not in mourning. She told us she had mourned the loss of her brother years before.

A paralegal from Sanchez & Sanchez called after they got Reba's fax and said the man in the photograph was not the man her boss knew as Alberto Ochoa. Surprise, surprise. After her call, I wanted to work all night, trying to nail down every piece of evidence we had against Vincent. Wade had a prior obligation to speak at a meeting of the Texas Bar Association, but promised we'd pull everything together and talk to the police in the morning. Reba told me I looked worse than leftover meatloaf and urged me to go home to bed. I couldn't remember ever feeling more sick, flu-like symptoms and anger building to a fever pitch. If Vincent Ochoa had anything to do with David's death, I would make him pay.

At home I popped another one of the stay-awake cold tablets and downed it with a Coke, then wrapped myself in David's flannel shirt and settled behind my desk. I would find that no-good, lying son of a bitch and. . . . I stopped, realizing I wanted to see him dead. Good thing I didn't own a gun. There was no statute of limitations on his crime, I reminded myself. Vincent Ochoa might be found guilty of two counts of murder, perhaps capital murder, and end up in jail for life. Maybe draw a death sentence. The thought comforted me, but I couldn't sit here and do nothing.

I picked up the phone and dialed Whispers. A syrupy voice answered.

"I heard the tragic news about Vincent's father," I said. "Isn't it the most awful thing? Would you be a dear and give me Vincent's address in Mexico so I can send my condolences?"

"He's not in Mexico, honey," the gooey voice said. "He's right here. You wanna talk to him?"

Before I could reply, a masculine voice came on the line. "I'll take this call, sweetheart." Ochoa must have been screening all the club's calls. He didn't speak until the other girl clicked off the line.

"I've been waiting to hear from you, Miss McKenna."

"Why? Who is this?"

"Don't play dumb." His tone was a blend of smooth sexual innuendo and condescension. "You know who I am, and probably exactly what I want. If I get it, you get your kid back."

"Kid?" My body began to shake. My sweaty palm

slipped on the phone receiver.

"You haven't missed your kid yet?" His laugh shot a chill of fear across the phone line. "What kind of mother are you?"

What was he talking about? I jerked around in the chair to look out the window. Midnite stood outside the back door wagging her tail. He wasn't talking about my dog. My gaze lifted to the house next door. It was dark. Kit! Did he think. . .? Atkins had been watching my house. Kit came over every day after school to play with Midnite. Oh, my God! He thought Kit was my daughter!

I willed my voice to stay calm. "What do you mean? I'm not a mother," I said. If I convinced him we weren't related, Kit wouldn't be in danger. He'd realize he had no hold over me.

"Right. Brave mama." He chuckled. "If you wanna see your daughter again, meet me at the warehouse. One hour. Bring my *garbage* with you. We need to talk. You know the game. Come alone."

I'm not thinking straight
Because I'm in a hurry.
God, I can't be late,
There's no time for worry.

CHAPTER 29

After getting no answer at Kit's house, I had to assume Vincent told me the truth so I raced to the office. I didn't waste time separating Wade's paperwork from Vincent Ochoa's effects. One sweep of my arm sent everything on the desktop into the garbage sack. No time to worry about paper with Kit's life at stake. He had taken her, and I would do whatever was necessary to get her back.

I ran to Reba's desk and dropped the plastic sack by her chair. I had to find her gun. Tonight I appreciated her philosophy about keeping a weapon handy.

Yanking drawers open, I shuffled notepads and various forms. Pushed aside hanging file folders. No sign of the gun. The desk drawers to the left of her computer were locked. The pencil drawer was stuffed with junk—pens, clips, makeup—but I finally found a key ring. I had to brace myself to keep a steady enough hand to try each key. None fit.

I glanced at the wall clock. My allotted time had dwindled to thirty minutes. Chances of making it to the warehouse on time were slim, unless a helicopter miraculously appeared on the roof, waiting to swoop me across town. Hoping Reba didn't keep the drawer key with her, I picked up the phone and punched in her home number.

The phone rang six times before she answered. I interrupted her hello drawl. "Where's your desk key?"

"Girl, didn't I tell you to go to bed? You sound pitiful. Are you at the office?"

"Reba! Where is it?" I screamed, stopping her short for a second.

"You lookin' for my automatic? Gawd almighty, is there a prowler? Did you call 911?"

"Reba!"

"Under the big planter by the window. What's goin' on? I'm comin' over there."

"No! Don't!" I cradled the phone between my head and shoulder, stretching the cord so I could reach the planter. As I tipped it, fishing around underneath until my free hand closed on the key, needles of the Norwegian pine scratched across my face.

"Ammunition's in here, too?" I demanded, jiggling the key in the lock.

"Sure, a full box. You know how to use that thing?"

"No problem." Hopefully, I'd remember something from one training session I'd attended eons ago.

"What's goin' down? You need help?"

"No, just your gun. I have to do this alone. Ochoa has Kit." I yanked the drawer open. The Werther lay on top of a stack of yellow legal pads. I clutched the pearl grips and raised my eyes for a split second in a silent prayer. "Found it. Thanks."

Reba yelled for me to wait, but I slammed down the receiver.

With twenty minutes left, I raced down the freeway. My sketchy plan wasn't foolproof, to say the least. Common sense told me to call the police, but I refused to take the risk. I was convinced Ochoa wouldn't hurt either of us until he made sure I'd returned all of his belongings, although I hadn't yet figured out if what we had was enough to incriminate him.

After Kit was released and safe, he could have everything back. Then it would be me against him—a more comfortable equation.

Thinking about Kit with Ochoa petrified me. She had to be okay. I had to get her away from him. Please, God, keep her safe.

I had to keep telling myself Ochoa wouldn't gun me down at the warehouse. Another dead body and crime scene tape would spoil his plans to auction off all that fine furniture in the morning—furniture that had probably occupied his father's home at one time.

He probably wouldn't blow up the building either, even though his M.O. was to create "accidental" explosions. Unless getting rid of me meant more to Ochoa than getting the money for the furniture.

In the back of my mind, I knew how simple it would be for him to shoot me and Kit, ditch his weapon, and dump our bodies anywhere in the city. We could easily become statistics on Houston's list of mysterious unsolved murders, but I couldn't think about that now.

As I turned onto Yale Street, a strong wind buffeted the Ranger. Slanting rain began to beat against the truck. I parked in a lot near the warehouse and dumped half of the sack's contents onto the passenger floor. Maybe I could exchange Kit for these remaining items.

Taking the garbage bag with me, I jogged down the sidewalk, then crossed the warehouse lot, staying close to the building. I squinted against the icy rain and noticed an old Chevy pickup parked next to the row of company vans I'd seen on my last two visits. Didn't look like Ochoa's style.

Parked in front of his warehouse was the shiny black Jaguar. I patted my jacket pocket, the presence of the Werther reassuring. I scanned the building front, but something wasn't right. The light fixtures above each office door created a regular pattern of dim circles down the row. Then I realized one of the overhead warehouse doors stood open. I dropped to my knees, heart hammering. Except for the howling wind and splattering rain, I couldn't hear a thing.

By opening the overhead door, Ochoa had given me an alternate entrance into the warehouse. I scooted ahead, crouched, trying to keep my eyes focused on the door despite rain dripping off my eyelashes. Beyond the doorway, it was pitch black. I reached the Jag and thought about puncturing the tires so Ochoa couldn't get away. But I hadn't brought a pocketknife. If not for Kit, I'd have happily shot out his expensive Pirellis. When the noise brought Ochoa around, I could shoot him, too.

The thought of Kit spurred me on. I decided to go in through the office door, using Suzanna's key if the door was locked. I hugged the dripping sack to my body, running toward the steps. Wind whipped around me.

Suddenly, a bright light snapped on.

"You're late."

My eyes followed the spotlight beam to inside the warehouse, somewhere higher than floor level, but I couldn't see past the blinding light. I swallowed hard. "Traffic—you know how it is." My voice seemed to blow away with the wind.

Ochoa didn't answer. If what they say about people's lives passing before their eyes is true, the frames of my past would soon be flipping swiftly. I tried hard to remember my plan. "Where's Kit?" I yelled.

"Come in," Ochoa shouted back, "so I can see what you've brought me. This way." The spotlight moved to illuminate another set of stairs leading up to the loading dock. I sprinted for the steps, eager to bring our meeting to a head and see Kit safe.

When I reached the warehouse floor, the spotlight switched off. I clutched the plastic sack to my chest as a makeshift bulletproof vest.

I straightened my shoulders, trying to portray a tough

image, even though Ochoa surely couldn't see me in the black room. "I can't figure out why you believe I'd risk my life for a child who isn't even related to me."

I inched farther into the building, pulling Reba's gun from my pocket. Should I try to hide, try to find Kit, or would we be safer if I simply faced him?

"You're here, aren't you?"

I took a deep breath. "But someone like you, someone with such little respect for family you'd murder your own father—"

"I did *not* kill my father," Ochoa shouted. His assured voice, echoing in the cavernous room, came from somewhere above me. He had to be sitting on one of the upper rows of shelving.

"We know you went to Mexico," I said. "And now your father is dead."

Vincent snickered. "That old man served his purpose, but he was not my father. My father died over two years ago. Heart attack, God rest his soul."

My heart lurched. Alberto Ochoa dead, two years ago? Had he hidden his father's death for control of the company? If Vincent continued admitting his crimes, he'd *have* to kill me, unless I got him first.

I sidestepped down the aisle, my eyes beginning to adjust to the eerie blackness around me. Where was Kit? What was Vincent planning? What if my stupid assumption he wouldn't blow up the furniture was all wrong? He might have insured the warehouse contents for a bundle. My teeth began to chatter, and I had to clamp them together.

"Let Kit go, Vincent," I said, tightening my grip on the Werther. "She's not my daughter. She's not involved in this. It's you and me. I brought what you told me to bring. I don't know what's so important about the stuff, why you had to kill Suzanna Kemp to stop her prying." I wanted Ochoa to talk, tell me facts I could use to testify against him if I made it out of the building alive.

"Who?" He sounded shocked.

"Mitzi's friend," I said. "You've killed everyone who's interfered with your grand plan, beginning with my husband." I continued down the aisle, squeezing back tears.

"You bitch! How could you know that?" The spotlight flashed on, then fell, followed by footsteps thudding on the floor. A gun fired. I jumped back, bumping into a piece of wooden furniture, then stumbling into a cushioned chair. Another shot zinged past me. The spotlight bobbed in my direction. If Vincent killed me, there'd be no one to protect Kit. Dammit, the man had taken everything from me when he killed David. He wasn't going to hurt the girl.

I crouched beside the aisle, aiming the automatic toward the light, when a clattering noise sounded in the far corner of the warehouse. I turned to look, and Ochoa tackled me from behind, throwing me down. Reba's automatic skittered across the floor. Vincent lost his hold on the spotlight, and it landed about five feet in front of us.

"So, you figured out about your husband." Ochoa had an arm around my neck, a knee in the small of my back. "Too bad. You might have gotten out of here alive, but you're too nosy, like he was. And stubborn. I told you to come alone."

"I did come alone," I mumbled hoarsely, trying to pry his arm off my neck. "If somebody's back there, he's with you, not me." No chance Reba could have figured out where I'd gone and sent for the police. The visitor was probably Leo Atkins, come to help his boss dispose of one victim's spouse. Ed Kemp was lucky he hadn't shown up for the party.

Ochoa's hold on my neck loosened. "Get up," he said, yanking my wet hair. Pinging sounded in the back corner, like someone was throwing pebbles to distract us. I shuddered, remembering the rats. Ochoa pulled me to a standing position, then shoved me. "Get going. We're checking this out together."

Up ahead, to the right of the spotlight beam, I saw the mounted deer antlers that had attracted Midnite's attention on our prior visit. I took measured steps, all too aware that Vincent still had control of his weapon. He'd need to pick up his light, though, to investigate the noise in the dark corner. I trained my peripheral vision on the black cylinder. When Ochoa's arm reached for it, I ducked to the right and grabbed the antlers, swinging my arm around to stab him in the knees. A soft two-note whistle stopped my arm in mid-flight.

I jumped back just in time to avoid the huge urn hurtling toward Ochoa. The pottery hit his head, knocking him down. Broken pieces of pottery scattered. Ochoa's gun slid across the concrete floor to my feet. As I stooped to pick it up, I saw blood pooling around his head. Fitting, I thought, remembering Suzanna's wound.

Then I raised my eyes, looking to the upper shelf. Kit peered over the edge with a shaky smile. "I couldn't have done it without Larry," she said. "He found me."

Footsteps echoed across the blackness, and Larry Rogers rounded the corner. "You got the bastard," he said, giving Kit a thumbs-up. "Good job."

It's time to leave the past behind,
Though they'll be always on our mind.
Right now it's time for closure,
Can't you see it's finally over?

CHAPTER 30

"Is he dead?" Kit whispered the question, as if she didn't really want to know.

"I don't think so, baby," I said. "Come on. Let me help you down from there." I climbed onto a wooden chair, then took a giant step to a dresser top, stretching my arms to guide her. Kit dangled over the side of the shelf, hanging onto the metal edge, agile as a monkey. I grabbed her and lowered her to the dresser. When she flung her arms around me, I hugged her tight, rubbing her rigid shoulders, blinking back tears of relief.

Larry knelt amid the pieces of broken orange pottery. He held his fingers to Ochoa's neck and looked up. "I feel a pulse."

"We better get the police over here pronto," I said, "and an ambulance." Though I wouldn't care if Ochoa bled to death right before our eyes, I had to think about Kit. Even though he had kidnapped her and she'd hurt him saving my life, no twelve-year-old should have a man's death on her conscience.

As Kit and I clambered down to floor level, Larry retrieved the two weapons from the floor and handed Reba's revolver to me. "Forgive me if I'm not in a hurry to save him," he said, fingering Ochoa's gun, "but I guess the law will deal with him. Ever since I figured out he killed Suzanna, I've had revenge on the brain. I didn't expect to see him at the club tonight. Thought he'd still be in Mexico. Then he left in a big hurry, so I followed him. I'll admit, I thought about killing him. But when I saw him pull this little girl out of his trunk, I knew I had to save her. Nothing I did to Ochoa could bring Suzanna back."

"Larry, you deserve a medal." I turned to Kit, putting my hands on her shoulders, searching her eyes. "Thanks to you, too. I'm so sorry you got messed up in this. Where did he. . .what did he. . .did he hurt you?"

Kit's eyes glistened with tears, but she shook her head. "I'm okay. Can we call the police now?"

Larry offered to make the call while Kit and I kept our distance from Ochoa, waiting silently, hand in hand. He stirred once, but didn't regain consciousness. It seemed like a long time before we heard sirens in the distance.

"Did he really kill your husband?" Kit said as a police car pulled up outside the warehouse.

"I'm afraid so, baby," I said. My chest felt so tight I'd have suspected a heart attack under other circumstances.

"Then I don't care about what happened to me today," Kit said, squeezing my hand. "I'm glad we got him."

***

I wanted to go in to the office Saturday morning and catch up on work I'd neglected over the course of the Kemp case. Wade insisted I needed rest to get over my cold. He meant I needed time to recover from the shock of finding out David had been murdered. Mother called, and I convinced her I'd be sleeping soundly all day, and no, she didn't need to bring me anything. My cold might be contagious, I told her, and I didn't feel like company. Jean Thompson had taken Kit to spend the weekend at her grandmother's house in the country. I missed her already.

I thought a lot about Vincent Ochoa and the extent of

his greed. Wade told me Ochoa had regained consciousness at the hospital and was in stable condition. The D.A. was busy gathering evidence for the grand jury. They would nail him for two murders, Wade felt sure, not including the imposter who died in the Mexico City explosion. I wondered if we'd ever know the true identity of the man who'd impersonated Alberto.

The police interrogated Leo Atkins and came to the conclusion he hadn't known Vincent at the time of Alberto Ochoa's or David's deaths. He would most likely be charged with arson for setting fire to Mitzi Martin's apartment building, even though it was Vincent's orders that led him to commit the crime.

I thought my hatred for Vincent Ochoa would burn like the flame at the tomb of the unknown soldier. Forever. Like Alberto's sister, I'd done my mourning long ago. Problem was, I had continued mourning, month after month. Year after year. It was time to move on. Running my angel back and forth on its silver chain, I stood on David's side of the walk-in closet in our bedroom. No, *my* bedroom. I looked across the row of hanging clothes, reached out and touched the silk blend of his favorite sport coat. Then I pulled the jacket off the hanger and laid it in the large cardboard box at my feet. David's clothes could be put to good use by Goodwill or the Salvation Army.

After a couple hours of packing clothes, I'd just taken a break and popped the top on an ice-cold Coke when the phone rang. It was Maggie Robbins, calling from her hospital bed.

"I heard you solved Mrs. Kemp's murder," she said. "Are you doing okay?" She didn't mention David, though news reports had broadcast the fact I'd brought my husband's killer to justice. I had listened to one network's version of the story. That was enough. I hoped Maggie wasn't fishing for an exclusive interview.

"Me? I'm fine. You're the one with the bullet wound. What's the prognosis?"

"Oh, Doc says I'm out of here later today. Then I'll be back on the streets, looking for a good story." Maggie was silent for a moment. I wondered if she'd ever set foot on the street again without worrying about stray bullets.

"I'm glad you cleared Ed," Maggie said. "I hated having dinner with the man, just to get an interview, all the while thinking he might have actually killed his wife."

I laughed. "You have a reputation for doing whatever it takes."

"Well, he promised to arrange a meeting with his father, and I'm holding him to it. I only hope Arthur Kemp's more personable than his son."

"Ed's not exactly big on charm," I agreed, "but I probably owe him an apology for judging him the way I did. Convicted him in my mind from the start."

"Now there's a story," Maggie said, laughing. "I'd like to have a minicam film that apology scene."

After we hung up, I thought about what Maggie had said. Obviously, she couldn't picture me apologizing. Maybe I was a hardhead, but I didn't like other people pointing out my faults. The more I thought about it, the more I realized Ed Kemp deserved an apology. He was the client, and I'd stubbornly refused to listen to his side of the story.

Around five, I left the house, stopped at McDonald's for a quick dinner, then headed to Kemp's neighborhood. Might as well get the apology off my chest. Something about the day made me long for complete closure.

Surprisingly, Ed Kemp greeted me with a big smile and invited me to join him and Eddie for a Domino's pizza supper. I supposed he might feel some kind of bond with me now. After all, our spouses had been murdered by the same man. Even though I'd just eaten, the smell of pepperoni lured me into the family room where Kemp and his little boy had set up their meal on the coffee table. I followed Ed's lead and sat on the floor, Indian style. The television set blared a Rockets basketball game.

"I gave Mrs. Hernandez the weekend off," Kemp said, picking up a slice of pizza. "I'm looking forward to spending some time with Eddie alone." He fanned the pizza with a magazine to cool it off, then handed a slice to the toddler. I cringed as cheese dripped onto the boy's shirt sleeve. I doubted Mrs. Hernandez would condone eating over the room's beige carpeting, especially feeding a toddler gooey pizza. The child should be in a high chair and have his pizza cut into bite-size pieces, but I wasn't going to tell Kemp what to do.

"I guess Wade filled you in on the details of what happened last night," I said, accepting a small slice. "I came to apologize for treating you so badly. My attitude isn't the best sometimes."

"Don't worry about it," Kemp said. "You're talking to the king of bad attitudes."

At least he realized it. I leaned over the table and took a big bite. On TV, one of the Rockets had made a three-point shot. The crowd cheered. Little Eddie yelled something I couldn't make out and jumped up to clap his hand with his dad's. The high five seemed to be one of the first tricks dads teach their sons. But Eddie tipped his other hand, the one holding the pizza, and the slice headed for the floor. I jumped to my knees and reached across the coffee table to make a heroic catch, saving the carpeting from a big pizza sauce splotch. Eddie giggled, staring at the front of my sweatshirt that had landed on top of the pizza still in the box. The look on the kid's face was priceless. Kemp and I burst into laughter.

I sat back on my heels, my side cramped from laughing so hard, and thought I saw someone at the window. Kemp had grabbed a handful of napkins and turned to dab at the grease on my shirt. He thought better of the close contact and handed the napkins to me. The guy wouldn't ever be my favorite person, but laughing sure felt good.

"I think you might have company," I said as the doorbell rang. "I'd better go."

Eddie picked up my piece of pizza and was trying to feed it to me when Kemp showed Vivian Coulter into the room.

"Well, what a cozy scene."

I looked up, starting to say hello, but the tone of her voice stopped me. It could have chilled an Eskimo's blood.

Kemp touched the elbow of her pink cashmere sweater. "What's the matter?"

Vivian turned a scathing look on him. "What's the matter?" Her tone raised to a high-pitched scream. "You have to ask me what's the matter?" I stood and scooped up Eddie, holding him protectively against my shoulder. I felt his lower lip quivering and knew the screaming had frightened him. I cradled his soft blond head.

Vivian turned to me. "Give me the baby!" she hollered. I stepped back, away from her.

"Give him to me!" She reached for Eddie, her eyes wild. "He's mine now."

Kemp grabbed her arm this time, angrily. "Vivian. Calm down. What the hell's wrong with you?"

She yanked her arm from his grasp and reached into her purse. Realization hit me suddenly. I dropped the boy on a sofa cushion and lunged across the room toward her. Not fast enough to stop her from pulling out a small nickel-plated handgun and aiming it at me. I froze.

"Vivian, in the name of God!" Kemp yelled. "Put the

gun away."

"No, Edward." She moved toward me. "I waited such a very long time, and I won't let her or anyone else take you and my baby away from me." Her eyes looked as though she'd been drugged.

Or had lost her mind.

I remembered Clay telling me about Vivian spending time at a private hospital with some kind of "emotional problems." Her family had sent her out of the country. Now I could see why.

"What are you talking about?" Kemp said. He looked confused but my mind was clicking, putting the pieces together.

"We're the ones who should have had this baby," Vivian sobbed. "He's ours—yours and mine."

"No," Kemp said, shaking his head. "You're confused. Here, let me help you. Sit down with me and we'll talk."

"Don't move." Vivian swung the gun toward him, but quickly aimed it back at me. "Talking won't help. You're never going to talk me into anything again."

Kemp slumped into a side chair, head down. "I'm sorry, Vivian."

"Sorry doesn't cut it, Edward." Vivian wiped tears from her eyes with her free hand and straightened her shoulders. "Med school was more important to you than life itself. Certainly more important than me. Well, that's behind us now, but I still want you. You and Eddie. If you hadn't insisted on that abortion, this would have been our baby. Now he is."

Kemp looked up in horror, realization clouding his face. "My God, Vivian, you killed Suzanna!" He gave me a frantic look, pleading for me to do something.

Eddie whimpered, but he hadn't moved from where I dropped him on the sofa. I inched over, putting myself between the boy and the gun.

"I love you, Edward," Vivian moaned. "We were meant to be together. You know that."

Kemp faced her with a stern expression, but spoke softly. "Maybe you're right," he said. "Let's all sit down and talk calmly. See how you're upsetting the baby."

When Vivian's eyes shifted toward Eddie, I pounced on her, knocking her to the floor. She didn't lose hold of the gun. I tried to pin down her right hand and grab the weapon, but she fought like a wildcat, scratching my face and neck with her left hand. She rolled on the floor, kicking at me with high-heeled shoes, snarling like a wild animal. The baby wailed behind me.

"Get Eddie out of here," I yelled to Kemp as I tried to control Vivian's squirming body by sitting on top of her. But he appeared next to me, bending over to try and remove the gun from her grasp. As he pulled, Vivian's wrist twisted and the gun discharged as it clattered to the floor. Vivian screamed. Kemp fell backwards, clutching his left arm where the bullet had grazed it. Vivian screamed again and didn't stop until I slapped her across the face.

Ed managed to stand and stumble over to the couch where he picked up the crying child. Vivian stopped squirming and looked like she might be in shock.

"Are you all right?" I said, glancing at Kemp and his son.

He nodded. Blood from his wound dripped off his elbow onto the beige carpet. Kemp brushed hair out of Eddie's face, leaving a trail of blood on the baby's cheek.

Then Vivian's stupor vanished and she threw me off of her, rolling out from under me with the skill of a wrestler who was about to be pinned. In a second, she had grabbed the gun and was up on her knees. I gritted my teeth, pulling myself up on one elbow, expecting to be shot. But Vivian's attention was trained on Kemp and his son, and her vacant stare turned to anguish.

"I hurt my baby," she whimpered. "I wanted my baby more than anything in the whole world. It's no use. Nobody will let me have my baby. I'll never have my baby now." She lifted her arm, aiming the gun at her own chest.

"Vivian, no," Kemp shouted.

She pulled the trigger, and her body slumped to the floor.

Kemp moaned and rushed to Vivian's side. He bowed his head, feeling for a pulse along her slender neck. Vivian's lifeless gray eyes stared at him as a red stain spread across the chest of her pretty pink sweater.

Time to move on.
The future's bright ahead.
Gotta carry on.
With hope and promise we'll be led.
As we carry on.

CHAPTER 31

Continuous lyric ideas rolled through my head Sunday morning, fed by the emotions I'd experienced over the past week. Country music focuses on love, hate, sorrow, and especially pining over the loss of a loved one. Depressing lyrics naturally sprang to my mind. I scribbled them all down for future reference. Scraps of paper and tablets with words scrawled across them litter my house. But I didn't want to dwell on sadness today.

Last night's scene kept trying to replay itself in my head. Learning Vivian Coulter gunned down Suzanna Kemp had shocked me, and the discovery had eroded my professional confidence. I had ignored Dad's rule and assumed too much. After Kemp explained the circumstances surrounding his and Vivian's broken engagement years before, pieces started falling into their proper place.

Though the Kemp and Coulter families had planned for and expected their children's union for years, Ed had refused to marry Vivian when he found out she was expecting their baby long before he was due to graduate from medical school. He'd talked her into an abortion, which had been botched and led to an emergency hysterectomy. Vivian showed no sign of recovering from her deep depression after the surgery. Her emotional problems, along with Ed's own desire for children, killed the engagement. Despite what

Vivian had done, I couldn't help feeling sorry for her.

As I sat on my piano bench, I forced my imagination to search for happy lyrics—something uplifting. Reba and I had composed some good stuff. Not Nashville material yet, but maybe I'd agree to make the trip just to get her off my case. I was humming and dabbling with chord progressions when the doorbell rang. Wade had offered to pick up the things I had packed and take them to a homeless shelter. I could have handled it myself, but he'd sounded so eager to help. Besides, it made me feel good to know he cared. The cardboard boxes were ready and waiting.

Even before he'd crossed the threshold, Wade pulled me into a big bear hug. "Corie. God, I'm glad to see you, alive and in one piece."

I couldn't talk around the lump in my throat, so I stood there, returning the tight hug.

When he stepped back, I found my voice, and my worries poured out.

"I've been wondering about my job security. Who's gonna hire an investigator who jumps to the wrong conclusions? I might single-handedly destroy your hot-shot lawyer reputation." Though trying to sound funny, I couldn't have been more serious.

"No wonder Vincent Ochoa looked at me funny when I mentioned Suzanna," I continued. "He really didn't know who I was talking about. There were clues—I should have seen them. Vivian told me she had a personal trainer who came to her house, but then Clay talked about her coming in to his gym. I should have realized she was following Suzanna around. Clay even talked about Vivian hunting with her dad. I should have at least considered her being the killer. She was everywhere I turned, following Kemp around, holding his baby. I'm sure she's the one who shot at Maggie, too, after *I* told her Ed and Maggie were seeing each other." I stopped, catching my breath, watching Wade's weird grin. "Maybe I ought to close up shop."

Wade took my face in his hands, and a change in his eyes made the grin turn serious. We stood almost chin to chin. "Stop rambling. All I care about is that you're okay."

I tried to ignore the warmth of his hands and the tug of his eyes. "But—"

"No buts." Wade held a finger over my lips. "None of this is your fault."

Yet another emotion swept over me. Afraid to acknowledge it, I changed the subject. "Everything's ready. You need to borrow my truck?"

Wade smiled. "I'm glad you're moving on," he said. "It was time." He turned to look at the boxes by the door. "I don't think I'll have any problem fitting them in my car." He picked up the box on top, tested its weight, and put it back down.

"So, Vivian Coulter thought you and Ed Kemp were interested in each other?" He turned, leaning against the boxes, staring at me.

"Apparently so." I felt suddenly uncomfortable under his scrutiny. "She must have watched us from the window. We were laughing at the baby. I guess it looked like something more."

"I see." Wade folded his arms across his chest. "You haven't changed your feelings about him, have you?"

"No way!" I knew the words sounded defensive. "But Kemp did explain to me he'd started drinking a lot lately, and that's why he was always in such a foul mood."

"No kidding?" Wade walked toward me. "You gonna offer *me* something to drink? Have any coffee?"

"Sure." I walked toward the kitchen, Wade close on my heels.

"What about this other guy?" he asked. "Clay something or other?"

"Mitchell. Clay Mitchell. He owns that gym, Total Fitness. The one over on Kirby."

"Yeah, I know the one. You two getting close?"

"Not especially." My face felt hot, remembering the back rub, so I changed the subject again. "You know, Kemp says he's going to AA starting next week. I guess all that's happened might change him."

I took the coffee can down from the pantry shelf.

"What's happened will change all of us," Wade said. "But especially you."

I scooped grounds into the filter and ran water into the pot without looking at him. I imagined I could feel his breath on my neck.

I poured the water into the coffee maker, hit the on switch, and turned around. "I know."

"How are you handling things so far?" His eyes looked even bluer than usual, maybe a reflection off my blue Formica counter top.

"Okay, I think. Fine."

"Mind if I say something personal?"

I shook my head, figuring he'd tell me what he thought no matter what I said.

"You've been through a lot," he said. "Whenever you need me, I'll be here." He reached out and touched my hair. "Snap your fingers, and I'll come running." He smiled. "You do know that, don't you?"

I nodded. The lump in my throat returned.

We stood like that for a while, then Wade headed for the door. "Guess I'll load those boxes while the coffee's brewing."

My heart thumped harder than usual as I watched him walk back and forth between the house and the car with the boxes. Midnite stayed at his side, her wagging tail keeping time with his steps. When he opened the back car door to put boxes on the seat, she jumped in and he had to coax her out before he could close the door. He stopped to pat her head. I stood at the back door, feeling warm all over despite the cool mid-November breeze and the remnants of my cold.

All of a sudden it hit me that there were other clues I had overlooked. Clues hidden in my heart. I had a feeling they were reflected in Wade's heart, too. Suzanna Kemp's death was a horrible tragedy—but it had headed me on the right path. One to a new life.

I went inside to fix Wade a cup of coffee, remembering he liked lots of sweetener, and took it out to where he was playing fetch with the dog.

"She's loving this," I said, watching Midnite race after a tennis ball. "Kit's only been gone for a day, and Midnite already misses her."

"That's natural," he said, "but I don't mind stepping in. New relationships can be even more special than old ones."

"You're right about that," I said.

As our eyes met, I had a hunch happy lyrics were only a notepad and pen away.

KAY FINCH

Kay Finch is a Pennsylvania native but, as her husband likes to say, she got to Texas as fast as she could. She has worked as a legal assistant in Houston for the past seventeen years, beginning in the criminal law arena at Richard "Racehorse" Haynes' firm before turning to a specialization in family law. Kay meets with clients at one of the worst, most emotional, times of their lives. Though the typical clients are law-abiding citizens, to the best of her knowledge, it's not hard to imagine them each with a motive for murder. And so the Corie McKenna series was born, beginning with *Final Decree*, a novel sparked by one particularly memorable client many years ago.

Kay is a member of Mystery Writers of America, Sisters in Crime, Private Eye Writers of America, and the State Bar of Texas Legal Assistants Division. She has recently become Board Certified in Family Law by the Texas Board of Legal Specialization. Kay lives in a Houston suburb with her husband and their family of Labrador retrievers.

Visit Kay on the worldwide web at:

http://www.kay-finch.com

Visit the Top Publications, Ltd. website at:

http://toppub.com